W9-AVG-061

THE FIND

To Gene

Enjoy Life

Dave

9/21/12

THE FIND

A Novel

Isaac J. Myers, II

Writers Club Press
New York Lincoln Shanghai

The Find
A Novel

All Rights Reserved © 2003 by Isaac J. Myers, II

No part of this book may be reproduced or transmitted in any form or by any means, graphic, electronic, or mechanical, including photocopying, recording, taping, or by any information storage retrieval system, without the written permission of the publisher.

Writers Club Press
an imprint of iUniverse, Inc.

For information address:
iUniverse, Inc.
2021 Pine Lake Road, Suite 100
Lincoln, NE 68512
www.iuniverse.com

This book is a work of fiction. The characters and incidents in this book are figments of the author's imagination. Any resemblance to actual events or persons living or dead, is entirely coincidental.

ISBN: 0-595-27018-2

Printed in the United States of America

I dedicate this book to my wife JoAnn.
You're the wind beneath my wings.

Acknowledgments

One of the things I enjoy most about writing is creating the characters and imagining their personal journeys. With each word that I write, I learn more about myself and the world around me.

I wish to thank my kids—Joe, Jordan, Shamika and Shivaughn. You're the greatest!

My family and friends—your support means everything.

Bonnie Spelman—for the many hours she spent reviewing the novel.

Bryan Aubrey—for his editing and direction. Your competence will always reign.

Beth Shipman—at Marshside Mama's Restaurant, Daufuskie Island, for sharing her local flavor and down-home setting. A good time was had by all.

Edsel Williams—at the Gullah Book Store, Hilton Head, South Carolina, for helping me understand the Gullah language.

All the special people on Daufuskie Island, whom my family and I have come to know.

The Gullah people for the riches they have brought this earth. Your spirits are endless.

Glossary for Gullah Words

Gullah is an English-based Creole marked by vocabulary and grammatical elements from various African languages. It is used predominately in the Southern States.

a'libe/alive
attuh/after
Ax/ask
ax'e/ask her
bin/been
'bout/about
cep/but
chickin/chicken
chile/child
crack 'e teeth/talk about
cyan'/can't
dat/that
de/the
dese/these
de't/died
dey/there
dinnuh/dinner
dis/this
doctuh/doctor
don'/do not, don't
duh/are
dun/done

en/and
'e/he, she, it
eb'ry/every
ez/as
farruh/father
fib/five
fry/fried
fuh/for
git/get
gib/give
gwine/go, going, going
hab/had
happ'n/happen
haffuh/have to
huccome/how come
hu't/hurt
I/I, me
leabe/leave
leh/let
look'n/looking
lub/love
luk/like

The Find

matt'r/matter
mek/make
mek'som'/make some
membuh/remember
miss'e'/miss her
murrah/mother
muse'e'hu't/must be hurt
nebbuh/never
notus/notice
oonuh/you
prey'd/pray
sine/since
sistubs/sisters
sump'n/something

tek/take
t'ings/things
tol'/told
t'ru/through
tuh/to
ub/of
wan/want
weh/where
we'n/when
wid/with
wor'y/worry
writt'n/written
wuh/what
you'own/your, your own

P R O L O G U E

▼ ──────────────

Katherine put on her sweater and headed towards the kitchen while Sarah laced up her shoes. Running her fingers through her untamed brunette locks, she took a final sip of her lukewarm coffee. She now had to squirrel away a couple of banned treasures. Over her shoulder, she noticed that the federal agent was suddenly within breathing distance. "Shit," she muttered.

"I know you don't want to do this, but it's the right decision," he said.

"Right for whom?" she replied, ready to do battle. The agent watched Katherine lather up the cup. A quick rinse and she turned off the water to face him head on, hips leaning against the countertop. She looked right through him then took one last view of the canary-yellow kitchen. Sarah's leaves from the previous fall's school project were still pasted on the wall. They made her think of the fun she and Sarah had trying to decide the right spot to display them.

In front of her, the oak country-top table with its two chairs only deepened her musing.

Katherine thought of Beth, her father's hospice nurse, and the morning they both sat at that table while she confessed that she was pregnant with Sarah. That was fourteen years ago, but it seemed hardly any time. The love that Beth laid upon her that day could still be felt in the room, and other places in the house.

Impatient, the agent edged closer still. "Katherine, I need to do this," he explained.

"Let's get it over with. I don't want my daughter to see any of it," she said. She looked up in disgust and stared, corpse-like, at the ceiling. She was frozen, and when the agent finished his cold frisk, she wiped the tears that rolled to her earlobes from her upturned face. The brief humiliation was over and she was ready to move on.

As Katherine returned to the living room, the sad look on Sarah's face worried her. Sarah didn't say anything but her eyes spoke for her.

"I just had to make sure you didn't take anything that might give your identity away," the agent said as he followed her into the living room.

"Now, why would I want to do that?"

The agent, standing next to Sarah and masquerading as a truant officer, looked menacing. Sarah looked hopeless, her eyes searching for answers. The last couple of days had taken their toll on her. Her thirteen-year-old mind was like that of someone who had just hit thirty. Experience can do that to you, Katherine thought, still refusing to believe that all of this was happening.

It was quiet except for the churning, dusty engine of the big black Suburban waiting outside. Katherine took one last look at the large sack in the middle of the living room floor. Pictures, Sarah's cheerleader trophies, and so much more piled there like yesterday's news. She collected each fleeting memory. Disheartened, feet glued to the floor, her thoughts unraveling, she thought back on her conversation with Detective Barnes days earlier.

*   *   *   *

"Katherine, we have to protect you. It's not safe as long as this Riggins guy is out there," Detective Barnes had explained as he sat down next to her.

Puzzled and emotionally drained, Katherine glared at him. "*Protect*—what does that mean?" she asked. The cold walls of the New York Seventeenth Precinct echoed as she rested her arms on the coffee-stained table. "Protect!" she repeated. "Do you realize the hell my daughter and I have gone through?" This time she expected an answer from him.

Detective Barnes, somewhat uncomfortable, moved closer, scratched the back of his head and tried to push his thoughts forward. "We have no choice, Katherine," he said, his hands locked together. "Riggins thinks you have the list. And, even though you don't and I believe you, he's convinced you've got it. You and Sarah are not safe until we can get him. You're gonna have to trust us. Will ya do that? Just give us time. We have to gather the evidence against him."

"I don't know," Katherine responded. She leaned forward and rested her head between her hands. "I just don't know," she said, shaking her head in disbelief. "I want to forget about it and move on with our lives. The names on that list mean nothing to me. That's your issue not mine. I wish I'd never seen it. This shouldn't be my problem."

"Just knowing one name can be deadly," Detective Barnes said as he placed his burly hand over hers. "You know too much, Katherine. You're a witness to a confession. That alone makes you a target."

"Confession," she replied, followed by a long sigh. "All I heard Detective Glen say was that he killed for Riggins, that's it. I don't know if that's true or not. And I have no idea who this Riggins is, except that he's some hot shot out to destroy our lives."

"Listen, I understand. But this guy, from what we can tell, is ruthless. He'll kill again. You're a bomb as far as he's concerned! That list included the names of powerful men and their indiscretions. I suspect some congressmen may have been thrown in as well."

"I don't know," she said, diminished. "The names on that list, besides John Walters, are unfamiliar to me. I'm not into politics."

"Katherine, that's what I'm trying to tell you. The fact that you remember anything and heard a confession makes you a target."

Brushing her hair away from her face, she said, "Detective Barnes, I'm still trying to get over the fact that my daughter's father wanted to kill us. When I left him in New York...let me restate that. When his father forced me to leave New York, Nick became different. His father not only threatened to kill me, he was going to disinherit Nick. I had no choice."

"I don't doubt your reason or how you got involved in any of this. All I want to do is help you and your daughter. The last thing I want to do is make this harder on you."

"I didn't say you were, but if something like this can happen to Nick and change him, I don't know if I can trust anyone. Right now, I can't remember a thing. I just want to go home. I never asked for this. I just wish..." Katherine paused. She found it difficult to finish her thought.

They both needed to gather their thoughts. Barnes waited. He hadn't yet told her everything about the full-blown witness protection program she was entering. He had to find the words to inform her, and while he wanted to assure her that it would only be for a short time, he just couldn't. There were too many unanswered questions surrounding the murders of the investment bankers and now the confession of a prominent New York City detective, also dead. Barnes knew that the hapless Detective Glen, who had finally confessed to the murders, had stopped short of killing Katherine and Sarah. But his account still didn't tell Barnes why exactly Riggins had paid him to kill those bankers—assuming, of course, that the detective's confession had been truthful. Barnes wanted desperately to believe and to think that this was the end of the story, but he just couldn't be sure. It didn't fit. And he was determined to find out why. For now, Katherine and Sarah had to be protected. He couldn't allow them to fall victim to a man who would stop at nothing. Without his protection, this was another homicide waiting to happen. That he was sure of.

He stared at Katherine's tired and bruised face. The mustiness and smoke from the basement where she and Sarah were rescued were still fresh in his nostrils. Challenged by his thoughts, he hadn't realized how difficult this was going to be. It was the first time he had ever had to deliver such a message. He thought of how painful it would be for them to take on a new identity and give up their past. He couldn't imagine it happening to his own wife and kids.

Man, this is not easy! he thought, shaking his head. "Katherine, we'll do our best to give you your life back, but for now you have to trust us," he insisted. "Some people from the Bureau are on their way here. They'll work with you. I'm really sorry, and for what it's worth—I know this isn't easy for you, but you're doing the right thing."

Katherine acknowledged him with tired, tear-filled eyes. She searched him wordlessly through her blurred vision. It was excruciatingly difficult—even if she had already reconciled herself to this well before Barnes had walked into the room. A few days ago, her life was normal; she worked at the library and studied for exams. But all of that had abruptly changed. After being stalked, after running like a hunted animal, she was told she had to assume a new identity. Her descent from dignity, she feared, might have a lasting effect on Sarah.

She needed another moment.

Detective Barnes's strategy was in her best interest. She knew that. If nothing else, her brains needed to become sunny-side up instead of scrambled like they were now. She had to bring a semblance of order to their life. She couldn't help it, though—she blurted out, "How am I going to explain this to my daughter? I'll have to explain to her why I never told her that Nick Walters was her real father. This is crazy! How do you explain to a child her father tried to kill her? I can't believe I'm here having this conversation."

After taking a good sip of water, Barnes pulled his chair closer to her. "I can't answer that for you. I can get someone to be with the two of you to help you through this. I realize this is difficult, but you're a survivor, Katherine. I promise I'll do my best to help." It was about the only promise he could make, but he felt good about it.

Exhaling, she looked over at the flag standing in the corner. The stars and stripes. *God Bless America* played in her head, and she pitied herself. Turning to Detective Barnes, she declared, "Telling Sarah the truth will be difficult. After that, it's easy."

*   *   *   *

Katherine watched Sarah being escorted out the door. Her only hope, beyond wishing all this had never happened, was that she and Sarah be allowed to return to their home in Alberville, New York. Tearful, she thought of her father. Though Al had died years ago, she had never felt separated from him. "Who will place fresh flowers on his grave in my absence?" she asked herself.

Drawing a great big breath, she stepped onto the front porch. The door closed right behind her, and she stood no more than three steps away from the vehicle that would take her and Sarah into a place unknown. Refusing to look back at the remnants of Katherine Oberman, she reluctantly stepped forward. She was now Jennifer Perry— though not a whit less uncertain of her future and what was in store for her and Sarah.

A deathly silence surrounded her and Sarah. She had allowed the doors to the casket to close, and now darkness was merging with the gathering clouds overhead as they were driven away.

CHAPTER I

▼

Four years later, Daufuskie Island, Hilton Head, South Carolina

Calabogue Sound welcomed everyone who plied her warm blue waters with gentle, rolling waves. Katherine watched the H-ferry leave the dock and the stillness of the ocean wash towards her hollow mansion. Only the narrow squeak of the rocking chair beneath her could be heard.

She sipped her tea. As the fluid warmed her insides and comforted her soul, she followed the flutter of a butterfly, whose wings threw a rainbow of gentle, dancing movements—until the lonely black-and-yellow maiden landed on the window sill.

She took another sip and prepared for a performance fit for a princess. But there was a sullen beauty in what she saw around her, a beauty eclipsed again by the battlefield erupting inside of her.

Her fingertips rimmed her cup and her mind kept traveling to places she was not ready to revisit.

Katherine placed her cup on the thick, antiquated mahogany table that was slightly cracked. Its etched lines reminded her of those embedded in her palms. There were so many stories hidden beneath the surface of this old table, she mused, secrets so unsettling that they could only be entrusted to someone certain to conceal them. As the rustic smell of the antiquated wood and spiced tea filled her sinuses, she covered her face. She needed to find the strength to bury her thoughts. To allow them to surface would only ignite her smoldering pain.

It was going to be another busy day at the mansion. There was a lot of work to be done, and failing to redirect her thoughts was not an option, if she was going to get through it all. As she struggled, the waiter-cook, Keith, arrived dressed in his colorful day outfit.

"Are you okay?" he asked. "Do I have to pick you up from that table and carry you?"

"I'm fine…just thinking about today," Katherine replied, caressing her cup.

"Jenny, people hate to hear other people complain, but I don't mind. You know how much I like gossip," he said sitting down next to her, his own cup in hand.

"That's good, Keith. Maybe you'll find someone that needs your ear."

"Don't get me wrong. I'm not looking for news, but if it comes my way I'm more than willing to write the story, details included, of course. You know, there is something unusual about the gumbo today. I put my foot in it and it still doesn't taste right," he said, smiling.

"There's your answer," Katherine remarked.

"No, really, it tastes funny. Not right today. I wonder if that new guy has been messing around with the sauce?"

"I hope so. After all, he is the head chef," Katherine said, rubbing her fingers over her cup. "I guess…I mean…that's what I expect when it comes to gumbo."

"You guess!" Keith exclaimed.

"You know what I mean. I really don't like gumbo anyway. It always tastes different to me. Maybe someday I'll learn to appreciate it."

"I wonder about you sometimes, Jenny."

"What do you mean?"

"Guess…you really don't seem like a Lowcountry kinda girl."

"I…I am," she responded, tightening her grip on the cup.

"Sorry, I shouldn't have said that. It's really none of my business. Just trying to know you better. I really didn't mean to pry," Keith said. Pausing, he sipped his coffee, aware he had hit upon a nerve.

Katherine cradled her cup in silence and looked away.

"I'm sorry—I've got to go. Been cooking gumbo since five this morning and I've got to make sure it's right. People are particular about their gumbo around here."

"Keith, remember, too many cooks will spoil the pot."

"I'm no amateur. I know what I'm doing. Hey, my pot is calling me…Later!"

"Sure, see ya."

"If only he knew," she whispered to herself as Keith walked away. She thought she had adjusted well to the Lowcountry, but maybe it was still obvious she hadn't. She wondered about her life and the four years she had spent on Daufuskie Island, trying to adapt. All her life, she had done nothing but adapt—and become more and more enmeshed in a tangle of trust, mistrust and deception. She longed for tranquility, not just her real identity. Was that too much to ask for? Why did she have to be cast away into a witness protection program? It had been four years now and counting.

It wasn't fair—just not right.

She longed for Alberville, and it really bothered her that she was not even allowed to visit Al's grave. *"What kind of a daughter does that make me?"* she asked, feeling the pangs of internal wounds that no one else could see. *"Maybe I really haven't adjusted to any of this, after all."* In one gulp, she took down the rest of her tea, now as tepid as her heart.

The whistle of the early morning H-ferry sounded—the first call of the day.

Katherine watched a flurry of people quicken their steps. Nineteen-year-old Jila was among them. She had become Sarah's friend, and hers too. A native of the island, Jila was proud of her Gullah heritage. Katherine watched from afar as Jila draped her red bag over her shoulder the way only she could do, predictably drawing the attention of other people around her. Her body was perfect and moved like a well-oiled machine. Katherine admired her—Jila was a rare gem who knew, like few others did, how to make her and Sarah feel at home. Maybe it was because she, too, didn't seem to fit in; somehow it didn't bother her at all. Jila just did her thing, working and speaking to anyone who would speak to her. Somewhat unusual behavior for a Southerner, but she didn't care. If you needed to know the truth she would tell you. If you wanted to know about the island she would dazzle you with her stories. She didn't hold back when it came to talking about the island. She wanted all those that cared, as well as those that didn't, to know that her people were the ones who nurtured this island.

Katherine watched as the ferry pulled away. The morning mist hovering over the ocean turned her thoughts back to Keith. *He's right!* she thought, still beating up on herself. She couldn't get his words out of her head. *I have to decide if I'm going to allow myself to fit in.* After all, she had only reluctantly welcomed her new beginnings, and their time on the island promised to be lengthy. The one thing she had going for her was that everyone on Daufuskie Island, including the guests, loved her. She hoped that maybe they, unlike Keith, couldn't see beyond her forced demeanor.

She picked up her cup and headed to the kitchen to prepare herself for the day. She had to welcome the new visitors to the mansion. It still amazed her how they had barged this mansion from a place far away. You'd never know it, except for the pride the owners felt in having purchased it so cheaply.

She powdered her cheeks, carefully attending to her image in the mirror. This was no longer Katherine Oberman. Being unborn was like not being born at all. The thought pained her. The motion of her hand on her cheek ceased as she found herself staring into the reflected eyes of a person she didn't know.

"Jenny! Jenny! Are you in there? Bob's here. He needs to see you." It was Helen, Miss Personality—the dutiful cook who, of late, was fond of playing middleman between Keith and the head chef, Bob. It didn't surprise her that Bob was demanding to see her. Somehow the word gumbo resurfaced. A smile lined her lips as she tried to picture the scene she was about to walk into. Keith had his ways and he knew exactly how to get under Bob's collar.

"Give me a sec, I'll be there," Katherine replied, completing her makeover. "I'm ready," she said to the mirror and took a deep breath.

CHAPTER 2

▼

The island was enveloped in the warmth of a typical Southern day. Unlike Katherine, Sarah—now Amy—had no issue with her new environment. She was into activities and people, especially Jila. The two girls had bonded like glue. This amazed Katherine. They were so different, yet there was something unique about their friendship that only they understood.

Sarah and Jila took their usual spot on the beach overlooking the great Atlantic and the shoreline of Hilton Head. High on the Richter scale, Sarah was in full bitch about her tennis match.

"I can't wait to play this afternoon. Alison thinks she's hot stuff. I almost beat her the last time we played. I hate it when I lose to her. She tells everyone and laughs as if she's done something big. You'd think she just beat a tennis pro. That grin of hers is, like, *so-o-o* annoying."

"Don' care for the game maself," Jila countered. "I'd rather walk on the beach. Ya see this here seashell? Beauty, ain't it? Look at all the lines. Sometimes I wonder 'bout 'em. Kinda 'minds me of the lines in ma hands."

"I never thought about them much."

Jila brushed off a few of the shells she had gathered. "Amy, I can tell ya ain't from 'round here."

"You know I'm not! But why do you say that? I like collecting shells—don't get me wrong. They're pretty. But I mean, do you want a public-service announcement from me?" Sarah asked.

Laughing, Jila quickly answered, "Thas' what I like 'bout ya. Ya speak ya mind. Never worryin' none 'bout what ya thinkin'. Didn't mean nothin' bad, jus' those that knows this island, well..." She smiled. "Ah, heck, I jus' love this place, I really do."

"I believe you, Jila. I can tell, but it's going to take a lot to make a geisha girl out of me."

"I think ya means *Gullah*."

"Whatever—you know what I meant. Jila, you're at home here. But I like this place, too. I just...I mean, I'm working on it. Whenever you look out on the ocean, I see a deep calm on your face. I feel you've lived longer than your years, if you know what I mean," Sarah said, her eyes wandering between Jila and the harbor town lighthouse as Jila lightly dusted off her shell with her fingers.

"Ya maybe right. At times I feel like I bin here before. My folks tells me I have. Guess maybe thas' why this place is so special. I don' know. I jus' believe there's a whole lot more to our lives than we understands. Look—ya young in body, but ya mind live a life twice ya age. Am I right?"

"I wouldn't say that," Sarah replied, shifting her position to cool her skin. "Jila, every time we come to the beach you seem different." They traded questioning looks. "I mean, this seems like a special place for you. The shells and everything. You're able to lose yourself in this place. I enjoy being here, but it's different for you, isn't it?"

"It *is* special. Ya probably lookin' at this here shell"—she held the shell in her hand for Sarah to ponder—"jus' like any ol' shell. Things to throw in a bowl and say ya collected 'em on the beach. They ain't so for me, though."

Sarah hung onto each word. The heat of the sand felt more bearable.

Jila continued, "When I find shells and hold them in ma hand, it's kinda like holdin' someone ya love. Each of 'em got life inside and they done helped shelter ma people." She brought several up closer before Sarah's eyes. "Yeah, 'em shells, they gots meanin' way more 'an anythin' ya or I can imagine. Mama tol' me stories 'bout how hard my people looked for 'em. They used 'em to put a roof over their heads. She even tol' stories she heard 'bout men dyin' or bein' overcome by the heat—they was all tryin' to build their homes. Here, hold this and close your eyes."

They sat eyes closed, Indian style, as they baked in the honeysuckle heat. The soft ocean wind whispered in their ears as birds flew high above. Sarah, feeling the heavy heat on her eyelids, waited. Jila had her full attention.

"Feel it? Amy? Jus' keep ya eyes closed. Let the waves talk to ya. There—feel it?" she asked again, her hands piled on top of Sarah's. Sandwiched between the two pairs of hands rested a hollow shell, soaked with perspiration. "Do ya hear it?" She closed her eyes again. In Jila's head appeared a day brighter than any that Sarah had seen, and surely enough, the soft sounds of drums began to beat. A vision of her native people spread before her mind's eye. They were happy, singing just for the joy of it, their clothes drenched in sweat. Women carried buckets of shells on their heads as they made their way back from the shoreline, their skirts soaked by the great Atlantic. Men, their bare feet deep in the wet dirt, piled shells one on top of the other, mixing them with a thick clay-like material. In the middle of the festive scene stood a ginger black man with pearl teeth that matched his shirt. His long gray ankle-length pants, wet to the knees, draped the earth beneath him. His smile was simple and comforting, and his eyes were fixed on Jila, his daughter. Like army ants the people worked on against a backdrop of rich green earth. Old oaks rose up majestically and their branches stretched almost to a city block in length.

"Amy, do ya feel it?" Jila asked. Her proud smile lit up her face as sweat dripped from their hands that were still pressed together. Tears of joy streamed down her cheeks. It was a beautiful vision, and her smile was that of the ginger man.

When Jila finally broke her trance, she opened her eyes to the blinding sun, but she felt peaceful. She had gone to Gullah Heaven again. Sarah, frazzled by the hot sun, felt her own calm.

"Ya see, Amy, them topless homes made o' seashells, marked HISTORIC LANDMARKS, those ones ya see when ya get off the H-ferry, at the end of the island dock? Ya know, the ones they call tabby homes. My people built 'em, jus' like they nurtured this land. They done picked Sea Island cotton till their fingers bled, but they made this ol' cotton-bearin' land what it is today. Without 'em, none o' this'd be here. Their souls lay deeper than the roots of 'em trees ya see yonder. And they all 'round us. I can hear their voices in the wind, day and night. I feel 'em with me all the time, especial' when I get up real close to the water. Ever' time I set foot on this here prepared earth, ever' time I feel the sand massagin' ma weary toes, ever' time I see a shell, I feel it and hear it all at once. Their joy proud, Amy! They gives me more strength than I reckon. They all 'round us. Guess I live fo' this earth. Them shells is souls waitin' to be found. Can ya feel it? They right here, lookin' over us, Amy!"

Sarah sat silently listening to Jila's calm, sage voice. She took a deep breath, and with one hand shielding her eyes from the bright sun, she found Jila's sparkling brown eyes gazing into hers. Her armpits pasted in summer sweat and her legs fried on the searing sand underneath her, she smiled. Like an egg cracking, their hands unlocked.

Sarah's hand cupped a shell like a baby chick, except this one had red crab legs sticking out. Jila's eyes searched her friend's face for an indication of what she intended to do. But the breeze just kept blowing. Then Sarah said, "Jila, I feel kinda strange. I'm beginning to understand why you love this land so much. I'll never look at a shell the same way ever again, or think of this place as just a place." But now, she couldn't bear the heat any more. "Boy, is it hot! Let's cool off."

CHAPTER 3

▼

It was a perfect—if stifling—summer day with a low constant wind. Everyone was out basking in the sun. The beach club was filled with children swimming and splashing in the tepid water. Seagulls, wings spread wide, hovered above waiting for an unguarded sandwich or crumb. The big blue seemed taciturn, a mirror image of the sky above. Not a plane in sight to obscure the clear sky that overarched the people of Daufuskie below.

At the mansion Keith was hard at work serving food with style. "Make them want to come back," he always said—he was a perfectionist. That's how well management had trained him. He was their good find, a natural at his job. He delivered with proud perfection and dressed his part. His creased pants and freshly pressed Hawaiian shirt iced his performance. Keith walked with a slight limp that became more prominent with the cold weather. If he had not told everyone about his injury, those who didn't know him better would probably have taken it as a proud man's walk. But as only Keith could do, he had to add special flair to his own ailment.

"The soup—it's really good today," Keith said to one of the golfers. It was close to high noon—the blistering bright heat baking the earth and lighting up the mansion confirmed it. Visitors and residents continued to flock in, keeping the H-ferry busy. Realtors were on high, selling the land as if it were gold. That's what everyone imagined it was. It was the land that sold itself. No one who traveled onto the island wanted to leave. And those that lived there had become somewhat selfish over time. They wanted to keep their hidden paradise to themselves. But the place hadn't been this busy since Melrose's golf tournament, and that was years ago. The word was out, everyone wanted a stake in H-Point. The island was not for everyone, but its marketing was so successful it lured many people that no one was counting on. On this day, the bar nestled in the center of the mansion held a standing-room-only crowd. Beer—that was the favorite, followed by the endless chatter.

Katherine was busy sorting papers and verifying receipts. Lowcountry humidity toasted the corner room where she had made her office. It wasn't her favorite task. It had become a part of the job and she was good at it, but the drudgery of reading name after name triggered some unsorted memories.

"Hey, Jenny!" Keith called. "Amy wanted you to know if she and Jila could escape."

"*Escape*, Keith?" Katherine asked with a quizzical look.

"Yeah, Jila wants to go shopping," he said. "You know, like spending cash for fun."

"I get the picture, thanks. I'd better give her a quick call."

"Honey, you'd better do something better than a call," he said. "If I were you I'd close my bank account. That girl looks like she can spend some money." Keith was grinning as he flirted dangerously with Katherine's patience. Just in time, he noticed the beads of sweat on her forehead. "Okay, okay, I'm reaching my limit for today, I know. Boss in heat. I'll back off," he said, still grinning, but then decided quickly to redeem himself with a message he'd forgotten to pass on to her. "By the way, some guy called for you the other day. He didn't leave his name."

"Some guy? What did he say?" she asked, curious.

"Just asked if Jenny Perry worked here. I told him you did. Said he would call back. Must have been one of those old geezers calling on you again. I'm sure he'll call back."

"Something to think about…"

"Anything wrong?" He leaned against the wall.

"Oh forget it, I don't have the time. You'd better get back there," Katherine ordered.

"Yes, I'd better…to find you some coolant. I think the heat is getting to you."

"Spare yourself the trouble. I'm fine," she replied, pulling the phone next to her as she sat at her desk.

"Later, then. Sounds like Mr. Hassel is upset about something," Keith quipped.

"Yeah, his beer glass must be empty, I'm sure," Katherine replied, but by then, Keith was well beyond earshot.

$$* \qquad * \qquad * \qquad *$$

"Hurry up, Amy," Jila yelled, holding her stomach. "Water-taxi leavin' in twenty minutes. We miss this one and we have to wait a whole hour. I got major shoppin' to do and I wanna make sho' I get me some of that fresh fish at Frank's. Ya hurry now—I'm salivatin'."

"Sure, Jila—shopping," Sarah sarcastically replied as she put on her make-up "This wouldn't have anything to do with Mike? My mom told me he was running the water-taxi today."

"Mike," Jila repeated with a devilish look on her face. "What makes ya think that?"

"Oh, nothing. I'm ready." Sarah emerged from her room, and Jila's expression changed to a smirk. Jila had on her hot red tank-top, hip-fitted capri pants, and perfectly polished nails and toes to match. Trading quick glances, the two headed out the door.

The pedal to the floor, their golf-cart couldn't move fast enough for Jila. "This is when I wish I had a car," she said, impatient.

"Calm down, we're almost there. Look—I can see Mike!" said Sarah.

"Where?" Jila asked, almost falling out of the cart before hearing an amused "fooled you!"

"Ya day'll come and I can't wait. How does that go 'gain? What goes around comes abound."

They laughed for a good while, but when all the humor expired, a solemn mood overtook Sarah. "How long have you lived here?" she asked.

"The island? All ma life. Ya know that."

"Nothing, just asking," Sarah said and parked the cart. "Sorry about fooling you back there."

"Like I said, ya day will come." Jila hid her smile, and they headed towards the boat.

*   *   *   *

"Careful, watch your step, folks," Mike said as he helped the girls onto the boat. Jila, wearing a before-glow, sat witless, watching his smooth lips and perfect whites. She practically went into a swoon looking at his head-to-toe white ensemble and ripped body; she sighed and watched him walk away, fixing her eyes on the briefs outlined underneath his pants. Sarah, holding onto her shoulder bag, chuckled as she watched them interact.

The quick ride across the short stretch of Atlantic Ocean was dizzyingly spectacular. A mist of cool water splashed their faces, and when they arrived, Jila was so refreshed she was ready to hop off the boat by herself. But with a quick wink, she signaled Sarah to go first, who in turn obligingly gave Mike her hand and returned Jila's wink. Jila, her Indian pattern bag hanging from her shoulder, followed and confidently shared a smile with Mike. Pretty soon she was strutting up the dock with Sarah in tow, wading through the crowd surrounding them. Only she knew how to do this. Masculine eyes from every direction were locked on her, though none more closely than Mike's—and she knew it. The only problem was that it embarrassed young Sarah, who whispered in her ear, "Jila, I don't know about you sometimes."

They both bid Mike goodbye.

"Actin'!" Jila replied. "Part of the enjoyment of bein' on this island. Sho' is nice gettin' 'way, ain't it?" Before Sarah could reply, Jila noticed another crowd gathering at a distance. "Amy, somethin' goin' on over there. Look—Channel Two News. Must be a star or somethin'. Les' go," she urged.

"I'll wait here, you go ahead."

"Come on, les' see what's happnin'. Ain't everyday ya get this chance. I remember, durin' the big golf tournament, that cute guy—ya know, the young black guy, one that wins all the tournaments—walks right past me and I almost touch 'im."

"You'd have to be dead not to know who he is, Jila!" Sarah was surprised and waited to see where Jila was going with this.

"I know ya right—I jus' didn't have the nerve to get his name."

"His name," Sarah repeated, rolling her eyes.

"Ya know what I mean. His name in the papers all the time. Maybe he's back. Come on, les' go together."

"Naw, you go. I'll wait...*Go ahead! Don't be shy.*"

"Come on, Amy, what's the matter with ya?"

"No, I said! I'll wait for you, Jila."

Repositioning the strap of her bag, Jila said, "Forget 'bout it. Les' get us somethin' to eat. Is that okay?"

"Yeah, whatever. Sorry, I just don't like crowds," Sarah explained.

"Fine. I'm sho' we'll find out later. Ya okay?"

"I'm fine, it must have been the ride over. Sometimes boats make me a little sick."

"I gotta have somethin' to eat. Ya look like ya need some food, too."

At the restaurant, they ordered fish and fries, and pretty soon they were deep in small talk. Jila, still troubled by Sarah's brusque reaction earlier, but trying to brush aside her changed demeanor, watched with concern as Sarah played with her food and fell completely silent for long moments while avoiding eye contact.

As they ate their meal and gossiped intermittently, a pair of interested eyes watched from outside. Nick Walters—tall, well tanned, speckled-haired, Italian-looking—was dressed in a perfectly tailored pale linen suit that blended well with the panoramic view behind him.

"Hey, waiting for someone, Good Looking?" a hot blond wearing a halter top that begged for attention paused a few feet away. His ears might as well have vanished; only his eyes were turned on.

He didn't answer.

In the restaurant, the waiter was asking the girls if they wanted some dessert, and didn't seem to want to take no for an answer.

"No, can't eat 'nother bite. I'm full," Jila said, holding her stomach.

"Me too," said Sarah. They both chuckled, having taken in more than their share.

"One last time, ladies: the chocolate cake is *really* good today," he said.

"I believe you, but I can't." Sarah said as she looked at Jila, who waved her hand in front of her face and said, "I wouldn't be able to shop."

"I'll bring you the check. But you're sure now, ladies?" he insisted with a mirthful look.

"Yeah, we're done," said Sarah.

"I tried. Be back in a jiffy."

"Jila, you're such a flirt. I saw the way you looked at him."

"Not interested. Jus' enjoyin' the conversation."

"What conversation, Jila? All he did was ask if we wanted dessert about a thousand times or more."

"Jus' wants to talk, and he's cute. I thought maybe the two of ya might make a nice couple." But when Sarah hit her with an impatient look, Jila knew she'd better move on. "Jus' kiddin'. But he sho' has a nice smile."

"They must have put something in your iced tea, or maybe the sun struck you. Maybe Mike will wake you up. I think we'd better get you back to the boat."

"I'm wide 'wake. But, Amy, ya don' seem interested in anyone on the island."

"Jila, ever think that maybe I'm okay with that? Let's go shopping before I change my mind and head for our boat."

"All right, I'm ready. Let me see that smile," Jila said, grabbing Sarah's arm. Each supported the other as they headed out the door. Neither of them paid any attention to the man standing before the window pane. They were back to their usual selves, chattering away as if their lips had been sealed for years. As they browsed the shops, Nick followed at a watchful distance. He looked down again at the picture he held in his hand. A saddened look slapped his face. It was a picture of Sarah—years removed.

*   *   *   *

"Amy, I'm tired. The boat should be here in a minute or two. Les' sit down. My feet are hot. I can't wait to take off these sandals. The more I walk the tighter they get."

"I know what you mean. I hate it when leather gets hot. That's why I put on something else. Let's sit over there—those rocking chairs are calling us."

"Next time we come over here, we need to eat *after* we shop. That food wore me out."

"Kind of like eating your mama's food. I feel that way every time I eat at your house."

"That's good, keep comin' over. That'll help me keep off 'em pounds. I gained 'bout ten this summer."

"Please, let's stop talking about food. It's starting to make me sick all over again."

Jila leaned back in the chair listening to the music in the background. "Oh, it feels good to sit down. If I kick these sandals off they might jus' land in the ocean," she said, legs stretched out, smiling.

"Don't get too comfortable, here comes the boat."

"Ya, shoulda never wore those jeans, Amy. Nice, but they look real hot."

"You're startin' to sound like my Mom." Sarah sighed and closed her eyes, trying to find the strength to stand up.

"Wake up, let's go! It's here," Jila yelled.

"I like that music," Sarah said, "and I really like this place, don't you?"

"I do, but I'm ready to git back to our quiet lil' island." Jila tried to get up but plumped right back into her rocking chair. "W-o-o…that's why I hate sittin' down on a hot one like today. I hate gettin' up," she said, before swinging herself to her feet and walking away, bags in hand.

"Wait for me!" Sarah yelled out feebly, slowly gathering herself. Jila walked briskly, and the next time Sarah lifted her head to see how far her friend had gone, Jila was getting onto the boat. But just then, in a split-second, she cleanly missed her footing. Luckily, Mike had been staring at her and caught her arm in time, then gently assisted her to her seat. Sarah watched with a pleased grin on her face, trying to figure out where Jila's burst of energy had suddenly come from.

Within seconds they were speeding back through the cool sprinkle of Southern ocean mist, ever closer to the island, their heads laid back. As the boat moved away, Nick watched from afar. He knew he had to get there.

CHAPTER 4

▼

"Mom, I'm back! I'm at home," said Sarah as Katherine listened intently on the other end of the telephone line. "I had the catfish, and it was out of this world. We ate like pigs...yeah, Jila, too. She was so full she almost fell getting on the boat." Sarah laughed and then listened to Katherine's tired voice. "I'll be here. I don't think I could do anything until I take a nap. Have to peel myself...out of these...jeans," she said, wrestling them down to her feet and then kicking them off. "I know, don't say it. I already heard it from Jila...No, she's not here; she went home. I'll see her later this evening. She wants to go down to the beach club, then we plan to go to her house...All right, I will. I'm gonna try to do some reading. I promised myself that I'd finish *Beyond The Umbilical Cord*. It's a great book. What? You gonna read it after I finish?...Okay. Later, Mom. Don't be late."

Outside, construction workers were busy casting roofs high above the greens and the big blue. Each new home looked different from the others. The days were long and arduous. Everyone on Daufuskie made the most of each minute.

Sarah went to the porch, book in hand, and sat at her usual place. She hoped to save her energy for that evening, with Jila, and it wasn't long before *Beyond The Umbilical Cord* slipped down onto her lap and she fell fast asleep to the distant tapping of hammers beating like woodpeckers.

*   *   *   *

"Excuse me, that boat you just got off—when will it be back? I want to see the island," Nick inquired. The tired old golfer, Mr. Hassel, removed his hat and wiped his forehead, his gut full of beer.

"The boat'll be back in an hour, but I don't think you can get on it. Private, you understand. For the Islanders—only people who can ride on it. If you want to see the island, there's a realty company over there." He belched and apologized, and then pointed to the realtor's office nearby. "They can arrange for you to take a tour. That's what I did, and next thing I knew I couldn't get enough of the place. They'd be able to help you."

"Thanks," Nick said as Mr. Hassel walked away. Friendly fella, he thought, and headed to the real estate office. "Hi, I'd like to take a tour of the island. A guy told me once you go there you never want to leave. That true?"

"Yeah, but we don't give tours. Are you interested in property?" the woman asked. "That's about the only way you can get on the island, 'less you live there."

"I'm interested, that's one of the main reasons I'm here. I heard about the place and couldn't wait to see it."

"What type of place are you looking for, sir? You can either buy or build? There're a few homes for sale, or you can just buy land and build when you're ready. You have a few options."

"Not really sure at this point...I'm just interested. How about you make arrangements for me to see the place?" he said, ready to go.

"We can arrange for someone to come and get you. Don't think anyone's available today, though. Give me a minute, I'll be right back—okay?"

"Sure thing, take your time," Nick said. He grabbed a brochure to browse through while waiting. He thought of Katherine. The last time he had a chance to talk to her, they were separated by bars. He had to explain everything to her, but she just wasn't a good listener. All she wanted to know was what in the hell happened to him. Maybe it'll be easier this time. As shaken as he was after overhearing a conversation between his father and a colleague of Riggins, the sheer joy of finding Katherine and Sarah again buoyed him. His father had mentioned that they were hiding somewhere in South Carolina and that Riggins was about to expose them. Just like before, Riggins and Barry were plotting, only this time he was not included in the plan. He knew he had to get to Katherine.

But there were so many apologies he needed to make to her it scared him. This unplanned reunion was important to him, whether or not she accepted his word, but it was even more important to protect Katherine and Sarah. Prison had changed him. It had restored his mental balance, which he had always had in him—it was just buried by the heady circumstances that had led to his incarceration. Wiping his forehead, he waited, wrinkled brochure in hand.

"Sir, I'm sorry, there isn't anyone available today. I spoke with Tom, one of the realtors, and he'd be happy to pick you up in the morning 'round eleven. It's really busy this time of the year. They've been swamped."

The disappointment showed on Nick's face. "Can't I just go over and take a look on my own?"

"I wish that was the way they did it. You have to be escorted by someone. I'm sorry, would you like to think about it?" she asked.

"No, I'll be here in the morning. Eleven, right?"

"That's right, sir."

"I'll see you then, thanks," Nick said.

"Sir, you forgot the packet. Take a look at it. It'll tell you all about the island and what property is available. If you have any questions, please don't hesitate to give me a call. My home number is on the card."

"Thanks, I'll do that," he remarked and exited.

"Just my luck," Nick said to himself, watching the people passing him by like yesterday's news. But he didn't care. His focus quickly shifted back to Daufuskie, and he gazed at the captivating H-Point lighthouse and the trees outlining the shore.

CHAPTER 5

▼

When Sarah came by, she and Jila relaxed on the porch. It was a quiet warm evening, disturbed only by the squeaks of their rocking chairs. The fragrance of healthy flowers filled their nostrils, but this couldn't compare with the heavenly aroma wafting from inside as Mama lifted the last piece of fried chicken from the large pan.

Deep in thought, Sarah rocked on. Hovering high above, twinkling lights filled her sight.

"Fib minutes, dinnuh gwine be dun," Mama yelled.

Laughing, Jila turned to Sarah and mimicked Mama's words: "*Dinnuh gwine be dun.*"

"Stop it, Jila, you're sick!"

"Amy, I ain't tryin' to be funny. I like givin' Mama a hard time; she used to it. I love hearin' her speak Gullah. It makes her more comfortable."

"I understand her when she does that. I'm just glad she feels comfortable around me."

"You bin 'round her long enough. She love havin' ya here. Tol' me herself she never seen nobody 'joyin' her food like ya."

"I love Mama's cooking. Wish my mom cooked like that."

"She a good cook, but so is Jenny. That fish we had the other night at ya house? Real good that was. Now, if Jenny'da added a little flour and dropped it into a fryin' pan, don' know if we be sittin' here tonight," she said, laughing.

"Jila, don't get me wrong. I like my mom's cooking. But if we brought Mama over for a few tips, I might actually love it." She smiled, satisfied with her play of words.

"I don' know what to say 'bout ya, Amy…" Jila began, before Sarah, without warning, fell into a trance-like state. Jila had witnessed this before, but every time it passed quickly and was easily forgotten in the effervescence of their conversation. Jila now wondered if something was not right. Sarah was too often beside herself.

"Amy, can I ask ya somethin'?"

"What now?"

"Is everythin' all right with ya?

"I told you I was fine?"

"You ain't talkin' much. Maybe ya think y'are, but—"

"Jila, I said I'm okay. Just thinking."

"Why y'all actin' like somethin's botherin' ya, then? I see it in ya eyes, especial' when ya get that strange look on ya face. The otha day on the beach—ya sho' lost me…like tonight. Jus' a feelin'…ya don't have to answer, I guess."

"I thought we were having a good time on the beach."

"*I* was—I didn't say I wasn't. But ya was all preoccupied with some-thin', I don' know what."

"You wouldn't understand, Jila. My life isn't as simple as yours…I'm sorry, I didn't mean it that way."

"Forget 'bout it. I'm sorry I asked—it's really no business o' mine. Ya remind me of ma brother; he get kinda moody at times. He likes people, but I think he loves bein' all by himself."

"I'm not like that at all. I like being with people. Don't try to label me," Sarah said.

"Sorry ya feel that way, but I'aint, really I'aint, Amy," Jila replied, laying a look on Sarah that spoke for itself. For the first time in a long while they stared at each other without a smile. The air was awkward. It had been so much easier the day they had first met.

"How would it make you feel," Sarah began pensively, "if you found out I was someone else, not the person I said I was? Would that bother you?"

Jila sat still on the edge of her seat. "Amy, I like ya. Ya my best friend, but—" Just then, Mama came to the window and stood there, grease-spattered apron and all, her hair dusted with flour. The smell of chicken had reached high noon, but Mama sensed that something more important was unfolding outside, and she turned quietly away.

"I know somethin' ain't right. What ya tryin' to tell me, Amy?"

Tearful, Sarah struggled to regain her composure. "Just that, Jila— I'm not who you think I am. I mean…You have to keep this to your- self—I'm really someone else."

Unsure of what to say, Jila pondered her best friend's words. She had never seen her like this before. "Ya can trust me. Ya know ya can," she said, masking her confusion. "Somethin's troublin' ya bad. Bin that way fo' a long spell, I know. Ya haven' bin yaself. Everythin' bothers ya. When we went shoppin', I really thought ya was mad at me 'bout somethin'—somethin' I did. Or maybe it's Jenny? I know she bin wor- kin' lotta hours lately."

"Everything's okay, I'm used to her working like that. Things will slow down after Labor Day." Sarah paused, but she didn't want Jila to think she was sinking into one of her trances again. It's a long story, but I can't keep it inside anymore. Promise me you won't say a word. Please," she begged.

"Whatever it is, I've learned a thin' or two of ma own in nineteen years. And trustin' 'n supportin' those ya care 'bout is two of 'em already. *Promise!*"

Sarah was too ashamed to look into Jila's eyes. Her secrets were bur- ied deep, and she struggled to pull out whatever she could. She wiped her eyes, hesitated for a moment and then began to speak slowly. "Jila, one day, some years ago, while coming home from school I found a bag of money in the woods which included a list of bad men's names. My school janitor called and told my mom that a strange man was searching for us. She quickly realized that he wanted that list we found, and we needed to get help fast. Especially after we realized that some of the men named on the list had been recently murdered. Anyway, the bad men were on our trail so fast we had no time to think. My mom trusted a detective she knew when she was living in New York, so she had to get to him, especially after realizing that detectives from Alberville—that's a town in New York state—were also named on that list. The next thing I knew we were running as if we had stolen something. We had to abandon our car, hide out in a strange home and hotel, and eventually we made it to New York. I was so exhausted, Jila. I remember it all so well. We rested for a while in an abandoned building—a dark basement. We were frightened to death! Then, we heard footsteps coming. A man yelled, 'I know you're down here. Come on out, I won't hurt you. All I want is the list'."

Sarah wiped some sweat from her forehead and went on.

"I couldn't stop shaking. When my mom saw the man, she jumped out and began fighting to protect me. I couldn't stop screaming. When she couldn't fight anymore, she yelled for me to run. But I couldn't, Jila!" Sarah looked intensely into her friend's eyes. "A gun went off. I didn't hear my mom, so I thought she was dead. I was hysterical—screaming out of my head. The next thing I knew this guy had me in his arms with a gun to my head and was shouting, 'Where's the list, where's the list!' Then I heard Mom moaning. I was so relieved she wasn't dead, but I could barely catch my breath. The man was holding me real tight and kept yelling, 'Where's the list, dammit? Shut up, shut up!'

"Then the backdoor to the basement flew open. It was a detective named Glen, and he shot the man holding me. I was trapped as the injured man fell. I couldn't move or scream. The next thing I knew this detective was standing over the three of us, holding a gun and a flashlight. And, Jila, you won't believe this, the detective then said,

'The only one getting a list today is me.' I couldn't believe it. I thought he was there to help us.

"I was in shock and the injured man held me tight. Then I saw Mom look straight in my direction and yell out at the top of her voice, 'Oh, my God! Nick! No, Nick, why? What are you doing? She's your daughter, Nick! Please don't hurt her!'" "This is how I found out that this Nick guy was my father. I later found out also he had a five-leaf-clover tattoo done on his arm, like my mom's pendant—when they were going out. Well, she had recognized it.

"I didn't know what to think. The basement was starting to fill up with smoke. The detective kept yelling for the list and then he snatched me away from Nick and pointed the gun to my head and shouted, 'I will kill her!' My Mom begged him not to, and kept repeating, 'Why?' He said it was because of the money and that some guy named Riggins was paying him. He even confessed to killing some other men on Riggins' behalf. Mom begged him not to kill us. But he refused to listen. He started counting—he said if we didn't give him the list by the time he got to ten, he'd kill all of us. I can still hear him counting and my mom's voice crying out for help. She kept telling him we didn't have the list anymore. We'd lost it when I almost fell into the Harlem River, but he didn't believe us. The last thing I remember is him calling her a liar and yelling out the number eight. Then I heard another shot. Detective Ganelli killed him.

"It was like a scene out of a movie. We were surrounded by police officers and detectives as they brought us out of that building. And that's why we're here, Jila. We were placed in the witness protection program, because everyone feared what this Riggins guy might do. They told us there were a lot of people involved in this and it would take some time to gather all the evidence. That's why I seem troubled sometimes. I'm still afraid. And it's hard knowing your name is Sarah and your mother's name's Katherine, and having to respond to Amy and Jenny. I guess we've grown used to it. Mom's better at this than I am."

Jila was agape. By the end of it, she could only marvel at how incredible Amy's—or was it Sarah's—story was.

Salty tears streamed down Sarah's cheeks. Her words had come straight from the heart. Jila stared with her brown eyes. So many questions she wanted to ask! But she now understood the pain that must have been gnawing at Sarah's guts.

As for Sarah, she couldn't even believe what she had just done. Yet she seemed relieved and reborn, now that it had all come out. No longer would she have to suffer alone with a secret that only Katherine and she knew.

But why now? Jila asked herself.

Sarah's heart raced, her chest throbbed. It was as if she had unzipped her skin. She wanted to run away but she couldn't move. "Oh, Jila!" she cried out, covering her face.

Jila held her in her arms and sobbed. "Amy, I'm so sorry. Would ya prefer I call ya Sarah when we're together?"

"No, it's not safe," Sarah hastily replied.

Other questions swam inside Jila's head that she dared not ask. Sarah's well-being was more important.

Sarah rested her head on Jila's shoulder.

"Lord, give me strength," Jila prayed silently as she held Sarah tight in her arms.

CHAPTER 6

▼

A new day began.

Sarah and Jila were back on the beach, searching for seashells and listening and dancing to the music. *Daylight come and me wanna go home*—the words rang out from Jila's music box. Sarah sang along, mimicking Jila's soulful strut. Twisting and gyrating as if they had a hula-hoop around them, their laughter was infectious, and boaters passing by whistled and screamed for more, thinking they were witnessing some authentic island culture. Jila, a natural, played for their attention. Teasing her thin cotton skirt she twirled and turned herself into a human umbrella. Sarah was enjoying the groove and trying to keep pace, but she was no match for her friend. She gasped for breath before her small frame fell into the warm sand, a bucket of shells sprawled next to her. She was laughing. In her playfulness there was joyful release.

"Jila, I haven't had this much fun in a long time. "*Daylight come and me don't wanna go home,*" she sang.

"Ya sick," Jila said, winded. "People must think we got nothin' better to do. Did ya see Mr. Gray drivin' by? He almost flip his golf cart. Musta bin that hip action and that twistin' y'all were doin'," she snickered.

"I don't think so. I'm sure it was that stack you were waving. The way he was looking at you, I thought it was Mike. Believe me, it wasn't me—my butt could use some help."

Grinning, Jila said, "Amy, ya need to be locked 'way, and the key destroyed." Noticing that Sarah did not respond to her joke, Jila added, "Ya know what I mean, don' ya?"

"Yeah. Just thinking."

"What 'bout?"

"It just made me think about how I felt when I first came to the island. Things have really changed since then," she said, shaking the sand out of her hair. "I feel good."

"I'm glad ya finally happy. Ya given this place life—them rich folks don' know much how to take ya. And they ain't used to seein' much of me, either. They probably thinkin', Why won't she stay over on the far side o' the island."

"Oh, Jila, why do you say that? You're as much a part of this place as me. Just 'cause you live outside these gates doesn't mean you don't belong here. Remember what you said to me—your family nurtured and seeded this island. Has anyone ever led you to believe otherwise?"

"No, don' reckon anybody did. Not really. It's jus'…when I look 'round, where do I see my people. They all cooks, grounds keepers, baggage carriers for the rich white folks. Not one of 'em livin' here. That don' bother ya any?"

"Sure, but that's today; tomorrow will be different. Look at me, I come from mixed blood. I live here and my mom runs the mansion. I hope you're not trying to say they're prejudiced, because I don't feel that way. I know I can be a little naive at times, but I don't think I'm missing something here."

"Ya life's different. What my family done seen tells me different. One thin' I *will* say, though: people is tryin'. The tryin' jus' needs to get harder."

"Wow, I guess it's your turn to lay on the heavy, huh? I wasn't expecting this. I want to understand. I just don't want you to think that I don't care."

"I'd never think that. I've come to know ya and Jenny too well. Aw, les' forget 'bout all of this."

"No, we need to talk like this sometimes, that's what friends are for. Don't ever think you can't talk about something with me. We're here for each other. There's a special reason why we've been brought together." Sarah rubbed her shell.

"There is," Jila echoed. Her smooth cocoa skin relaxed as she gazed upon the big blue.

"I have an idea, let's travel," Sarah suggested, excited. "I think we both need a trip."

"Travel," Jila repeated in a toneless voice.

"Yeah, let's visit Gullah Heaven."

"Do ya really mean it?" Jila asked, surprised.

"Of course, I do," Sarah said, reaching out for Jila's hand. The two of them, eyes closed, began a soft chant. Their hearts felt lighter as their minds entered the place that heals troubled souls.

*   *   *   *

The water-taxi was at full throttle, ready for its short journey to Daufuskie. The captain, half his face hidden behind his sunglasses, hummed his favorite tune and ignored the first mate. He was trying to catch up on the news, the pages of his newspaper flapping in the wind. Outside the cabin, smelling the salty ocean air, sat Nick and Tom, glancing at dolphins tirelessly swimming their welcome dance.

The trip took barely twenty minutes. As they approached the other side, the engine's pitch suddenly plummeted and they began pulling up next to the dock. Nick watched as passengers boarded the H-ferry. Compared to the water-taxi, this was the Titanic. They disembarked and walked the long dock towards the cart barn, the smell of oleanders in the air.

"Is it always this peaceful here?" Nick asked, awed by the huge oaks and quiet beauty.

"You haven't seen anything yet. Ain't for everyone, but we want to keep it that way. You'll see—kinda like living on your own estate."

"It feels that way," Nick said. "I'm sure I'll have lots of questions."

"I'm sure you will, and I'll do my best to answer them. We'll have plenty of time," Tom said. "Here comes Brian. He's been with us for a couple of years."

"That's a good sign," Nick said, preoccupied.

"Brian, this is John. He's thinking about buying here." Nick felt somewhat awkward hearing himself being called John, his middle name, which he never used in normal circumstances.

"Good place, John. Anything I can do to help, this is where you can find me."

"Thanks," Nick said.

"Brian, if anyone comes looking for me, let them know I'm with a client. I'll be back in a couple of hours."

"Will do. See ya later," he yelled as Nick and Tom drove away.

"Everyone this polite?" Nick asked.

"Our company prides itself on customer service and making everyone feel at home, especially our guests." Tom was conscious about the stereotype of the garrulous salesman, so he drove on quietly for a few seconds, then he couldn't hold out any more. "By the way, I've been meaning to tell you I really like your hat. Looks kind of European."

"It is. I get sunburned easily."

"I keep a sunscreen on all the time this time of year. I've been burnt a few times and it's painful."

"As I was saying, I heard about the island while strolling along the boardwalk over on Hilton Head. A golfer told me about it."

"That doesn't surprise me none. We have a lot of golfers visit the island and they're all in love with us. Do you golf?"

"No, not really. Occasionally, I go out and hit the ball, usually for the business. That's it."

"Maybe if you lived here you'd play more—it's addictive."

"If I lived here, I'm not sure what I would do besides relax."

"Sounds like you need a break."

"You might say that."

"So what do you do?" Tom finally asked.

"I run an investment firm. Took over the company's business from my father."

"I bet that's challenging. I always wanted to know more about investing. I dabble in it. I ain't very good, though."

"It takes time. You never know what's going to happen. The market can hurt you if you're not careful."

"I can believe that. Say, if you bought here I could learn a few things from you. Maybe I can get rich and buy one of those homes on the ocean." He grinned.

"I guess so," Nick replied, looking around and paying no particular attention to the conversation. "Nice house, who lives there?"

"A professional hockey player and his wife, nice couple. We have all kinds of professionals living on the island. I tell you what I'm going to do, since we have some time. I'll take you over to the other side of the island. This will give you a feel for the whole island. When we come back, we'll have lunch at the clubhouse and I can answer any questions you have. Okay?"

"Sounds good. I'm sure I'll have a few. I'll throw some of them at you while we're riding around."

"That's what I'm here for," Tom replied in typical salesman style, despite himself.

"That big house we passed when we first got on the island—what was that? Looks old and interesting."

"Oh, it is. The mansion was bought for a buck and barged here from St. Simons. A lot of history to the place. It has guest rooms upstairs, a bar, and the general store. It even has a few historic items on display. A lot of people eat there during their lunch hour and watch the boats go by. I'll take you for a tour when we return."

"That's okay, just curious. Who runs the place?"

"Well, let me think about that. There's a great cook and waiter—his name is Keith. Really does a nice job. There's a gal named Jennifer. She's the manager. I guess, now that I think about it, she runs the whole place."

"Jennifer," Nick repeated.

"Yeah, Jennifer Perry. She and her daughter moved here about four years ago. Real nice people. They live in that small yellow house we passed earlier. We don't build too many that size on the island."

"I see," Nick said. "What about her husband, what does he do?"

"Jennifer's husband? Oh, she's not married. Would be a nice catch for some lucky guy. Comin' to think of it, I don't think I've ever met a guy on Jennifer's behalf. She sort of keeps to herself."

"What about her daughter? How old is she?" he asked.

"About sixteen or seventeen; beautiful girl. She's a cut-up. Every-body knows Amy. She's always the life of the party down at the beach club with her friend—a native girl named Jila. Those two sure know how to dance. A couple of weeks ago when we had our ice-cream social they were in full bloom. Never a dull moment around here. It's kinda what you make it, I guess. You want to golf all day, you can. You want to enjoy the sun and fun at the beach club—that's a lot of fun, too. If you're like me, though, you'd enjoy riding around just admiring the place. Up ahead there's an equestrian center. The horses are so clean you can't even smell them. You'll see—we're almost there."

Nick ended his questioning as they neared the gate, his hazy view of the island becoming clearer. He tried to listen some more, but his mind kept taking him back to Katherine and Sarah. He had to find a way to warn them that their hideaway was no longer safe, that Riggins knew where they were. He felt so close to accomplishing this. He had it all planned out, yet it wasn't that simple. It frightened him how Sarah might react if she saw him. He could still hear her screams as he held her in a choke hold, demanding that Katherine hand over that damned list. How could he have been so foolish? A thousand times over that question had haunted him. How? And what did he expect to achieve exactly short of chasing them back into Riggins's arms? But there had to be a way!

"We're almost there. Are you okay, John?" Tom asked. "I bet it's the sun. It relaxes everyone around here."

"Yeah, must be it," Nick replied. "It's been a long day and it's only one o'clock." He sighed. "I can't believe I said that. I'm starting to sound like my father."

"Welcome to the club. Isn't it strange how we become so much like our parents. I can still remember promising myself I'd never think that. What can I say? That's life, is what I keep telling myself."

"Yeah—life," Nick repeated somberly.

*   *   *   *

After hours of riding around, butts sore from sitting so long, Nick and Tom were at last at the clubhouse for a hearty lunch. Tom's salesman instincts were telling him that Nick was more than interested—this was a man looking for something. He may bide his time and look as distracted as he wanted, but there was no mistake—he had the tell-tale signs of a buyer. So Tom invited him to return and stay on the island for a weekend. Without a second thought, Nick accepted and went on chomping on his sandwich and looking out over the pond.

*   *   *   *

A soft Southern breeze alleviated the fierce swelter of the sun and made napping and tanning everyone's favorite pastime.

At home, Jila was washing her hair, and thinking about her conversation with Sarah. She had shared almost as much with her as she did with Mama; their friendship had become a sisterly bond that allowed them to be open with each other. But Jila shuddered at the memory of her best friend's despairing eyes while Sarah was sharing her innermost secrets. What's more, Jila never thought there were any secrets between them—until now.

She lathered her hair.

Jila was thankful for the cleansing they got from visiting Gullah Heaven earlier that day. They had been so refreshed they resumed their hunt for shells. But now things felt different. A strangeness had descended between them on that beach. Their hearts were, in a sense, sullied and it pained Jila to think this.

She sat herself on the bed, swathed in a heavy towel, but it was Sarah's burden that weighed her down. She tried to imagine how she'd feel not only if she discovered that a strange man was her father, but if the hands of that same man had grabbed her throat in a death grip. Jila prayed as she looked out the window. The sky was clear and she understood why—all the clouds were imprisoned within her.

CHAPTER 7

▼

Nick decided to take up Tom's offer to spend a couple of days on Dau-fuskie Island. Just short of noon, As the sun burst through the clouds like fireworks, Nick was dressed in his Jamaican blue shirt and knee-high khakis. He lugged his oversized leather bag as he readied to board the water-taxi.

"*I think we got everyone!*" the captain called out and then locked the waist-high gate to the boat. "Sir, you're welcome to sit inside, if you like. The water is a little choppy today."

"That's all right," Nick said. "It's hot. I welcome the shower. Just take your time—I'll enjoy the breeze." He removed his hat and placed it at his side. Now he was ready. His eyes, shaded by sunglasses, fell on the Haig Point lighthouse that stood unwavering directly in their path. The big blue was iced with perfect waves, each floating a welcoming melody to all that chose to ply its waters. Jet skiers, some in couples, rode the waves, their minds racing away from the pains of this world.

"Up to you. But if it gets too bad there're plenty of seats inside," the captain repeated with a smile.

"Will do, Captain. By the way, just curious, but is the mansion open on the weekends?"

"Every day," he cheerfully replied. "The dinner hours may change, but it's open all the time. When the general store, bar and grill are closed, you can usually go inside and enjoy the view or read. Ever been inside?"

"No, I was here the other day, looking around for the first time. Didn't have a chance to go in, so I thought I'd check it out this weekend. Kinda nice to have a whole weekend to decide if you want to live here."

"That what you fixin' on doing?"

"Yup—possibly."

"They been doin' that the last couple of years. Keeping the place open on weekends. I think it's helped—economically, I mean. Well, have a good time. I'm sure we'll run into each other again this weekend," the captain said, making his way to his post with a grin of acknowledgment along the way to the passengers inside the cabin.

Despite the promised bounces and sprinkles, the ride was uneventful. Then, as Nick stepped onto the dock, a hand extended uneasily towards him. "Good to see ya again," Tom said, eager to shake hands again. "I'm glad you decided to take me up on my offer. How was the ride over?"

"Nice," Nick replied. "Really nice. On a day like this, I could spend all morning and afternoon on the high seas."

"You'd need to throw on a nice thick fifteen sunscreen, though. What do you say I take you over to where you'll be staying. I've arranged for a nice two-bedroom plantation home overlooking the golf course. You'll like it. There's also a golf cart available to give you a better feel for this place. I'll be on the island all day—so you can call any time if you want to get together tomorrow or have questions."

"Sounds good. I think I'm going to get lost today. I'm sure I'll have plenty of questions by lunchtime tomorrow."

"I've already got you registered," Tom said as they approached the golf cart. "Here's a guest pass. Keep it with you in case anyone stops you. People on the island know each other. Hop in," he said before taking control of the tiny car's steering wheel.

"I understand," Nick answered lamely and listened to Tom rattle on. *What a talker!* he thought.

"We had a young couple on the island the other day..." Tom began again.

Ahead of them rose an ancient oak tree, its branches seemingly as long as a whole city block. Sitting on a bench in front of it was an elderly lady and a laughing little girl. It saddened Nick that he had never had the opportunity to entertain Sarah, his own flesh and blood. *How could Katherine keep such a secret?* he always asked himself. The little girl's mellifluous giggles faded behind them.

"John, are you still with me?" Tom asked.

"Yeah, just enjoying the scenery, watching the young girl having a ball."

"This is a real family place, you know. Have you got kids of your own?"

"One," Nick replied, with a distracted grin. "Just one—about seventeen."

"We have a few teenagers on the island," Tom said as they pulled into the drive.

"That's good," Nick replied, checking out the scenery, trying to imagine what a true father-daughter relationship would be like—or just a close relationship, something he had not known in his own childhood. It was all foreign to him. Obtaining wealth pretty well defined the essence of parenthood in his family. He was the heir apparent. Any love and attention he had received as a child had been bestowed by people other than his parents. It took him years, but he had finally reconciled himself to this reality—until now. Suddenly, he has lapsed into a world he has never been warned about; he felt defeated. He, too, was a parent. His only solace was that it wasn't by choice.

Again, Tom's voice pierced through his solitude. "We're here. I don't think I showed you this place the other day." Nick just sat back, a half-grin still engraved on his face. The well-cared for townhouse, with its wide stairs and covered porches had ample shady areas that were ideal for relaxation. Nothing short of a *Better Homes and Gardens* picture for the taking. The colors and fragrances of the flowers blooming amid the green leaves and tendrils washed his senses. The ironic part was that he was actually tempted.

"Here's the key. There's a bottle of wine and cheese for you in the kitchen. Will you be needin' any help?"

"Nope," Nick hastened to assure Tom, removing his bag from the back seat. "I'll be fine. Looking forward to getting to know this place better."

"Be sure to call if you have any questions," Tom repeated for the umpteenth time. "I left my number next to the phone."

"I'll be fine. Much obliged," Nick said.

Tom backed out of the driveway, but the salesman hadn't given up on his hope for some company. "You get too lonely tonight, give me a ring. We'll have dinner or something…my wife is at her mother's."

"Sure thing," Nick sniggered.

Standing alone in the doorway, he took a deep breath. It was impressive. The matching striped sofa would have been enough. But the Southern hospitality was fit for a king, with its mint-green walls trimmed in white and, beneath his feet, the floral welcome mat. Martha Stewart would have been proud. He was overwhelmed.

He set his bag inside and stepped out on the back porch. Golfers dressed like professionals were making their way along the course, seemingly anchored by the velvet green that cushioned their spikes. Closing his eyes he sucked in the air, let it out, and headed for the shower.

He had to find a way to warn Katherine about Riggins. He wasn't exactly sure what that man was up to, but it wasn't hard to figure out. The warm water traveled down Nick's anxiety-ridden face, his hands pressing tight against his eyes.

CHAPTER 8

▼

Sarah and Jila were up to their usual, entertaining themselves down at the beach club. Sporting her new two-piece California ensemble, Jila was busy drying off, shaking her wet hair over Sarah's sun-hot skin just to irritate her.

"Wake up! Water real nice. Ya tan faster if ya got in," Jila voiced. "I'm goin' inside an' gettin' me a slurry—want one?"

Sarah turned over to defend herself. "The only thing I want from you is to stop dripping your wet hair on me. That water is cold."

"Cold! ya jus' too hot. Come on, les' go get somethin' cool to drink. I promise to leave ya 'lone."

"Promise?" Sarah asked. "You do and I'll take you up on your offer." She groped around with her small fingers. "Have you seen my shades? Where's my towel?"

"Ya'll layin' on ya towel and ya shades is ridin' high 'cross ya big head. Ya bin sittin' in the sun too long."

"Give me a sec, I need to put some sunscreen on. Jila, would you do my shoulders and back?"

"Sure thin' if it get ya up an' movin'." The two pampered each other while enjoying the ocean breeze on a usual busy Saturday. The pool was filled with many people escaping the bristling rays of the sun; even the kiddie pool was running on overload.

*   *   *   *

Finally Nick was ready to go. He was a just about to shut the door when he realized he had left the local directory behind. His agenda was long but time was short and he knew he had to make the best of each minute. He picked it up and headed off to the beach.

Riding along the beach trail, he spotted two familiar souls. Jila and Sarah were running in and out of the big blue like school kids, neither paying any attention to the man on the short bridge looking out.

Their laughter was infectious. It was picked up by the waves and lifted up above the magical little island. It changed Nick's grin to a smile, despite his pain. He longed to laugh, to be a youngster himself.

He wished he could enjoy the fun with them—after all, it was Sarah. But would he ever be allowed?

The shutters of his camera winked out of control. For the first time he performed what he always knew was a parental duty but had neither had it done for him as a child nor been able to do it as a parent himself; he captured a precious moment deep inside his soul for safekeeping.

Then the pain returned—the pain of being an absentee father, hated and feared. It lurched his innards and pulled him back. He fought for a way to patch the wounds he had inflicted in their lives.

But how? How could he do it without interrupting the beauty surrounding this child before him?

And then the moment was gone. Nick stood, once again, at a great remove from the pleasures of life beaming from the two girls' faces.

How could I? he murmured. It was too much to ask. And yet there was no turning back. He would have to disturb their peace another time. For their own good. All he wished for was that their reunion would be an orderly one.

As he drove off, Sarah and Jila caught a quick glimpse of the man. At first, they thought it was Jim, a native of the island, doing his usual—bird watching and taking pictures. Shaking out their towels, they offered their bodies again to the sun and plumped down on the sand, oblivious to all that lurked around them.

As the ocean breeze caressed her body, Jila scrutinized Sarah, who lay on her back with her eyes closed. Sarah couldn't see the tug-of-war in Jila's watchful eyes, although things were changing between them. Their conversations felt more scripted, and the quiet moods were growing longer. Jila wondered whether Sarah regretted having shared the secret with her, but she wanted to find a way to let her know she could be trusted.

"Amy, I want things to be like they used to be."

Surprised, Sarah lifted her head up off the towel. "What on earth are you talking about, Jila? What have I done again?

"No, it jus' seems like things are different since ya tol' me 'bout what happened to ya and Jenny. I don' want it comin' 'tween us. Ya my best friend. I'd never tell anybody. I'd sooner die!"

"I know that, Jila. I trust you. It's just…" Sarah gasped for breath, overtaken by what she was about to say. "It's been a long time since I talked about what happened. I have so many questions inside my head."

"Questions?" Jila asked, puzzled.

"Yeah. I listen to you talk about your father and how much he means to you…how much you still love and miss him. Well, I have a father out there and I don't even know or care to know him. I never had the opportunity like you to ask him a single question. Everything I heard about him came through Mom."

"Ya sayin' ya don' even care to know 'im?"

"I guess I am. That's what bothers me so. Here you are, the kind of person who'd do anything to talk to your father one more time, to hold him in your arms. But I couldn't care less."

"Amy, do ya mind if I say somethin'? Ya won't get mad with me, will ya?" Jila asked, sitting up.

Sarah replied uncomfortably, "Why should I?"

Jila exhaled. She grasped for the right words, and ended up thinking of the prayer she had made earlier, her stomach lurching from the anxiety. "I don' know how to tell ya this, Amy. I can't imagine how I'd feel if I were in ya shoes. The one thin' I do know is ya gettin' older. And I ain't much older than ya no more. But with age come change. What I'm sayin' is, as I get older, I look back on some decisions and realize…well, that if I had to make 'em all over 'gain today, it be different. Real different, Amy. I ain't sayin' this is what's happenin' to ya," she said defensively, then hastened to add, "but maybe it is. I know ya still hurtin'. Maybe ya reached a point in ya life where ya jus' need mo' answers. Answers that only come from talkin' to ya father."

Sarah looked away and focused her eyes on the tiny shell she had dug out of the sand. This time, Jila was bothered by the uncertain quiet that descended, but she waited. "I could never do that, Jila. My mom would never forgive me."

"Ya sayin' ya thought 'bout it? Have ya ever talked to Jenny 'bout it?"

"Jila, I really don't want to talk about this anymore," Sarah said tearfully.

"I'm sorry, Amy. Didn't mean to hurt ya none. Jus' tryin' to help bes' I can."

"It's not you, it's me. But I'm fine for now." Sarah resumed her stretched-out position on her towel and closed her eyes.

Jila fell silent as she drew figures in the hot sand.

*   *   *   *

Nick couldn't figure out what was harder: seeing Sarah and not being able to identify himself or meeting Katherine without ever talking to Sarah. He stood outside the mansion, hidden by the trees and watching Katherine as she moved about, alive yet sheltered from his touch. Watching her conjured up a thousand different variations in his mind of how he could begin a conversation with her without provoking her fear or loathing.

He had to help them somehow.

In the end, there was no good way to begin—too much had gone wrong in their lives. Yet there was still hope, if only he could muster the courage to talk to her. His actions may lead to his own funeral, with all that Katherine and Sarah would demand to know from him, although he didn't necessarily have all the answers. The gist of it all was that he was selling out his father. There were so many things Nick still wanted his father to tell him, especially concerning his relationship with Riggins. Something wasn't right.

Well, that was impossible—for now.

Nick went back to the house and into the shower, struggling ceaselessly with thoughts that all but crushed his head. After lathering himself, he stopped and beat lightly against the wall with his fist, begging for forgiveness. He stood for long minutes in the smothering heat of the shower room, drenched in tears. Life had given him a deck that no one but he could shuffle. No one understood the game, no one was left. And having paid a steep price, he knew exactly how he had to play his hand.

There was no turning back.

CHAPTER 9

▼

Keith rushed into Katherine's office, pissed. "Jenny, I'm going to bitch slap him. He doesn't know his ass from a hole in the ground. Where did you find this guy?" he asked.

"What are you talking about?" Katherine asked.

"What am I talking about?" he exclaimed, "If Bob's going to act like a bitch, someone needs to put him on a leash and walk him. 'Cause if I have to, I'll use it to choke the hell out of him." He stopped, breathless.

"Close the door," she ordered, pulling a chair out for Keith. "What are you two fighting about now?"

"Oh, we're not fighting, because if we were, his ass would have been gone a long time ago."

"Then tell me why you're so mad?"

"Jenny, he must have gone to the *School of Cordon Undue*. He just doesn't get it. He thinks he's cooking for a girls' club." Keith pushed his hand into his hip.

"I can't read between the lines. What happened?" she asked, leaning against her desk in resignation.

"I fixed the curry just like our customers like it—hot and spicy. You know that mix I created?"

"Yeah?" Katherine responded.

"Well, the better cook than thou took one taste and right there and then insisted we weren't gonna serve that to our customers, 'cause *it was too hot*. We needed to freeze it and serve it to the guys on men's night, after they'd had a few drinks. This is the South, for heaven's sake. Doesn't he get it? People like their curry hot! I swear if it wasn't for Helen, I woulda cooled off the pot with his head."

"Now, Keith, the two of you have to work together. Bob is good at what he does. I know you two don't agree on a lot of things, but you can't get yourself upset each time he wants to change something."

"Well, I'll tell you right now, I'm not taking responsibility for his screw-ups. If he wants to chase the customers away and you're happy with that, so be it."

"That's not how we're going to work together. I'll talk to Bob and then I need to talk to you both. Is he in the kitchen?" Her thoughts were interrupted by the ringing of the telephone.

"Hello."

"Hi, Mom, what's going on?"

"Nothing much, just talking to Keith. What are you up to?"

"Just got in from the beach with Jila. I was thinking about getting a few personal items. I checked the general store, but it didn't have what I needed. One thing I still haven't gotten used to here…"

"What's that?" Katherine asked.

"This island has no real stores," Sarah said. "Wanna come?"

"No, I have to work late tonight. Is Jila going with you?"

"She was, but she says she has to work."

"I see. Are you sure you don't want to wait until tomorrow? You know I don't like going over there, but maybe I can take a few hours off."

"That's okay, Mom, it won't take long. I need them tonight, I'll see you when you get home."

"Be careful. Love you."

"Me, too, Mom. Later."

Katherine hung up with a grin before redirecting her attention to Keith, who was pouting. "Okay, wait here. Let me talk to Bob. This fighting has to stop." She really was fed up with their sparring. Keith was about to make some comment, but the closing door hushed him and he just sat there alone.

*   *   *   *

With a towel wrapped tight around his waist and another catching the water dripping from his hair, Nick glanced outside and happened to catch sight of someone in the distance driving along the golf path and heading his way.

It was Sarah.

She was on her way to the H-ferry, singing and happy as only she could be. Nervous, feeling like a pathological criminal, he stumbled back and glued himself to the wall.

He scurried for something to wear and checked his watch. He realized he had twenty minutes before the H-ferry's departure. He dressed in a flash, plopped his old reliable on his head, and rushed out the door.

The golf cart couldn't move fast enough.

Iced by his tight stomach, he observed Sarah from afar. She was about to embark the ferry. He had to get to the boat. He parked his ride abruptly, planted his feet on the dock, and rushed forward. The same captain he'd met before gave him a thumbs-up as he held the gate open with a friendly smile.

By this time, Sarah had made her way to the upper deck to gaze at the lights and bustle of Hilton Head. A warm breeze blew. The captain asked everyone to take a seat and then turned to Nick and asked, "So, you decided to leave already?"

"No," he replied, breathless. "I have to pick up a few things. Don't plan to be gone long."

"I understand. The boat leaves every hour on the half-hour from the other side. If you shop fast you might be able to catch the next boat back," he said.

"Thanks," Nick replied, eyes fixed on the door leading to the upper deck. His shirt was already pasted to his body in the heat, though the sun was just about to make its final descent.

"This is crazy," he muttered to himself, uncertain about what to do next.

CHAPTER 10

▼

What a day! Katherine thought as she locked the door to the general store, found her favorite chair, kicked off her shoes, and aired her throbbing feet. She sprawled in the oversized chair like a drunken hillbilly.

The mansion was quiet except for the humming of the dishwasher. Katherine nodded off.

When she woke it was to the soft sound of the night breeze sweeping the ocean. She pulled herself together and gathered her strength before noticing that the little watch on her wrist said a few minutes after midnight. She rose from the chair and made her way out through the mansion, the soles of her irritated feet planted firmly on the wood beneath. It was better than leather she thought, her shoes dangling from her hand. A mystic darkness cloaked the area outside the ornate windows. The bright stars seemed to dance to the soothing refrains of the ocean waves. It was unusual, though welcome, that there should be no overnight guests to worry about. Anyway, it was Keith's turn to get there early and start breakfast. Tomorrow was women's day and the ladies loved having a long, luxurious breakfast before teeing off.

Reflecting on the day, she turned off the last light in the kitchen.

Keith and his incendiary temper! If he could just relax, she thought, he and Bob would become a great pair. The kitchen was quiet, but she imagined excited souls all around her. Keith's garish excitement was palpable. His words were still bouncing from wall to wall. Realizing that she was too tired to stay there, she took a deep breath and exited.

A warm breeze caught the top of the trees and caused them to shimmy. Katherine strolled down the wooden ramp leading to the cart barn to the accompaniment of crickets. She had to tread carefully to avoid catching a splinter in her foot. Her armpit held the shoes her feet didn't want to feel, and then quickly, as if walking over hot coals, she darted over to her golf cart and turned on the lights.

Primal fear.

There was no one in sight. Only her fear—slithering like a snake. But basic instinct is a funny thing. Every shadow, every dusky tree stoked more fear and made her heart race faster than the golf cart could move. She and Sarah had been on the island for quite some time, and traveling down a road without lights was still downright creepy. She never got used to it, but it was even stranger that there were absolutely no cars on the island.

Her feet held the pedal to the floor.

Eyes on alert but now exhausted, she arrived at her door. Avoiding everything, including the lights, her body drooped and then sank into the sofa like a heavy rock, her shoes cast away on the floor. The house was quiet, which Katherine always welcomed after a long day at work. She closed her tired, aching eyes, knowing she had to find the energy to check on Sarah.

Without warning, the normally adoring Hurricane pounced on her wildly, jolting her. Then the startled cat recognized her and began to purr insistently for comfort. Katherine took him, stroked his fur, and soothed him with her voice.

Something was not right.

Hurricane was all wet and he smelled funny. Inching toward the lamp, Katherine switched on the light. What met her eyes was devastating. Traces of blood were all over the sofa and, she saw to her horror, all over herself too. Her eyes fell on the matted, blood-soaked fur of her cat, now at her feet. Gasping, eyes and mouth opened, Katherine's fears finally burst out. "Oh, my God. *Sarah!*" she screamed, "Sarah…Sarah answer me, goddammit!"

She dashed through the hall, brushing helplessly against the walls on the way to Sarah's room. The door was closed. Katherine burst into the room.

"*Sarah!*" she screamed.

But she could tell in the dark that Sarah's bed was unoccupied. Her head swirling, Katherine flipped the lights on violently and looked downwards. There were tracks of blood leading to Sarah's bathroom. "Sarah!" she frantically cried out.

Suddenly, she let out a horrific scream, her body slamming itself against the door. She covered her mouth. At her feet, Nick lay prostrate in a pool of blood.

"Katherine…" he moaned, his trembling hand pressing against his blood-soaked shirt. His shoulder was pierced.

"So…sorry, Kath…erine…forgi…forgive me," he begged her, His eyes looked faint.

"Nick! What in the hell are you doing here?" she shouted, her head rocking in denial. "Where's Sarah?" she demanded.

"Katherine," Nick replied, grimacing and struggling with each breath. "Don't…be afraid. I won't…hurt you…Kath—"

"Sorry?" She backed away, baffled. "Sorry? Where the hell is Sarah, Nick? And what are you doing here?"

"I tried. Please…they…ha…have her. I tried," he stammered.

"What are you talking about? They…they who? Oh…oh, no!" she moaned, falling backwards, hands pressed against her head.

"I'm not…sure, Katherine. Ah, ah," Nick moaned, taking a deep swallow. "I was following her…wanted to see my daughter." Pain was etched on his face, but he fought to go on. "Two guys grabbed her. I tried…tried to save her, Katherine…I'm sure it's Riggins." His head lolled forward over his chest.

"Oh, my God!" Katherine screamed. Her knees still pressed against the floor as she hovered over Nick. "Dammit, don't do this to me," she demanded as she fought to revive him, but even she couldn't breathe in the sweltering heat of this once cool abode. The events of four years ago returned ominously to hang over her head—Sarah and Nick prostrated in an abandoned basement, Nick unconscious. This time no one was towering over them, gun in hand and ready to kill for a list—a lousy list that included the names of everyone involved in the investment scandal. It was worse this time. Now they had Sarah, and the inanimate figure—a shadow of the man she once knew and loved— lying before Katherine was the only man capable of helping.

"Dammit!" she shouted, bruising her thighs with her clenched fists. She staggered down the hall towards the phone, her hands pressing against the pastel walls and leaving bloody imprints. She entered a room and groped around breathlessly before pulling out a drawer and ransacking it, then doing the same to another.

Nothing seemed to fit.

It was as if she had stepped into another world. Her mind was fogged up; she had no confidence in her own ability to act.

She knocked over the lamp and grabbed the phone. As she dialed, her heart seemed to beat even more uncontrollably but she managed to regain enough of her composure to wait for someone to answer.

First ring. Second ring.

"Come on, come on. Pick up the phone…. Hello, hello! They have Sarah. Help me, please!"

"Who is this?" an anxious woman on the other end replied.

"It's me, Jennifer Perry. I mean, Katherine Oberman…whatever. You told me you'd protect us. They have my daughter, dammit! They have Sarah!"

"Are you okay?" the woman coolly asked.

"No, I'm not. Two men kidnapped her! Don't you understand? Please…I need help now."

"Where are you?

"I'm at home, on Daufuskie Island. Please! I need to talk to some-one that can help me," Katherine pleaded.

"One second please." The woman eyed the computer screen and quickly dialed. "Ray, Jennifer Perry's on the phone! Hurry. Someone has kidnapped her daughter. Case code ZOD. I have it up on my screen."

"I got it, connect me," he ordered.

"Right. I'll stay on the line with you," she said.

"Jennifer?" the hefty agent sounded, gesturing others in the office to stand by. "Are you all right?"

"They have Sarah! They'll kill her. Please, I want my daughter back."

"Some men are on their way right now. Are you at home?" he asked.

"Where else should I be but in this safe haven you sent me to? You were supposed to protect us!"

"Jennifer, we'll help you. I promise."

"Promise?" She was infuriated. "I heard that before. Now look what happened. I don't believe anything you say. I don't care about your promises. I want Sarah! Do you hear me?"

"Jennifer."

"Dammit, call me Katherine. That's my name. To hell with Jenni-fer."

"*Katherine*, please, try to calm down. I know this is not easy. But we'll find her. Is anyone there with you?"

"No, I mean yes. I'm here with a Nick Walters. He tried to save her."

"Nick Walters?" he responded.

"Yes, you know him well—read my file. He's been injured." She glanced at the darkness that loomed outside the windows.

"I understand. How bad?"

"He's been stabbed in the shoulder and he's lost a lot of blood."

"Keep the doors locked. Here's the number to my direct line." He clearly pronounced every number. "Don't move until the men get there. I'll arrange for medical help. Please, don't go outside. Listen, I want you to make sure all of the doors are locked, then come back and let me know. Just be careful."

"Okay." Katherine fearfully eyed her immediate surroundings and put down the telephone. She got to about three feet of the front door and then bolted forward to lock it. Her eyes glancing back at the open phone, she stumbled towards the screened porch, hesitated and looked back down the hall towards Sarah's room. Everywhere outside, on the porch, in the front yard, there were shadows.

She edged back and wrapped her hands around the telephone. "They're locked."

"That's great. We've placed a trace on your phone. If they call—I mean the guys that have Sarah—before we get there, try to keep them on the line as long as you can. Don't agree to anything. Do you hear me?"

"Yes, but hurry. If anything happens to Sarah I'll never—"

"Katherine, listen to me. I know this isn't easy. Just remember that these guys want something. They won't do anything just yet. I've been down this road before and I know how they operate. It's hard for you, I know, but please try to hang in there with us. We'll do everything we can to find her, okay?"

But Katherine felt defeated. She covered her face with her hand, trying to reconcile herself to whatever the agent said. "I hope so," she replied and then placed the phone back in its cradle. Down the hall the door stood open. The stillness of the house belied the turmoil she felt inside her. Everything seemed larger than life. She jumped at every noise. Every closed door, locked or not, only heightened her terror. She couldn't help it. She imagined the worse—anything or anyone could be prowling behind them.

Meanwhile, Nick came to slightly and waited for Katherine to return. He was in terrible pain. He tried to call to her, but faintness muffled his cry.

Katherine, the phone still in her lap, sat motionless, staring at a picture of Sarah. She could only see her gregarious smile and hear her infectious laughter. Tears beaded down the side of her face, ready to turn into a torrent, a torrent of saltwater from the ocean that surrounded their beautiful island. There was imminent doom in the air.

"Why is this happening again?" she asked herself. "Why are you doing this to me?" She lifted her head to the firmament.

She wondered, as she had many times before, if it would have turned out differently had she resisted Nick's father, who chased her out of New York, and had she not told Nick that Sarah was his daughter. Had she done the right thing—trying to bury the past, and then having it explode in her face?

She questioned her wisdom and her self-worth. What would happen to her only daughter now? She wished she had never been born into a world so confusing and unjust. "Oh, Sarah, I'm so sorry!" she sobbed.

She wept alone.

CHAPTER 11

▼

Gagged and blindfolded, Sarah was held captive in a car, her face buried in the backseat She struggled to free herself, but her tears only soaked the cloth band covering her eyes. Exhaust fumes seeped through the seat. It was sickening her, but her garbled pleas were either inaudible to the two men in the car, one of them right next to her, or else her captors choose to ignore her. She couldn't tell which.

Then one of the men, whose name was Paul, "That little bitch is a fighter. She tried to bite me. Did you see that?" He chuckled.

Jeff, who was driving, looked though the rear view mirror. "Ah, forget about that," he said, "we have her now. Who in the hell was that guy that came out of nowhere?"

"Hell if I know," Paul answered. "He was two seconds away from a bullet. And the other guy heading towards us, he was clueless. You should have let me play target practice on their asses."

"That other guy was just parking his car. He might have heard her scream. But I don't think you had time to use your gun—she had you going," Jeff said, smiling as he turned the corner. "It was my knife that saved your ass."

"What do you mean 'saved my ass'? He was closer to you than me. I don't think you had much of a choice! Besides, it was kinda fun watching you. I'd forgotten what that was like," Paul said while securing his hold on Sarah. "I had things under control. I was going to slap her and come and help you."

"Sure, I'da loved to see that. The guy never saw it coming—he was so focused on you," Jeff responded.

"I'm glad for him, 'cause I woulda had to fire a few shots and placed everyone in the parking lot on alert."

"Like I said, Paul, the Boss knew what he was doing when he put me on this job."

"That's a bunch of bullshit. All he knew was he had to save his ass, and we were fool enough to help," Paul said.

"Fool? "I don't think I could make this much money in ten years. Plus, the job is easy, that kiss-ass Barry did most of the legwork."

"Yeah, his nose is stuck up the Boss's ass," Paul said, slowing down the car.

"Anything wrong with that? He seems to be living well and I don't hear him complaining," Jeff responded.

"I think there's a lot we don't hear about. But as long as I get paid, I don't care. It's only a job, nothing more."

"We're going down a road that I'd rather deal with another day," Jeff said. "This could get ugly if we don't move fast. We need to get this over with and then we can talk about all that other stuff. We're here." He turned into a long driveway. "Barry was right—this place is spooky. Not the kind anyone would want to live in. Man, is it dark! Don't look like it's been lived in for years."

"That's the idea. You afraid? Do I need to call the Boss and tell him you're scared?" Paul said, laughing.

"Cut the bull. The only thing you gotta do is get her outta the car, and hope she doesn't lay something on you," Jeff said as the car came to a halt.

"Let's get serious here. Do you want to call the Boss to tell him we're here, or do you want me to call him?"

"You get her checked in, then I'll call the mama. Bet she'll be happy to hear from us! Ha, ha!" He stepped out and opened the rear door of the car.

"I'm sure mama's worried about her little baby. What do you think, sweetie?" Paul said as he pulled and then lifted Sarah to her feet beside the car. She had been listening to their conversation. Her hands desperately needed relief. She could no longer feel them and stood there dizzy, afraid to take another step without help. Paul led her towards the door, while Jeff worked on opening the garage.

Their nest in the woods was perfect. There was not a house in sight. Feeling a little anxious to get this job done right, Jeff hurriedly lifted the solid garage door. The early morning darkness was not something he enjoyed. He was more of a big city boy who liked to make big bucks, but unlike Paul, he wanted this ordeal to be over as soon as possible. Paul was more like the Boss. He enjoyed seeing others beg and plead, especially after he'd had a few drinks.

Jeff positioned the car in the middle of the two-car garage and bolted the door shut. As he crossed into their inner sanctum, his mind was fixed on the call that he needed to make to the Boss.

CHAPTER 12

▼

It was early morning and the sun had just breached the horizon. At the Riggins estate, it was business as usual. The daily briefings were about to begin. Riggins' trusted confidante, Barry, a thin tall man with crooked teeth, had just walked in. Those who knew him called him Glue. His nose was so far up the boss's ass Riggins couldn't shit properly. The word "no" was just not part of his vocabulary when it came to the Boss. Besides being Riggins' flunky, though, he had a certain flair. He wore out-of-his-element expensive suits that showed some sense of style. Which in turn enhanced his satisfaction with Riggins, his benefactor. And that was all that mattered to him.

On this day, Barry walked with a bounce. His perfectly polished brown-leather shoes matched the shine on Riggins' desk. Rumors were in the air.

"Boss, John was questioned again by the FBI, I've been told."

Riggins tapped his cigar on his desk. "John Walters?" he asked.

"Yeah, Walters—that's it. They think he knows more than he's telling. I heard they spent a couple of hours questioning him."

"What else did you hear, Barry?"

"Not sure about this, but it seems Walters felt he had to come clean. He'd been in contact with someone that tipped him off on the whereabouts of Katherine. Ya know, that smart one, AKA, missing in action."

"What about his son—Nick? I heard he was laying low since he got out of jail," Riggins said. "That spoiled son-of-a-bitch was lucky as hell. His daddy bought him time."

"I didn't hear much about him. The fact that the old guy he shot lived saved his lucky ass. Other than that, I'm not sure what's going on with him," Barry responded.

"That's interesting. John is protecting him again, I'm sure of that," Riggins said. He was molded to his stately leather chair. Adjusting his glasses, the tall, tanned, heavy-around-the-middle Riggins, dressed in his imported cuffed cotton shirt, took a moment to shuffle through a few papers.

Barry, unsure what to say next, kept watching the dark-haired man with gray around the edges who seemed to be ignoring him. Being familiar with Riggins' erratic behavior, he decided to reopen the conversation. "What do you have in mind, Boss?"

"He knows enough to pose a risk, but he's not a threat."

"No?" Barry asked, perplexed.

"No. Besides, finding that girlfriend of his is a priority. As long as she's out there we have a problem." Riggins puffed on his fat cigar.

"I'm sure you know what you're talking about. I just feel she's protected, though. Don't you?"

Riggins responded in a brassy voice, "She's *not* protected! She's as good as found! I need to get my hands on her. That bitch has caused me more trouble than she's worth. I can't shit without those Feds smelling it—all because of her. The sooner she's put to rest the better."

"You better be careful, you've already blown one opportunity, Boss."

"Bullshit, I haven't blown a damn thing!" he bellowed. "That fuck-up Glen did! Remember that!"

"All I'm saying is to be careful, Boss. You never know what—" Suddenly Dan walked into the room with an anxious look and a phone in his hand.

"They found her," Dan shouted. All six-feet-three of him towered over Riggins' desk, his black silk ascot neatly tucked.

Riggins sprang to his feet before the words were completely out of Dan's mouth. "I knew my source was right," he vented. "It's about time. Ever since her pathetic ass was rescued, the Feds have been all over me. Where is she?" His cigar smoldered in the silver ashtray.

"Just where they said she would be. She's on an island called Daufuskie. They have the daughter, but the guys ran into some trouble," Dan advised as he handed Riggins the phone.

"Jeff, what's going on?" Riggins asked, excited.

"We're on Hilton Head at the farmhouse. I have the girl," he said. "I've been trying to call, but I couldn't get through to you, Boss."

"Good job!" Riggins was elated and explained, "Last night a thunderstorm knocked out the power. But now we're talking, so what happened? Where's the mother?"

"Close. She's on Daufuskie and we'll get her—don't worry."

"Did the girl say anything, Jeff?"

"No, not yet. We had some trouble."

"Trouble?" Riggins repeated, an expression of anxiety appearing on his face.

"Yeah, some joker tried to stop us when Paul grabbed her. We were in the parking lot and this guy comes out of nowhere," Jeff explained.

"Is he dead?" Riggins ran his stubby hands through his hair.

"I had to knife him. I don't think he'll be getting' in our way again."

Puzzled, Riggins asked, "Is he dead or not?"

"If not, pretty close to it. We had to leave in a hurry, Boss. We had no time to find out."

"Jeff, don't fuck around. I need to get this mess cleaned up. I'm paying you and Paul big for this."

"No problem, Boss. Don't worry, I know what I'm doing, unlike our ol' friend Glen."

"He's pushing up daisies. Forget about him and do what you have to do, but do it right."

"I will. I'll call you as soon as I have something. I won't let you down, Boss."

"And I want to make her *suffer*—do you hear? I want her to feel the pain I've had to suffer. Call her now, and make her wait. I want her to think long and hard about this. I'll be waiting. Be careful."

"Sure Boss," Jeff replied.

"And Jeff!"

"Yeah, Boss, did I forget something?"

"No, I forgot to ask about Paul. How's he coming along?"

"He's keeping a close eye on her. I think he likes this spooky place; it's quiet. I guess this is the best place for a hideout," Jeff said, looking around at the barren walls.

"Watch him," Riggins instructed. "I'm sure you know what I mean."

"I do, Boss, don't worry."

"Good, call me right after you talk to her," Riggins stressed, rubbing his head.

"I will, I'll call you. I'll let her stew for a few hours. Later, Boss," he said.

Riggins was on the whole pleased. He drew a short puff from a burnt cigar, flashed a deceptively jovial smile, and poured himself a stiff one.

"It won't be long, Barry. It won't be long. I've been waiting for this moment for a long time—four years!" Riggins said, polishing off his drink.

Barry was concerned enough, though, that some words of advice escaped his mouth. "She sure is smart, Boss. We gotta be careful."

"Barry, do I look worried? Those bastards don't have anything on me. Once I have her on mute all of this will be over. Get Walters on the phone," Riggins demanded. "I want to see what he's up to. That son-of-a-bitch better not be fucking around on me." With an artful smile, Riggins poured himself another drink and walked out of the room.

Barry tracked Riggins' scent, then stood speechless, searching for a cigarette and pondering all that had happened. He had reason to be worried, and he didn't want any of this to last too long. The last couple of months had not been easy. Behind Riggins stretched a trail of investigators longer than the distance to eternity, watching his every move. Barry was aware this entire fiasco had begun long before Katherine came into the picture, but he had never felt this fearful before.

The calm inside the darkened walls of the study had vanished, possibly for good.

Barry knew how tired Riggins' Wall Street buddies have grown of doling him money just to keep their businesses alive. What started out as a get-rich-quick scheme had become an obsession. At first, they needed to pay him a few bucks to make a few, and then the few bucks turned into big bucks. Soon, they were trapped like caged animals, hounded by Riggins, who threatened to expose their darkest secrets and destroy their businesses.

Barry looked up at the impressive painting of Riggins hanging over the fireplace.

He knew how Riggins basked in his clients' respectful dread of him. He left them with no option but to keep on paying him. The chore of covering up their dirty bank books was prohibitively expensive, yet any hidden transaction exposed threatened to unravel them. The noose continued to tighten around their necks. But then, Katherine discovered the list accidentally. It had names and types of transaction. Enter Detective Glen, the man Riggins had paid a hefty bankroll sum to silence that woman forever.

This whole ordeal could have been over years ago, Barry thought. His feelings were increasingly unsettled as Riggins' plot reached its climax, because so much was riding on Detective Glen. What a screw-up!

Glen had failed either to retrieve the list or to eliminate Katherine. Those who cared remembered him now not only for what he couldn't achieve but for his big mouth—which happened to spring from overconfidence. Unfortunately for Riggins, Glen's failure had become the shit pile that the investigating flies hovered around. The authorities couldn't wait to take multiple bites out of his boss's ass, depending on the evidence being uncovered piecemeal.

In fact, the FBI might well be planning to bring this long case to a head in less than a few days. More witnesses, vindictive by choice, had been lining up to help close Riggins' chapter. The missing link was an actual confession that could directly link Riggins to the murders. Katherine's testimony was key and the Feds knew that. She, unlike a few others, was a direct ear to Glen's boastful confession and her testimony had merit. With all the other information that had recently surfaced, Riggins' tight-knit world of treachery was getting close to cracking.

Riggins was aware of how things worked inside the FBI. Without her testimony, the case against him would amount to nothing. Katherine needed to become dead meat. Being unsure of exactly what she knew, he was quite troubled. Thankfully for him, a relentless search had turned up the find of his life. Jeff and Paul had delivered—but only partially so far. The complete package was a must.

All these thoughts swam inside Barry's head, before Riggins reentered the room. "Why are you standing there?" he asked Barry. "I asked you to get John Walters on the phone. What in the hell is wrong with you? Has that brunette-turned-blonde been screwing with your head again?" Riggins approached his desk.

"I was just thinking about things. I really haven't had time for that. Just wondering—" Barry said.

"Barry, loosen up—you worry too much. It's my ass they're after, but do I look worried? Do you think you're going to miss out on something?"

"Why would you think that? I've earned my keep," Barry defended himself.

But Riggins just leaned back in his chair, clasping his hands behind the back of his head. "Why would you think I was thinking that? Maybe I hit a nerve, huh?" Riggins was proud of pushing Barry's buttons again.

Ticked off, Barry gave him a harsher look than he ever thought he could and headed towards the door. Just before exiting, he paused, but without looking back. "You'll regret treating me like this someday. I'm the only one you can depend on."

"Bullshit!" Riggins shouted. "Bullshit!" He scrambled to find his glasses and poured himself another drink. He searched in his desk drawer and pulled out his black leather book. Then he popped a couple of tiny white pills and stared emptily at the doorway through which the miffed Barry had passed back to the real world a moment ago. *Why do I put up with this shit?*

He polished off his drink.

Puffing on his oversized stogy, he threw a glance at the phone, his thoughts focused on his conversation with Jeff.

CHAPTER 13

▼

Jila was dressed in her oversized nightshirt. Hovering over the kitchen sink, she felt nauseated. Sweaty, weak, consumed, she held on to the porcelain sink just to maintain her balance.

Jila's spewing awakened Mama, who rushed into the sunlit kitchen, her head wrapped in her floral scarf. "Wuh de matt'r, Chile?" Mama asked, alarmed by Jila's ashen gray appearance.

"Somethin' happen'…somethin' wrong, Mama," she explained, cringing as she held her stomach. "Ah, Mama, I've bin feelin' sick all night."

"Wuh do oonuh mean sump'n hab happ'n?" Mama placed her arm on Jila's shoulder. Jila had her face within six inches of the drain. "Chile, wuh de matt'r? Leh I help oonuh chile. Oonuh muse'e hu't, gwine call de doctuh."

"No, Mama, it's Amy. Somethin' happen' to her—I know it. I gotta get over there. Somethin' bad, Mama." She took a deep breath.

"Chile, oonuh cyan gwine no weh luk dis," Mama said, her face etched with concern, her eyes darting between Jila and the phone that hung on the wall.

"I'll be okay…jus' give me a minute. I'll be fine, Mama." Jila rocked her head over the sink. She looked like she had a bad case of the flu.

"Chile, I gwine tuh call de doctuh. 'E won't tek long."

"No, Mama, please," Jila begged. "I'll be all right. Don' need no doctor. It happen' before, don' ya remember?" Jila fought to lift her head.

"Chile, wuh duh oonuh talk'n 'bout?" Mama asked in puzzlement.

"I felt like this the day Daddy died. I knew then somethin' real terrible was gon' happen and I know now…jus' give me a minute, will ya."

"Oonuh nebbuh tol' me 'bout dat. Leh I help oonuh. You' own farruh git dese spells w'en 'e a'libe. Eb'rytime 'e happ'n I prey'd." Mama gently rubbed Jila's back.

Jila held her hand tight to her stomach and took a deep breath. "I know, Mama, I hate to see ya worry. I remember hearin' ya and Daddy talkin' 'bout it. I guess he done passed this on to me." The pain untied its first notch. "Amy in trouble. I don' know what kind. I jus' know she is." She reached for Mama's hand. "I'll be all right, though. Don' ya worry none, okay. I jus' have to get over there." She washed herself quickly and began dressing.

"I gwine wid oonuh. Uh don' understand, huccome oonuh don' call?"

"I need to be there, Mama. Please, trust me. I'll be okay. I'll call ya as soon as I find out what's goin' on, I promise."

"Oonuh wor'y I. Bin 'long time sine dis hab happ'n," Mama said as she turned on the faucet. "I don' notus de two ub oonuh hab become luk sistuhs."

"Mama, she ma bes' friend. We bin through a lot together. Don' ya worry, I be okay. I'm feelin' much better now—see?" Jila sipped from a glass of water. "I jus' gotta find out what's gon' on." Her big browns searched for Mama's understanding.

"Chile, cep gib I call ez soon ez oonuh git dey."

"Thanks, Mama, I love ya."

Mama was worried to death, but they shared a tender moment as Jila held her tight. Mama didn't want to let go. When she did, she stood helplessly by the kitchen sink watching Jila make her way to the door. She had seen the disquiet on Jila's face. In her private despair, she turned around to resume her washing, then just as quickly, shook the soap from her hands and ran to the doorway to watch the golf cart vanish in the early morning haze.

After closing the door, she looked across the room at a picture of Jila's father. It was nestled on the thick wooden mantel, and his eyes connected with hers. A sullen smile interrupted his stony face. Mama felt again the sad gentleness of his soul. He was trying to tell her something, she thought. "Ben, prey wid me," she whispered in a lonely voice and then, opening her tear-filled eyes, she walked over to her easy-chair next to the phone.

Morning birds were chirruping outside, but even they could not put her mind at ease.

*   *   *   *

Katherine beat water against her face as she looked into the bathroom mirror. She had just spent the longest night of her life in heart-wrenching guilt. The dark circles around her eyes hardly showed the true depth of her emotional turmoil. Her forehead and eyeballs ached. She could only think of Sarah.

In the kitchen, two agents had set up camp. She tried to ignore what was going on in the room down the hall, where the doctor was still treating Nick. She approached the open kitchen door. The agent, a big muscular man with a deep voice, was speaking to someone on the other side of the porch door.

"Can I help you?" he asked in a stern and resonating voice. He didn't sound pleased. His muscles rippled under his close-fitting white shirt; his steel blue eyes stared through the screen. "Can I help you," he repeated, stepping onto the porch, his hand glued to the doorknob.

"Yeah, um, I'm Jila," came a surprised, nervous reply. Jila's words had caught in her throat. She stepped back and took a deep breath. "I'm lookin'…for…Amy and Jenny."

"They're not here," he curtly said just as Katherine was walking into the kitchen.

"Who's there?" she called out and rushed to the door. "Please, let me handle this," she demanded, waving off the other agent, who was about to step in front of her. She struggled to break the Big Guy's hand grip on the door. His stature was like a brick wall obstructing her view. "Excuse me," she said as she fought for her position. "Who's there? Jila!" she cried out, relieved.

Jila reached out with a big sob. She and Katherine barely touched each other when Jila's soggy salad legs buckled and Jila grabbed on to Katherine's right shoulder for support. "Jenny, I know somethin's happen' to Amy. I bin sick all night. Please, I gotta know," she begged. Katherine's eyes were filled with pain. Jila had never before seen such a look of remorse on her face. Her frazzled hair and beaten skin added years to her normally polished appearance.

Impatient and uncomfortable with this unexpected reunion, the big agent decided he had to do something. "Katherine, you have to come inside."

But Katherine ignored him and extended his order into an offer to Jila. "Come on in, Jila," she said. Wiping the tears away from her aching eyes, she backed into the stone-faced agent.

"No! Not a good idea," the agent warned, refusing to let go of the door.

"Please, the hell with your rules. You're a bit late if you're trying to protect me." Katherine was really pissed. She held on to Jila's hand and tried to pull her in.

"Look, Katherine, I'm just doing my job. We need to keep this place clean. The fewer people the better. I'm sorry," he said sternly. By this time, Jila's mind was on overload and the tug-of-war made her feel like a ball between two tennis rackets. Having never seen Katherine's temper before, she was taken aback. But she knew she had to do something to help Katherine.

"Jenny, I know…I know ya Katherine," she said haltingly, afraid of divulging what she knew before the four eyes that now glared at her in surprise. Katherine was totally startled by her admission. Jila gazed and waited for Katherine to give some sign. Thankfully, her big quiet browns spoke a language familiar to Katherine. Clearly, Sarah had shared their secret with Jila. Katherine felt relieved that she didn't have to explain her situation from scratch to her; only she had no idea exactly how much Jila knew. It had been years since she had allowed herself to be, simply, Katherine. Starting again troubled her, because it put her face to face with a past she preferred to forget.

"You see what I mean—not a good idea," the big agent asked. "She needs to go."

Katherine gave him a murderous look. "I said, come in, Jila!" Her bitchy eyes cut the agent down to her size. Then she reached for the door.

"Jenny, I'm so sorry. I'll go," Jila said, suddenly in the line of Katherine's death-grip stare.

"Don't, Jila," Katherine said. "We'll talk about this later. I'm glad you're here." She held up her hand in front of her and grabbed Jila for another hug. By then, the Big Guy was pretty pissed, but he didn't say a word. His crossed-arms look said it all, and he looked to his partner for support.

Jila glanced meekly at the other agent sitting at the table. The leather strap that belted his shoulder and the heavy metal piece in his cowhide holster gave her a chill. This wasn't real, she thought in her naive way. This only happened on TV. Her racing heartbeat sounded like the thunderous hoofs at a Kentucky Derby finish.

Tearful from the joy of seeing Jila, Katherine admitted, "Sarah is in trouble. Kidnapped. It happened sometime last night. I don't know what I'll do if anything happens to her, Jila. I just don't know." Despairing, she gazed into the young woman's eyes for comfort.

"I'm sorry, Jenny. I didn't mean to come over here and make things worse than they are, but I knew somethin' was goin' on. I can't explain it. I jus' get these sensations ever' once in a while, Jenny. I knew it somethin' real bad happen' to Amy. Don' ask me how—I jus' knew it," she cried, and then held her face in her hands.

"I'm glad you're here. Come on," Katherine said. She looked over her shoulder at the two agents. Both agents threw them a cutting glance, but in the end the smaller one nodded in acknowledgment.

"Just move away from the window, will ya," the Big Guy threw in his two cents' worth. "We're expecting a couple of our men here any minute. It's not safe. Why don't the two of you have a seat in the living room. We'll call you as soon as we hear something." But these words only grated on Katherine's raw nerves. She simply didn't care to hear anything he had to say, unless it was some good news about Sarah.

"Come on, Jila, don't be afraid," Katherine tried to soothe her.

Jila walked in without saying a word. She found it hard to detach herself from the agents' stares or to keep from contemplating their gear. They just didn't seem like they were there to help—at least, not the Big Guy. His partner, the one with the salt-and-pepper hair, looked younger and less intimidating.

"Oh, don't let them get to you. This is my house," Katherine said reassuringly.

"Jenny, she's 'live. I know she is. I feel it in here," Jila said, holding her hand firmly to her chest.

"I want to believe…I have to believe, Jila. If anything happens to her…"

Jila reached for her hand and suggested, "Oh, Jenny, let's pray. God will take care of Amy. It will be all right." Jila recited a Gullah prayer similar to the one given her on the day her father had died. So many visions went through her head, so many tears, but she prayed on.

Amy, she thought. Her friend's smiles and laughter were as Jila remembered her—they were running again all along the beach, the wind lifting their spirits.

*   *   *   *

In the back room, the doctor at Nick's side pitied his patient, who was wounded in an area that had no vital organs and yet was so easily sensitive. Nick struggled to stay conscious. He felt humiliated: he could have saved Sarah but he didn't. It was devastating.

He fretted and turned to reposition himself on his side and stared out the window, hoping to ignore the doctor. All he thought about was Sarah and Katherine, and the frantic hope of another chance to tell them how sorry he was. He needed their forgiveness. He had been only seconds away from succeeding—it just wrenched his gut. It was worse than that ignominious moment when he had heard Katherine's voice pleading with him not to hurt Sarah, his own daughter, as he held her tight in his arms four years ago in that godforsaken basement. But then he had no idea she was his girl.

What haunted him now was the sight of Sarah being carried away by two men and his failure to save her. Could he have done anything different, or was this his just desserts? He could only hope that some of it was truly beyond his control.

"Ah," he moaned and then took a deep breath before sinking his head deeper into his pillow. All he could do was shake his head in dismay, cry, and wonder if he should ever have come to the island. He'd been following Sarah for days, afraid of his own shadow. Maybe stepping forward would have prevented all of this. "*Oh!*" he cried out. "Sarah, forgive me!" he groaned, grimacing with pain as he lay in his own sweat.

This time the stubbed-faced doctor stood up. "I need to give you some more pain medicine," he said and reached into his bag. "You have to take it easy. This'll help," he promised, injecting Nick.

Nick stared at the bold-colored, flowered valances nestled above each window. He wished he had been the one on the ladder hanging them and looking into those beautiful browns of Sarah's. The cheerleader trophies, fallen-angel poster, and polished leaves in the room merely augmented his pain. There was no relief.

On the nightstand rested a majestic picture of Sarah in horns and pom-pom—a straight brunette with shoulder-length locks. Through the blur of semi-consciousness in his searching eyes, Nick caught her beautiful perpetual smile, which reminded him of another woman— her mother. But the tears of shame did not cease and he drifted off.

CHAPTER 14

▼

"Katherine!" Frank—the smaller, less offending agent—interrupted the two women.

Startled and unaccustomed to any of this, Jila sat expectantly on the edge of the sofa. Katherine held her hand to reassure her.

"I just want to let you know that the two men have arrived," Frank said. "They'll watch things on the outside—okay? We'll do our best not to draw attention to ourselves. When you have a moment, though, I'll have you meet them. Anything I can do for you?"

"Yes, why haven't you done anything to find Sarah? You've been here for hours. You've both talked to more people since you've been here than I do in a month, and I still haven't heard a word about Sarah's whereabouts. I really don't understand. My daughter is young and defenseless. The longer you wait, the less—" Katherine's voice broke as Jila comforted her and looked speechlessly into Frank's dark blue eyes that stared down upon them.

"Katherine, I know this is hard for you, but we're checking every lead we have. I expect news at any moment. These guys are not going to do anything to Sarah. I don't mean to upset you, but they want you and they'll use Sarah to get to you. Believe me, we're doing everything we can at this very moment. I assure you."

"I'm trying to believe that!" she answered. "I just want to trade my life for hers. Those bastards need to give me the opportunity and you have to make that happen! I trusted you—all of you. This should never have happened. How could you let it happen to Sarah?" She raised her voice again. "How could you?"

"Jenny, I know this is killin' ya," Jila said, wrapping her arms around her, "but ya gotta stay strong. Amy needs ya. I need ya. We all need ya. And I'm here to help—ya ain't 'lone anymore."

Frank had approached the sofa ready to throw in a few more words of comfort. "Katherine, I know none of this makes sense, but please give us the opportunity to help. We'll find Sarah; they won't harm her. They want her alive, trust me on this."

"Ya have to let 'em help," Jila said.

"But right now, I have to ask you to do something for me," the agent said. "We need a couple of better pictures of Sarah than we have, and anything else you think might help. You said you didn't know what she was wearing, but now you've got to check through her things. Check her jewelry for her necklace—anything that's missing."

Lifting her weary head off Jila's shoulder, a beaten Katherine muttered, "I'll do what I can. Just, *please*, find Sarah. Bring her back to me."

"Jenny, I think I can help," Jila interjected. "I know what she bin wearin' since yesterday. We was together. Had on her blue skirt and white tank top and those lil' bird earrin's ya gave her for her birthday."

"That's real helpful," Frank responded, obviously pleased.

"I'll check," Katherine said and turned her head toward the closed door down the hall.

"One of us will be glad to assist you," Frank said, pointing to his partners.

"I can handle this. I'm not afraid."

"I know you're not, and the doctor is in there," he replied. "One of us will go with you just to make sure."

"Nick doesn't scare me anymore. Just find Sarah, that's all I want from you."

"I'll have Doc wait outside the room, if that's okay with you?" Frank asked.

"Whatever," she said, feeling resigned. With those words she turned back to Jila with a vacuous look in her eyes. She stared directly at her, and yet her troubled soul was elsewhere, like a ghost of her previous self. It was as if she had gone into a trance.

Jila let Katherine's spirit rest, and Frank was understanding enough not to utter another word.

*   *   *   *

The bedroom door opened. The doctor stepped out quietly. "All done," he reported. "He should do fine. Just needs some time to recover. I gave him a shot of pain medicine. That should help, along with antibiotics," he told Frank through the open door of the bathroom while washing his hands.

Katherine made her way to the room. The smell of alcohol perked her nostrils. Nick silently watched from behind as she searched the closet and drawers. Katherine avoided looking at him.

"I'll check on him tomorrow," the doctor finally said, as he dropped a few of his belongings into the old black bag. Katherine didn't say a word. Instead, she contemplated the fact that within seconds she would be alone with Nick.

"I'll see you later. I'm going over to the mansion to freshen up. Call me if you need me sooner," the doctor said, walking past Frank near the bedroom door.

"Will do," Frank replied. "You okay, Katherine?" he called. He pushed the door gently ajar for a better view.

"Fine. I'll be out in a second."

He looked at Nick, who was trying to sit up, before the pain told him otherwise.

"Guess they don't trust me, Katherine," Nick said in a low monotone. The tension between them was as thick as molasses.

Why would he say this? thought Katherine. It infuriated her.

"Please, call me *Jenny*," she said.

"Jenny—I don't know a Jenny," he replied, puzzled.

"You're very astute, 'cause you don't know Katherine, either, and I don't know *you*. What in the hell do you want from me?" She was ready to do battle. "Do you think you can just pop back into my life after all you've done and I'm supposed to forgive you? I guess luck was on Sarah's and my side and we should be grateful."

Nick held on to his shoulder and desperately tried to sit up. "Katherine...I didn't know it was you...I mean...I didn't—"

"Look, folks," Frank interrupted, "this isn't the time."

"Please—let me handle this," she shouted to Frank, who continued to glare at Nick. She wasn't yet finished with Nick. "So, spare me. I never thought you could do something like that. The Nick I knew was different. You're no better than your pathetic father. The best thing he could have done was to get me out of your life. Do you have any idea the hell Sarah and I have been put through because of you and your father?"

"Kath—"

"I don't think so! Every day for four years, I've had to look into the mirror and repeat *Jennifer Perry* just so I don't make a mistake and forget. Every time I hear my own name, Katherine, I flinch. And my daughter—she's had to feel one name and call herself another. All this just for the sake of saving your poor daddy's fortune. I was just that black chick from the other side of the tracks who wasn't good enough for the Walters. Your father thought I wanted his money. He was too stupid to imagine that I really loved his son and would have loved him the same if he were penniless. Well, congratulations, Mr. Heir. I hope you and your father are happy."

"I didn't know, Katherine. And I didn't mean for this to happen. You have no idea what kind of hell I went through after I lost you. I looked and searched everywhere. I still recite the letter you left me—word for word. I would have protected you from my father," he protested. He was drenched in sweat again. He took a deep breath and grimaced from the sharp pain in his shoulder. "The day I found out what really happened I was devastated. But I was sitting in jail. My mother, yes my mother, finally told me the truth. She couldn't live with the guilt anymore. She overheard my father talking to Bobbie."

"Big Bobbie—now there's a real woman's man. Who's he beating up on these days? Don't tell me: the next punching bag your father doesn't approve of. I really pity the Walters. None of you are worth the trouble you've caused. Sarah and I have learned to cope with this trapped life. I really don't need your injured apology."

"But Katherine, I need—"

"Save it!" she said, waving him off.

"That's enough," Frank said. Nick stopped his pleadings. Enraged, Katherine charged past Frank and raced down the hall to her bathroom, where she fell to the floor and wept uncontrollably.

"Katherine!" Frank called out and turned the door knob. "Katherine, are you all right? Open the door."

"Jus' give her a moment," Katherine heard Jila say. "Let me try—*Jenny, it's me. Jila.* Open the door," she requested in her soft voice. "I'm here, if ya need me." Frank was at a loss for words. But Katherine wept on in drunken self-pity and colliding impulses and fears. She had once tried to alleviate the pangs of her broken life. She thought she had found some peace, but in the last twenty-four hours, the woman she used to know and had buried four years ago had come back. It was too overwhelming for someone who had had to change her very identity just to protect her and her daughter's lives. Now, with Sarah's disappearance, the unknown had come rushing back in. The most precious person in her life was missing and there was nothing she could do. Her own inevitable death, knowing Sarah was safe, would have been bearable, but even that was no longer an option.

Protection.

That's what they called it. *What a meaningless word!* Her once quiet home was a Fort Knox-in-waiting. She was enslaved by circumstance. Helpless. She knew there was no way out of having to follow someone else's lead. The price has been horrendous. She wondered what more she would have to pay.

"Jenny, please open the door," Jila pleaded. Inside Katherine's head was utter confusion, but she wanted so much to dig herself out of her hole, which felt deeper than a grave. But her reflexes wouldn't return. Her drenched armpits felt uncomfortable, and however much she wanted to release her buried face from her lap, she couldn't.

Katherine was sinking into an abyss. She was paralyzed.

"Sarah! Sarah! I'm sorry. I'm so sorry." Tears of regret salted her lips. She rocked back and forth.

Nick was pasted to the sheets in a room that felt like a tomb, but he heard Jila's troubled pleas. Maybe death would help ease the pain he had caused Katherine. But then, even death may not be enough, he thought. No one would ever distinguish the selfish man who had been molded by his father from the man who had emerged after losing his beloved Katherine.

He hoped that Katherine would listen to those who were trying to help her. It killed him to know that she was reliving the pain he had already put her through. Nick had lost all that really mattered in his life and Katherine's double jeopardy was ripping him apart. His erstwhile tan, now a mass of pale skin, showed the signs of his agony. He had become the man he hated the most: his father. Seeing Sarah again made him understand, for the first time in his life, what it felt like to love a child who would never love you back.

The man he had once promised himself never to become now lived inside of him. "Open the door, Katherine…they can help," he muttered feebly in panic to himself. He had to save her.

CHAPTER 15

▼

Anxious, Frank was back at the kitchen table. He was at pains to apply the Bureau's directives to the precarious situation at hand, and it was simply not a good idea to have Nick stay in the house.

He looked inside and was surprised that his partner had abandoned his post. The door was partially open, and he overheard voices outside. His partner was on the porch talking to the other agents.

Frank was about to pick up the phone when the Big Guy returned. "What's going on?" the Big Guy asked.

"What do you mean what's going on? Didn't you hear all that shit in the back?" Frank was ticked off at the other agent's casual attitude.

"Yeah, I heard. But you had everything under control." He parked his butt in the cool chair he had abandoned earlier. "I don't like that look on your face. Who are you calling?"

"Listen, we have to do something about Walters. We can't keep him here. She really doesn't need this. I'm going to call the Bureau and arrange to get him out of here. I'm sure they can work something out."

"Not a good idea, Frank. He's as much of a witness as her. I'm not sure we can protect him anywhere else."

"What in the hell are you talking about?" Frank said, throwing his hands up in the air. "There's enough of us to cover his sorry ass."

"Frank, I'm not challenging what you're saying, I'm just saying this guy is dangerous. Riggins' little entourage is thicker than many of us give him credit for. Who in the hell woulda thought he'd find a nameless woman on a sparsely populated island? Scary, huh? I've been involved in a lot of cases, none as screwed up as this, let me tell you."

"What do you mean?" Frank said, walking over to the sink. "Help me understand."

The Big Guy stood up. "Frank, think about it. Katherine is one in a million. Someone like her should have been put in protection and forgotten about. I never thought we'd be dealing with a situation like this. I put this case to rest a long time ago. Who ever thought she'd become a problem before the trial. The timing is too perfect. I'm not getting good vibes."

"You may be right. Might be someone on the inside…Hey, forget what I just said—I can't believe I said that. All this shit is starting to drive me crazy."

"Frank, I wasn't going in that direction, I just said I don't like the vibes. This is getting crazy. Let's not forget that Katherine has her issues, too."

"What do you mean by that?" Frank said, unnerved, setting his glass on the counter.

"I'm just saying, maybe she was after the guy's money. Marrying Nick Walters would have given her a lot of clout. I'm not saying it's true, but you never know."

"I can't believe you said that. You of all people; you studied the files. Where's this shit coming from? I'm getting a big disconnect here. If that's what you're thinking, maybe this isn't the right assignment for you."

"I'm doing my job and just being honest. You're right, I'm very familiar with all of this. But there's a lot going on here. Do you think this whole Riggins debacle is easy?" The agent backed away, feeling somewhat ruffled.

Leaning against the counter, a placid look on his face, Frank pursued him. "You really surprise me. You're one of the few people I wouldn't have suspected of entertaining such screwed-up thinking. I think we better end it here."

"That's not what I'm trying to do, Frank. I'm dealing with reality here. Take a break, will you. Why don't you go check on Katherine? Maybe that girl will let you get closer."

"Fucking funny…very funny," Frank said, heated. "You're starting to scare me."

"Not my intention—just a reality check. Frank, this is really starting to get to you, isn't it? I'm not used to seeing you like this."

"Maybe, but not to the point that I can't do my job or think straight."

The Big Guy tapped his pen on the table, refusing to respond, which would only give Frank the satisfaction.

"There's a reality base here," Frank said, pointing to his forehead. "I'm a father with a teenage daughter. I can't imagine what it would be like if something like this happened to her. It would kill me. That woman is hurting and there's not a thing we can do but wait for that phone to ring. The bastards!" He was shouting now, and pounding his clenched fist on the counter top.

"Take it easy, man," the Big Guy said and twirled his pen on the table. "They'll call—" A loud crash suddenly broke into his words and startled them both. "What the hell?" he said, grabbing his gun and looking around.

"Oh, shit, it came from the back room. Katherine! Jila!" Frank yelled, running down the hall. "Are you all right?"

"Oh, my God!" Jila exclaimed. She cupped her face in disbelief as she looked on. Nick had fallen out of the bed and pulled everything on the nightstand down with him. His face was chalky white, his eyes half open, and his body stretched out next to the bed, motionless. "*Help!*" Jila screamed.

"Damn! Call for help," Frank ordered. "Get the doctor."

"I heard you. I—phone's ringing," responded the Big Guy.

"Answer it! I'll look after this," Frank shouted. Katherine rushed out of her room. "Katherine, don't come in here," he ordered and hovered over Nick.

"The phone," she shouted, moving her legs faster than her muscles seemed to permit. Then breathless, she stood next to the big agent who had picked up the receiver, and she hung on each word escaping his lips. Her mind was racing out of control, but she listened on with Jila.

"Yeah, ah-ha," he said. "I understand. How long? Things are getting kinda crazy here. Yeah, she's all right. Call me as soon as you hear something."

"What's going on?" Katherine asked. "Who was that? Did they find her?"

"Not yet, our men are on their way to Riggins' house. Things are picking up around there."

Katherine had no idea what was going on. "Picking up! Who in the hell cares about Riggins? I want to know about Sarah! Tell me something—anything!" she shouted, desperate and confused. "You have to know! You have to know!"

"Please, Jenny, please," Jila pleaded. Everyone was exhausted.

"We've been staking out Riggins' house for a long time. With Sarah missing, my guess is he's trying to figure out what to do next. This may be the opportunity we've been waiting for."

"Are you saying he's responsible for Sarah's disappearance and you knew about it? That bastard is a killer, he'll stop at nothing."

"No, I'm not saying that. I don't know. We figured the closer we get to bringing him to trial the greater the chance he might do something, but—"

"And you knew he was coming after us?"

Pausing, the Big Guy gave Katherine a foreign look. "No! I didn't say that," he replied in a firm voice.

"You liar! I don't believe you! You're liars! All of you." Katherine kept shouting as Jila tried to pull her away. Jila guided her to the living room and sat her unsteadily on the sofa. Katherine's look was unforgiving when Frank entered the room and pulled up a chair.

"We're doing everything we can. I promise," he said.

"I don't want to hear about it. You're just wasting time. Sarah is out there. Those bastards! Please, forget about Riggins. Find Sarah. Why haven't they called?"

Preoccupied, Frank acknowledged Katherine's pleas. While Jila's eyes stared questioningly, creaks were heard from the porch and the faint shadows of the buff agents crossed the window. Frank shook his head. He wasn't at all sure how Katherine would manage. And it really troubled him that there were no clues yet as to Sarah's whereabouts. His thoughts then shifted to the closed door down the hall. There was nothing more he could do. Nick was again in the hands of the doctor. Rubbing his forehead as he leaned against the wall in his anxiety, he watched the two women. Jila had ably calmed Katherine. The dark beauty of her young face showed lips that only Picasso could shape, but she clearly took on responsibilities beyond her years.

Frank gazed with his midnight eyes at the polished handle of his gun. The clock on the wall was silently inching to eleven. Katherine played eyeball tennis between the clock and Sarah's picture that sat in the middle of the coffee table. Innocent beauty enveloped her. Her cream de-cacao skin was highlighted by brunette locks. Things were deathly quiet but Sarah's picture seemed to flicker with life.

The little house on Daufuskie nestled between the great oaks and pines hid more drama that day than any of its rich neighbors could ever imagine. Daufuskie's big news had invariably been about some resident professional hockey player, an occasional visit from a tennis pro, or all the millionaires enjoying their wealth. Katherine, a New York girl turned suburbanite and now an Islander, had traveled the gamut. Put five bucks in her hand and ask her what might make her happy and her only answer would be her daughter at her side, her birthright, and a humble place to live. That was all.

The phone rang again.

Shaken, eyes fixed, Frank answered. "Hello."

"Yes," said an unfamiliar voice. "I have the girl."

CHAPTER 16

▼

The old-school doctor wiped his brow as he exited the room, his stethoscope hanging crookedly across his wrinkled white shirt. He was drained, but he quickly ran into the hysterical exchanges between Katherine, who was throwing questions faster than anyone could comprehend, and the agents assigned to her protection. He approached without saying a word.

The Big Guy was in charge. From his seat, he commanded the mental traffic, but his bulk blocked the doctor's view. "Excuse me," the doctor said, steadying his stethoscope, "may I have a moment with you?" His words were quickly lost in the mayhem. One agent signaled him to lower his voice, before Big Guy pulled him aside. Towering beside him, he listened to what he had to say.

"He has taken a turn for the worse," the doctor announced.

"Listen, I need to know, is he gonna be all right or not?" The Big Guy whispered, looking over his shoulder.

"It's the infection—it's gotten worse. He's running a high fever. A little disoriented."

"You can take care of him—right, Doc? We can't move him. What do you think, Doc?"

"It's your call, he's on antibiotics. He'll need to be watched closely. Do you think it's safe here?" He sensed the agent's agitation.

"As safe as can be. Listen, we need to keep him here. We're not sure who might be watching."

"I'll make sure he's well taken care of. If things get worse we'll need to get him out of here, though. If we don't, next news you hear won't be good, and I'd rather not have my name attached on that end." By then, Frank was staring at them, but the doctor didn't tarry. He turned right around to resume his medical duties.

Katherine's view was obscured by a six-paneled chunk of wood and she was too preoccupied with thoughts of Sarah to notice this exchange.

*   *   *   *

"Barry, have you heard from Walters yet? I need to make sure that son-of-a-bitch isn't up to his old tricks again. Remember what I said earlier. Any more on what happened with the Feds?"

"Boss, I went over—thought it'd be safer to do that. These guys are making me nervous. I sure will be glad when this is over." Barry slapped his pack of cigarettes with his finger and positioned himself in his usual spot next to the window. The plush pines blocked his view of the gates, but so many new questions were filtering through his mind, the most important of which had to do with what was going on at the other end of the iron rods.

"But what did you find out?" Riggins asked, lighting up a cigar.

"Walters claims the Feds were there checking up on Nick and had a few questions. From what I could tell he didn't anticipate they'd return."

"Did you see Nick?" Riggins asked.

"No, I never left the study. I'm sure he didn't want my presence known."

"Do you believe him?" Riggins sucked on his cigar.

Barry didn't respond. He wasn't a mind reader, but his looks said it all. "My thoughts exactly," Riggins concluded. The two men traded stares—Barry with his back against the wall, Riggins molded to his chair and tapping out his cigar. "I haven't heard from them," Riggins remarked, his eyes pinned to the phone.

"May I suggest patience. Not hearing from them is good. They're big boys. I don't think you need to worry, Boss. They understand what needs to be done; plus, you told them to make her sweat," Barry said, certain his words had barely registered.

"I'm sorry, did I ask for your advice?"

This time Barry answered back, saying, "I believe you were talking to me."

"I was talking, but I didn't think I needed any direction," Riggins replied.

"Boss, let's clear the air. I'm here to help you. But whatever I do, it's never right with you is it? Help me understand." Barry put out one cigarette and fired up another with a slight tremor of his hands.

"All of you are screwing with my patience. Look around this place. I'm living in a tomb. This wasn't supposed to turn out this way. I'm the one that needs protection, I'm the victim. All I did was help those sons-of-bitches make some bucks. Shit, I deserve to get paid for my work."

"Things got a lot deeper than just helping out a few friends. Four of them are now dead," Barry reminded Riggins, then buried his cigarette as he exhaled.

Riggins opened his silver pill box and popped one. With a quick wince he drained his drink. "They only got what they asked for," he said in a thick voice. "If you want to play with the big boys, your balls better be thick enough not to crack under pressure. I don't regret a damn thing." Riggins' words belied his worried, distant look.

"Do you think this will ever get to trial, Boss? I think they will keep searching in this direction until they find something."

"Not if I find it first," Riggins quickly replied. "That Katherine chick is only one piece of the puzzle, it's apparent they need more. I know they're trying to confirm what she has told them. The others aren't talking, they're afraid. But Walters concerns me. He'll do anything to protect that son of his."

"There you go—talking about Walters again."

"I don't have time for this shit," Riggins scowled.

"Sorry Boss, I didn't mean to upset you. I mean…I don't think we need to worry about him, he's on autopilot," Barry said reassuringly.

"That bothers me even more. Because he's quiet doesn't mean he's asleep. Remember when I told you I didn't trust him? I've since confirmed his son's been looking for Katherine, too."

"I don't understand," Barry replied. "What would old Walters want with her now? It's my understanding that he wanted her as far away from his son as possible. I wouldn't think he'd do anything to have her surface again. It doesn't make sense."

"That's why I'm the boss," he said with pride, pouring himself another drink and sitting up in his chair. "Listen, she can help clear his son's name and make things look bad for me. Without her, it's all hearsay. Believe me, I know what I'm doing."

Riggins positioned himself in Barry's usual spot next to the window. The stub of his cigar was just short of singeing his fingertips. He watched as the groundskeeper mowed the velvet grass in the courtyard. His mind returned to an old friend—Manelli. At least that was how he thought of him then. Manelli weighed on his mind for a reason.

Riggins knew Manelli's banking business was going sour. But he had heard it through the grapevine, well before Manelli had told him that things weren't going well. Manelli was no doubt aware that Riggins had made a lot of money helping other bankers after leaving Wall Street. When Manelli reached out to Riggins, it didn't take long before he was trapped. He had expected to make money for the small fee he had to pay Riggins. But he was greedy and in over his head, and then, like the others, Manelli wanted out without having to pay his debts. However, his inability to repay Riggins as promised and Riggins' subsequent blackmail forced him to continue stealing from the institution—and bit by bit the noose tightened. Riggins, aware of Manelli's activities, used this knowledge to his advantage; there was no letting go. Riggins thought of himself as nothing more than a middleman trying to help an old friend in trouble, but the money was good.

Feeling uncomfortable, Riggins stared through the glass menagerie that he had built, as Manelli's face, filled with pain and horror, became more distinct to his mind's eye. It was like yesterday and Riggins could see it clearly.

A shot rang out.

Riggins was jolted out of his trance, but the smoking gun was only in his imagination this time. He backed away from the window, dazed from thinking so much about Glen's killing of Manelli. He staggering to his desk and searched for his little box, his hand trembling slightly as he placed another pill into his mouth, followed by a gulp from his drink.

Barry had no idea what Riggins was seeing—to him, his boss seemed a little delusional. In fact, Riggins' terror made Barry shrink back. But he, too, recalled Glen's description of what he had done that afternoon to Manelli, even if for him it had never been more than that: a description.

"Boss, are you okay?" Barry asked. His words might as well have been addressed to the dead. There was no response.

CHAPTER 17

▼

The hours passed since their initial call. It was dark, close to eleven, and still no word. Paul anxiously traveled the floor, thirsty for a drink. The acid that rested at the bottom of his stomach told him something was wrong. "Why haven't they called back?" he asked, observing the troubled look on Jeff's face.

"It's getting late, we shoulda heard something by now. I think something is up. Maybe I'll call the Boss. He'll know what to do," Jeff said.

"He might, but that's not the issue right now. They said they needed some time. Those bastards are plotting, but we have the upper hand—we've got the girl. They won't let anything happen to her. I know I wouldn't," Paul said with a grin. "She's our ticket outta here. Maybe they need to understand we're not bullshitting."

"I think they know that."

"What makes you think that? They haven't responded. It's in their hands, isn't it? They're planning something, I know it. I'm not getting good vibes. This is a time bomb and I don't plan to be around for the explosion."

"What are you thinking?" Jeff said, but Paul was already almost out of the door. "Hey, where are you going?"

"Give me a few and I'll get their attention."

"Paul, don't screw around; our asses are on the line."

"Do you think they aren't already?" he replied and left the room.

*   *   *   *

In the corner of the bed, Sarah was cowered in an upright fetal position with her frazzled brunette locks hanging heavily over her face. Sounds and a persistent light beaming beneath the door alerted her that someone was approaching. Terrified, she inched closer to the wall and stayed there, cupped by the bare mattress that supported her. With her eyes closed she began to chant, "Jila, Jila, Jila, Jila," which she continued as the door opened. This was something she and Jila had done many times before, especially when they traveled to the protected land of Gullah Heaven.

*   *   *   *

Jila's eyes opened. She lay in her bed looking up at the white ceiling that sheltered her. She cranked her head, clutched the wrinkled sheets and, in seconds, her body was gyrating back and forth on the bed. "Father, Father, Father," she chanted. A large black man dressed in a dingy white shirt, gray ankle-length pants and with cotton-wool teeth reached out for her with arms spread wide and a welcoming smile. A peaceful warmth spread across her skin and magically filled her room.

"Father, Father," she repeated. Her body relaxed at the sight of his smile.

"Father," the man's voice soothed. "Have no fear, child." Jila found herself in a lonely darkness, but now she was comforted and at peace. She had taken an unexpected trip to Gullah Heaven, certain her prayers had been answered.

*　　　*　　　*　　　*

"I'm not going to hurt you, just do as I say," Paul ordered after walking in as stealthily as he could. "Now, come here." But Sarah was too frightened to respond. "I said come here, dammit!" His knees pressed against the foot of the bed. "You're going to tell them they're running out of time. Now, get your ass over here!" he shouted. This time, he took hold of her ankle.

Sarah's eyes gaped wide and she chanted desperately as she struggled to free herself.

"Shut up!" he ordered and pulled her towards him. The next sound that escaped his mouth was a startled, "Ahhh." He relinquished his grip and his mouth opened wide to complete the utterly dismayed look on his face. He felt nausea, his vision blurred, and his head throbbed. "Aah!" he yelled out again, and gripped his head tightly. "What...what's hap...?" But his body fell forward limply, writhed for a moment, and then lay quietly splayed in front of Sarah. Sarah's chanting slowly tapered off and she backed up against the wall.

Paul was writhing some more when Jeff rushed into the room. "What the hell—Paul, what's going on?" Paul moaned, his hand reaching helplessly for his head. Sarah did not stir. Her breathing slowed down as a peaceful warmth enveloped her.

"What did you do to him?" Jeff demanded.

Paul was weaker than a wet noodle, his unfocused eyes looking somewhere between his shoes and the bed. In a tired, faint voice, he pleaded, "Get me out of here."

Jeff helped him to the sofa and asked, "Are you all right? What happened in there?"

"What...happened?"

"Yeah. Man, you don't look good."

"In there," Paul pointed. "The room—"

"You're all screwed up. Now, leave her alone. Listen to me. They called. That's what I was coming to tell you. They're bringing her to us. So, just relax."

"About time," Paul replied in a flustered tone. "When?" he remembered to ask. "Give me a drink."

"I don't think that's a good idea, but you look like you need something," Jeff said. He placed his spent cigarette in the ashtray and headed towards the kitchen. Paul groggily placed his head against the back of the sofa and waited.

On the other side of the wall, Sarah stared at the door in disbelief.

Jeff quickly returned to sit on the sofa. He leaned forward, hands locked around his knee. "Now, let's talk about what we need to do. Are you okay?" Jeff asked.

"I'm okay. Light me one. What did they say?" Paul asked and gulped down his drink.

"We need to call them with the final instructions, but this is the plan."

CHAPTER 18

▼

"They're here, Boss. What should I do?"

"Just relax, Barry. I can handle this. Those bastards don't have anything on me. Close the door."

"Don't you think they would have found something by now—anything?"

"No! Don't bitch on me now. Maybe it'd be better if you weren't around. The last thing I need is a weak cock waving a guilty sign while I'm being questioned. The bottom line is I haven't done a thing. You remember that. I've never stolen anyone's money. I never murdered anyone. My hands are clean along with my conscience."

"All I'm saying is these guys are smart, not your coffee-and-donuts type. Just be careful. You'd think after all this time they'd give up."

"Apparently you haven't been listening to a thing I said. You of all people should know those guys won't rest until they have something. I've been through this before and so have you. Now, look at me: do I look worried?" He flailed his hands in the air. "Just follow my lead," he said, ending the conversation with a hefty drink.

While Riggins prepared himself for the inquisition, the two FBI agents arrived at his front gate. The men drove past the gothic walls of black iron on the earth-colored marbled road leading up to the front door. The glistening driveway wove among a concourse of trees and flowerbeds.

Barry nervously waited as the Westminster chimes sounded.

The agents examined the leaded glass door. It was so dazzling they would have needed sunglasses to examine it properly. They watched the brass handle of the door as it turned.

"Please come in. Mr. Riggins is in his study. May I offer you gentleman something to drink?" Dan asked.

"No, thank you," the agent responded. "But we appreciate the offer,"

Continuing his military strut, Dan flashed them a quick grin and said, "This way. Follow me, please."

Riggins and Barry had been hovering around the desk. Barry finished his cigarette and crushed its remnants in the ashtray as the agents entered the room wearing unyielding expressions.

"Mr. Riggins, your guests," Dan said with a false smile.

"Thanks, please make sure I'm not interrupted."

"Yes sir, will that be all for now?"

"Yes," Riggins replied, before turning to the two agents with his own unwelcoming stare. A game of words and body language was about to begin. Silent stares lingered for a few seconds, although it seemed much longer, as each man maneuvered into position. Riggins then took command from behind his desk. Barry, on the other hand, assumed his usual sheepish pose. He loosely tucked his hands in his pockets as he deliberated over what to do next.

After the introductions, Agent Armstrong was the first to speak. "Mr. Riggins, we are here to ask you a few questions about a missing girl and a few other matters."

"Missing girl?" Riggins responded, willing himself against looking at Barry, who was just short of pissing in his pants.

"Yes, that's correct. Is there a problem?" the agent asked.

"What do you mean? Did I say there was? I'm not sure what you're getting at."

Impatient, Armstrong replied, "Listen, let's cut the bullshit. All of us in this room are aware that your name has been linked to the investments bankers' murders and you've been questioned by us in the past. Is that correct?" He leaned closer to Riggins.

"Just because a man is questioned doesn't make him guilty," Riggins replied.

"Make him guilty?" Armstrong repeated. "Interesting choice of words. But you haven't been charged with anything, Mr. Riggins."

"So what in the hell are you here for? I don't believe you drove up here just to tell me I haven't been charged."

"I think I made myself clear earlier—a girl is missing."

"So what the hell does that have to do with me?" Riggins asked. "Young girls come up missing every day."

Angered by Riggins' statement, agent Rodriguez interrupted them. "As you recall, the mother had some interesting things to say about you. I'm sure you were made aware of this fact."

"I seem to recall something about that, yes. The chick lived in upper New York and was being banged by Walters' son. I recall that, too. But that's yesterday's news. Anything to add to what I already know?" This time Riggins threw a quick look to Barry, whose frightened eyes told him he needed to get those agents out of there.

"Are we gonna play games here?" Armstrong asked. "I understand there were allegations that you had ordered the murders by the detective who was killed—you know, the one named Glen. I would think that deserves more than a recall response."

"Listen, I don't have time for this crap today. What do you really want from me?" Pointing a finger at the agent, he continued, "Let's not waste taxpayers' money."

"Do you really think that's what we're doing?" Rodriguez asked.

"Do you think I care?" Riggins replied.

Armstrong stretched out his arms, placed his hands on the desk, and said in a controlled voice, "Listen, Mr. Riggins, you're well aware that this mother and daughter were believed to have the goods on you.

Somehow, you've managed to elude us. But now the girl is missing and I believe you know where she is."

"Really, what crystal ball are you looking into? You'd better back up, buddy. Your deck is short of fifty-two, and I have more important things to do than to worry about some girl and her mother. That chick was nothing more than free pussy for Walters' son. Besides, I heard they were protected. Did the Bureau boys screw up?"

"So, you're saying you don't know anything about the missing girl."

"You're sharp," Riggins replied. Sensing he was getting under the agent's collar, and enjoying it, Riggins turned to face his underling. "Barry, what do you think? Do I need to say it again?" Barry said nothing.

"Mr. Riggins, you're a smart man, but even Hitler was buried. On second thought, I'm not sure we have a comparison here."

At that point Barry found his voice. "Ha, that's an understatement," he sneered.

"Excuse me, did you say something?" Armstrong asked, shooting a murderous look at Barry. Then he turned back to the object of his scrutiny. "Mr. Riggins, I'm through for now, but somehow I don't think this is the last time we'll see each other."

Riggins replied, "I'm sure it isn't. I'll be watching out for you on TV. I'm sure at this rate you'll be one of the FBI's finest." His smirk was almost unbearable.

Armstrong flashed a professional smile and backed away from the desk. "Time—it's an amazing thing when it's not on your side."

"I wouldn't know," Riggins said. "I have better things to do than to sit around watching the clock."

Before leaving, Armstrong decided to use the phone. "Do you mind?"

"Why should I, if that's all it takes to get the two of you the hell out of here," Riggins directed.

As Armstrong made his call, Barry whispered a few words into Riggins' ear. He still had that troubled look on his face, which he tried unsuccessfully to hide as much as he could.

"Thanks," Armstrong said, after he hung up.

"Anytime. Next time make sure you have your facts straight before you waste my time again."

"Let's get out of here," Rodriguez directed, while glaring at Riggins. Armstrong paused, his hand on the doorknob. But Rodriguez quickly nudged him. Armstrong settled for a final good look at Riggins before exiting, under the watchful eye of Barry, who then wiped the sweat off his brow, although he could do nothing about the sweat that had had already soaked the top of his collar. Riggins gulped some air and stood tensely watching the heavy Suburban pull away.

"Barry, we've got work to do," he said, reaching into his pocket for his pill box, then popping a couple of pills from his shaking palm.

＊　　　＊　　　＊　　　＊

"Man, that Riggins guy is a work of art. He did everything he could to provoke you."

"That's because he knows a lot more that he's letting on," Armstrong said.

"I was watching that other character while you were talking to him—he looked real nervous. He must have smoked four cigarettes in the short time we were there. I thought he was going to say something when you mentioned the murders, but the look on Riggins' face seemed to silence him pretty quick."

"That son-of-a-bitch knows exactly where the girl is—I'd bet my career on it. But we haven't much time," Armstrong said.

"What do you mean?" Rodriguez asked.

"If he doesn't get what he's looking for, they'll kill just to get rid of the evidence. That bastard's smart. He's a pro at this, but I intend to nail his ass. The last thing they have a hope in hell of doing, if I can help it, is putting their hands on Katherine. We're running out of time."

"They're supposed to make the trade sometime today. What do you intend to do?"

"To do?" Armstrong flashed a devious smile. "Do," he repeated again for emphasis, "or did?"

"You did! You son–of–a gun. You already did it!" Rodriguez said.

"What do you think? I needed to make a phone call like a roach needs insecticide. That fuck thinks he's smart. As I said, he and I will meet again real soon. He's mine."

CHAPTER 19

▼

A false calm hung in the air. Southern dew had formed on the rows of flowers lining the short driveway of the house. Everywhere colorful blooms camouflaged the mortal danger that lurked.

Frank stood in the doorway, arms outstretched and inhaling the smell of the earth. A couple of trucks loaded with pine mulch drove by. In the distance, avid golfers were already making their way along the course; a father stood over his son to redirect his swing. It was all so picturesque—Frank couldn't help but reminisce about his youthful outings with his dad.

Everything deceptively innocent, Frank thought. Hidden were the sufferings that had engulfed the family they were supposed to be protecting.

Frank drew in a final breath of fresh air before closing the door. Inside, everyone was just waiting for the phone to ring. This investigation has taken its toll on everyone, especially Katherine. Frank remembered the first time he saw a picture of Katherine and Sarah—the same one that rested on the coffee table. It was four years ago, shortly after their rescue. Now, her clothes tainted with blood and soot, Katherine seemed a shadow of the woman in that picture. She lay wrapped in an army blanket, as if she had just been released from a refugee camp. The terror on her face haunted him.

Frank ran his hands through his unruly hair, trying to control his emotions and thoughts about everything that had happened over the last couple of days.

"Frank, you look a little—" the Big Guy said.

"Naw, just a little tired."

"Been a long night."

"What in the hell is taking them so long?"

"Who?"

"Anyone, it's driving me fuckin' crazy not hearing a thing."

"Frank, call the Bureau, or I will. See if they heard anything. You'd think someone would have called back. You did make it clear these guys were serious—right?"

"Exactly what I did yesterday morning. They were planning to question Riggins today. The last thing I want to do is to lose Katherine. I wish we could have traced that fuckin' call," he said, pouring himself a cup of coffee.

"These guys know what they're doing. They want Katherine and will not stop until they get her," the Big Guy said.

"What I want to know is how in the hell they found out we were about to close the curtain on Riggins? It doesn't make sense. The only thing that could have made him go after Katherine is if he knew something was going down." Elbows anchored to the table, Frank held his head and looked across the room with an empty expression on his face. "This shouldn't be happening. That woman is right, you know!"

"These things happen," the Big Guy said, taking a seat across from Frank. "She wasn't put into the 24-7 program, just protected. Who in the hell would think someone would find them here? And why would they take her daughter instead?"

"Why should that surprise you? Katherine rarely leaves the island— makes her nervous. It would have been pretty difficult to drag her away without being spotted. If they did, someone else would have been killed in the process. That would not have been a smart thing to do."

"You're right, Frank," the Big Guy said perfunctorily. "I'm going to step outside and have one. Call me if you hear anything. And remember, this is no different than any other case. We're just doing our job."

"You do that," Frank replied, dissatisfied with his colleague's easy attitude.

The Big Guy stepped outside and closed the door behind him. In reality, he couldn't let go of the conversation he'd just walked away from. The agent on duty outside said to him, "You look like you just saw a ghost. Have you heard something?"

"Naw—I need some fresh air," he answered in a detached tone of voice.

"We made sure someone stayed on the dock. The guys took turns last night. I've also arranged for someone to be on the ferry. That should help," the agent informed him.

"Good," the Big Guy replied. "Do they think we need more men?"

"Not yet. We have a couple of guys on Hilton Head watching that end. We're okay for now."

The Big Guy noticed that the other man was moving listlessly back and forth, acting like he was carrying the world on his shoulders. "Sit down, will you? You're making me dizzy." Then he paused. "Hey, I'm sorry. Guess I'm just tired. I'm taking a break." He made his way down the drive.

His eyes directed at another agent standing in the wings, the first agent said, "Something's spooking the Big Guy. I don't like the way he looks."

"Aw, let him be. Just tired like the rest of us," the agent said. "Quiet—here he comes. Just let it go, will you," he urged. "That was quick," he told the Big Guy.

"I need to take a deep shit," the Big Guy grinned.

"Don't funk up the place," the agent quipped. "If I'm going to die I'd rather it be of natural causes."

"I'll be back; hold down the fort."

*   *   *   *

"Hey, guy, wake up!" Frank shouted and pushed the bathroom door open. "Good news. Riggins' place has been bugged, finally."

"Shit! Close the door, man. Can't you see—"

"Wipe your ass and get out here, things are heating up."

In no time, the Big Guy was out, and was tucking in his shirt as he entered the room. "What's happening?"

"We're going to bust that bastard's ass wide open," Frank said. "Where did Katherine go? We need to let her know."

"Maybe she's taking a nap," the Big Guy said.

"Cut the crap. I'll go and get her," Frank said.

Katherine had been sitting quietly in her room, praying, resting her exhausted body, though not her mind. She desperately wanted Sarah to know that she was doing everything she could. She kept seeing a little eleven-year-old girl with braces, eyes closed, surrounded by her tiny friends, and about to blow out her birthday candle. The image haunted Katherine. If she could only go back to that innocent day of Sarah's birthday party and stay there forever! She saw it as clearly as one would a Polaroid picture. Tim Oberman, Sarah's stepfather, was there. He had accepted her as his own and stood by her in her trials. His face glowed in smiles that day as he held two gallons of ice cream, ready to serve it. He loved to spoil her and on her birthdays he was at his best.

Katherine wondered if any of this would have happened had they not separated.

The money, the list, their brush with death, Nick's reappearance, their exile to a sparsely populated island—and now this. So many things had punctured the tranquility of her life. And so much guilt—particularly about her decision to flee before John Walters' blackmail. She could still hear the exchange on that fateful day that John Walters had sent his crony Bobbie to her apartment. "Miss Mills!" Bobbie had said in a stern voice. "Nick Walters knows nothing about this, but you are very astute. There's something, however, that John Walters wants from you."

"Mister Bobbie, or whatever your name is," she pluckily replied, "I think you should leave, and please take your money with you! I can't be bought. Oh, it all makes sense now! John Walters doesn't think I'm good enough for his son—I'm just some poor girl after his money. Now, I know why I never got invited to the Walters'. Me, that black woman from the wrong side of the tracks, trying to woo their son. I can't believe the audacity of that man, that family! He never had the guts to meet me. He's probably sitting *right now* on his throne thinking, *That poor girl, what an embarrassment to my family! How can my son care for such a girl?* It must be eating him alive knowing that Nick loves me. That's why you're here! Well just leave. Get out and take—"

"Wait a minute, you little lowlife black bitch! I've tried the nice approach, but you don't seem to understand. Now it's time to give you the big picture, you little slut. Listen to me: If you don't break up this relationship and leave New York, Nick will be disinherited. Do you understand what I'm saying? Disinherited! He'll have nothing. All the hard work he's put into the business will have been for nothing. He won't inherit a red cent of the Walters' millions. Do you think for one moment that'll make him happy to be with you? He'd never forgive you, no matter how hard he tried or how much he loved you, as you claim. Every time he looks at you, he'd feel nothin' but resentment. He would despise you. Could you live with that, bitch?" Bobbie paused for effect. "You better wise up and do it now! Take the money and help your poor dying old man go in peace. You can do that for him, at least. If you don't break up the relationship, Mister Walters will get rid of your little ass! I hear you're smart. You'd better put your brains to work!"

He looked down at the envelope in his hands and continued, "Inside, you'll find instructions on what you should say to Nick when you end this farce. Remember, if you tell him anything about any of this, he'll be disinherited and I'll be coming after you."

"Are you threatening me?" Katherine couldn't believe her ears.

"Let me put it this way—you won't get the opportunity to see your old man cold. Here. I'm leaving you the money. When your father is discharged from the hospital, I expect you to leave town and never set eyes on Nick again. If you ever do, you'll regret it. I promise you that. You'll also find some of your father's medical records in the envelope. Don't bother to make any contacts once you leave."

That was eighteen years ago.

Katherine wondered what the outcome would have been had she been brave enough to tell Nick what his father was up to.

Would it have made a difference?

Maybe Nick, instead of Tim, would have been at Sarah's birthday party? But would Nick have willingly sacrificed everything for her, and would he have been able to protect her from his father?

Katherine was buried in sorrow. What's worse, a puzzling concern for Nick's condition was creeping up from deep inside her. "God, please get me through this and bring Sarah home alive," she begged, and then buried her head in the pillow.

Her thoughts were interrupted by a knock on the door. It was Frank.

"Katherine, hurry! Good news!" He could hardly contain himself. "Open the door."

She did and immediately faced him. "Did they find Sarah?"

"We're getting close. Riggins' place has been bugged. It's gonna tip the balance of the evidence. We've been trying to do it for some time and we finally did. He'll know where Sarah is."

She brushed her hair out of her face.

"Frank, it's them on the phone," the Big Guy yelled. Frank and Katherine ran towards him, and Frank quickly grabbed the phone, waving them to hush.

"Ah-ha, Ah-ha…Where? What about the girl? I'm not comfortable with that…What do you mean she has to come alone? What guarantees do we have? Listen…" He thought for a moment. "It has to be in the open. I'm not going to accept anything else. What do you mean I don't have a choice! You—"

"Frank." the Big Guy touched Frank's shoulder, but Frank brushed him aside with a wave of the hand. He continued to listen. By then, Katherine was terrified; she hung on Frank's every word.

"Don't tell me whom I should listen to. You're playing with fire. You'd better not harm her—I mean that…She'll be there." When he finished, he shook his head in disbelief and looked at Katherine's worried eyes, wondering if he had failed her.

"So, what do they want?" the Big Guy asked, but Frank's eyes were locked with Katherine's.

She understood.

Somberly, Frank replied, "They want to trade Katherine for Sarah. It's the only option they're giving us," he said. "We knew it would come to this. I don't like it."

"You know what that means, Frank, don't you?" the Big Guy said, and they both looked at Katherine.

"I'm not afraid. I just want Sarah to be safe. If you can make that happen, I'll be okay. Just help me get Sarah out of this alive." Whatever their anxiety, Katherine's determination was reassuring. To her, Sarah's safety was all that mattered.

"Let's talk about this," Frank suggested.

"No! I won't go along with that. It may cost Sarah her life. Listen to me—that's not an option! I've been through this a thousand times before. I vowed I'd *never* abandon Sarah. I won't! Let's just give them what they want."

"Katherine, I don't know if—" Frank hesitated. A lump formed in his throat as he collected his thoughts. So much had happened over the last few days, but Katherine was now clearly ready. In fact, it was Frank who needed to draw on her strength.

"Read my lips: IT"S OKAY," Katherine said. "I won't blame you for anything. I won't, as long as you get Sarah out of this alive. I mean that."

"We'll do our best," the Big Guy said, and with this they all stood silent for a moment. A lone phone, half-empty coffee cups, and crumpled papers covered the kitchen table.

The Big Guy had never seen Frank so emotional. He felt awkward, because he couldn't share Frank's feelings. *Why can't he just take this as any other job*, he thought. And Katherine's resolve disturbed him even more; it seemed almost foreign to him. It wasn't supposed to be this way.

He was about to say something when Frank declared, "All right—I understand what we need to do." He rubbed his head. "But let's make sure we all understand." He called the other agents inside.

After a lengthy discussion, everyone was ready to proceed. The next phone call Frank expected would detail the meeting place.

✳ ✳ ✳ ✳

The Big Guy looked out the window. "She's back," he said. Jila was rushing towards the house as if her life depended on it.

"Let her in," Frank directed.

"Frank, with everything going on, we can't have her around anymore."

"Dammit! Let her in," Frank yelled. "This could be the last time—" He choked on his words. "Just let her in."

The Big Guy angrily opened the door and glared down on Jila, who brushed against his chest and passed him by as if she owned the place. She refused to be intimidated and her eyes searched for Katherine inside.

"It's okay, come in," Frank said.

Uneasy about the live beef standing behind her, she still managed to turn and ask him, "Where's Jenny?"

Frank's eyes told the Big Guy to back off. "She's in the back," he replied, pointing grudgingly.

"She'll be glad to see you—go on," Frank said.

Without saying another word, Jila marched in. It was still hot, of course, and the air was heavier than the last time she was here, but Jila felt that something was amiss. She tapped on Katherine's door. "Jenny, are ya in there? It's me—Jila."

Katherine was still stretched out on the side of the bed, her pillow tightly under her abdomen. But she didn't respond. She couldn't.

Jila opened the door, took one look at Katherine, and was horrified. Dark circles surrounded Katherine's puffed-up eyes and her hair was straggly. "Jenny, what they do to ya? Somethin' happen to Amy?"

Jila sat herself next to Katherine on the bed and wrapped her arms around her shoulders. Tearful, she had to know. "Ya heard from Amy, haven't ya?"

Scratching her arms as if bitten by mosquitoes, Katherine answered in a muffled voice, "Yeah."

Doubts suddenly began to gnaw at Jila. They brought back her earlier chills, when her friends in Gullah Heaven had to help her. But she valiantly refused to believe that Sarah could be anything but alive. "I'm 'fraid, Jenny. Is Amy all right?"

"She's okay," Katherine finally announced.

Jila burst into tears. "Thank ya, Lord!" She pressed her hands tightly against her face.

"Jila, listen to me," Katherine said in a decisive tone, clasping Jila's wrists. "You have to stay strong. I need you. Sarah needs you. I'm so sorry I dragged you into this."

Katherine now had to think about what she had to do next.

Jila thanked God that he had not let her down and wiped her eyes.

"I'm really glad you came back," Katherine said, hugging her again. "I think the years are catching up to me. Listen, Jila, you have to do me a favor."

"Anythin'…I'll do anythin' to help ya, Jenny—ya know that," Jila assured her. She was naturally fearful of what awaited them, and her first impulse had been to look away. But now she was filled with the same kind of determination that permeated every fiber of Katherine's body.

Katherine held Jila's smooth, dark-chocolate hands and felt her breath of youth. "I know you will, but this is a big favor."

"Jenny, is there anythin' else ya not tellin' me?"

"I want you to leave now and forget that this ever happened. That's what I need from you, Jila. You gotta be strong! Because the last thing I need on my conscience is for something terrible to happen to you, too. Do you understand what I'm asking?" Katherine was apprehensive about what she was requesting. She didn't want to torment Jila—possibly for the rest of her life—if either she or Sarah should never return. She could only beg for understanding.

"Jenny, no," Jila pleaded. This wasn't happening, she told herself. "Jenny!"

"Jila, please, I love you like a daughter. And Sarah and I will never forget what you've done for us. What I don't need now is to think what harm you might be bringing to yourself or your family. Promise me you'll do as I say. I want to hear it from you."

"Jenny, oh, Jenny! I'm 'fraid."

"I know, Jila. So am I," Katherine replied. They embraced, dreading the uncertainties that would follow. Each said silent prayers for the other, before their minds drifted toward Sarah. She had to be saved.

CHAPTER 20

▼

Saying farewell was hard. It was a monumental decision and it wrenched Katherine's guts. She prayed. The soft yellow valance decorated with a floral print hung above her bedroom window, but it was dull and stagnant. She fought to relax her troubled soul. Armpits tacky, stomach on empty, and heart on full, she looked out upon the sea of old oaks and natural greenery. The soft trickling of water made her want to run, play, perhaps even turn the hands of time back to a yesterday full of happiness. The laughter of a child's voice, the feeling of being loved unconditionally—such things were all so distant it seemed to Katherine that only the dead could feel them.

But she persevered. Shaking her head, she prayed for strength, safety, and understanding. And then, a feeling of peace came to her, as welcome as the morning sunrise. Everything seemed to make sense—to fit well in the scheme of things. But was this merely another false awakening? As she brushed the hair away from her face, she searched for other options. But there weren't any; that's basically how it looked from her vantage point.

She nudged the door open.

It was quiet, except for the low hum of a radio heard from the kitchen area. Right now, she hated the sorrowful gaiety of country music, even on low. The sounds seemed so out of place. Her legs took her down the hall to the room where Nick lay.

Once inside the room she was overcome by emotion, and just gazed at him. The smell of rubbing alcohol seemed to add to the sickness in the air.

"He's sleeping," the doctor said. He sat next to the bed, like a faithful guardian dog. "Seems a bit more comfortable. But he's restless and talks a lot in his sleep."

"Will he be okay?" Katherine asked.

"Hard to tell," he said, trying not to look defeated.

"I see," Katherine said, pondering. By this time she was standing next to the doctor, gazing above the top of his bald head. Nick's once dark, slick hair, now weaved in gray, rested untamed on the soft pink pillow. He was unshaven; his ashen dry face begged for color. His arm, stretched across the sheet, displayed the five-leaf clover tattoo that made her think of the last time she saw it. But now he lay in a bed, not on the floor of a dark basement after being shot by Detective Glen. "I need a moment with him," Katherine requested.

The doctor got up and left without a word.

Alone, Katherine could only reminisce about the man she once loved. She struggled with her emotions. There were so many questions and so few answers. Drained as she was, she nevertheless placed his hand in hers and stroked his fingers. She listened to his labored breathing. She had to say goodbye, more gracefully this time.

"Nick...I don't know where to begin," she said as he lay there expressionless. "The last time we were together it was so much like this. I knew I was leaving and thought I would never see you again. I can't tell you how much that hurt or how much I wanted to tell you the truth about your father. But I loved you too much to cause your father to disinherit you. I came back to visit you in jail because...I just had to know what changed you. You said that you searched for me for years after I left. I didn't think you would, but I still told Sarah all about your good side—your gentle side. I had to. You're her father, Nick!"

She paused for a few seconds to wipe her tears.

"I'm having a hard time with all of this, because…because I don't know if I'll ever have a chance to say it later. It's really hard…but…I do forgive you. I hate to see you like this. You've got to be strong. I'm afraid, Nick. I'm really scared, but I'm ready. I have to try and save Sarah." She wiped away more welling tears. "I wish you could help," she finally confided.

Sarah's picture stood on the nightstand, and there, on the edge of the bed, Katherine wept uncontrollably. "She is so much like her father," she said between sobs. She held the picture tightly to her chest, rocked her head, and refused to let go. Then she wiped her eyes one final time. "Goodbye, Nick, I'll never forget you. I think you know that," she said, and placed the picture next to him. *I can do this. I can do this*, she steeled herself.

She had to leave quickly, because Nick was drifting back from his dormant state. For the second time in his life, repeating what happened eighteen years ago, Katherine was about to walk out without letting him say his piece. However, Nick's mind was present as well as his body. He had heard her voice, almost every word she uttered, and for once he understood how much she cared. He wanted to beg her to stay.

Here I am! I can hear you he tried to say, to no avail. He was trapped inside a weak body. He had to tell Sarah that he was here for her, too. She deserved an explanation. Sarah's eyes kept stabbing his dejected soul. He wondered if he'd ever be able to make her understand. A father's love was supposed to be eternal and unconditional.

A few of his muscles twitched. But it wasn't enough to alert Katherine that he was present, let alone to ask her to deliver his long overdue message to his daughter.

Katherine walked out, but the door opened again and the tired doctor walked in. Nick couldn't confide in a doctor, but he had to do something, despite his almost complete absence of motor control. Maybe death was the answer.

*   *   *   *

Meanwhile, Katherine prepared herself. She stood next to the antique mahogany dresser. The five-leaf clover pendant given to her by her father rested beneath the silk scarf. She wished her father, Al, were there to help out, as he used to do in her hours of greatest need. When he passed on that pendant to her, his eyes sparkled, just like they did when he gave it to her mother on their wedding day. He was her guardian angel. She desperately needed his strength.

Holding the pendant tightly in her hand, eyes shut, she summoned his spirit. "Daddy, can you hear me?" she asked. She gazed into the light and placed the pendant in her pocket.

*   *   *   *

Riggins wore out the carpet pacing back and forth, hands behind his back. Waiting was not his favorite pastime. It had been hours and still no word. Paul's erratic behavior concerned him, but he knew he was good at what he did, and he usually delivered. Riggins hoped things wouldn't be different this time. Finally, he stormed over to the phone and dialed from memory.

"Hello, what's going on, Boss?" Barry asked.

"How did you know it was me?" Riggins asked, irritated.

"You're the only one that calls on this phone. Have you heard from them?" Barry asked.

"No, where are you?

"I'm on my way. I had a hard time getting the passports. It cost a little more than we planned."

"Why in the hell are you worrying about money? I've told you...Listen, get your ass over here. Are you packed? We don't have a lot of time."

"Packed? Why? I wear my clothes," Barry said, with a hollow laugh.

Riggins ignored his remark. "Just get here. How far away are you?"

"Hold on, I'm having a hard time hearing you. Must be a bad connection. Are you there? Can you hear me?"

"I can hear you. Where are you, dammit?"

"A couple of miles away. Are you ready? Is Ralph going with us?"

"No, he's making sure Nick is taken care of."

"Nick?" Barry was dumbfounded. "What's happening with him?"

"Dammit! Just get here, Barry."

"I'm on my way. See you later."

Riggins chomped on his chunky cigar as he searched for his pills. His alligator bags, piled up like library books, decorated the hall next to the front door. He checked his safe for the third time and locked it again.

CHAPTER 21

▼

High noon was in less than an hour. The winds were low enough to halt sailboats but strong enough to carry the pollen drift all about. Frank prepared himself. Instructions should be coming any time. The other agents—new agents—stood their posts waiting impatiently for the instructions, and the Big Guy was busy checking on Nick.

Someone approached from the other room. Frank was sure it was Katherine, so he adjusted his belt and stood up to greet her. When she appeared, the shadow of one of the agents on the porch startled her. "It's okay, just the guys," Frank quickly reassured her. "I'll tell them to stay away from the window."

"I guess I'm a little jumpy, I'll be all right," she said. She could tell he had not heard anything yet; the awkward silence confirmed that, so she plumped down on the sofa.

The Big Guy quietly eased his way back into the room. "Man, you look worn out," he told Frank. "Take a break. I'll watch the phone— it's more interesting than hanging around the sick. I tell you—I'm not getting good vibes about any of this. It's taking too long." But Frank hushed him. The Big Guy wasn't even aware that Katherine was lying on the sofa; she had a deathly silence about her. "Oh, sorry," he told Katherine, embarrassed. "I shouldn't have said that."

"That's okay, I feel the same," she said.

"I'm going to call the Bureau to see if they have any news. I'll use the other phone. You, watch this one," Frank said, as he walked over to the sofa." The Big Guy didn't say anything, but he was clearly disturbed. He popped a piece of chewing gum into his mouth and rested his rump at the table, facing Frank.

*   *   *   *

A car pulled up the stately driveway. Riggins watched Barry in his white business shirt, affecting his usual chipper façade, playing catch with his keys as he approached the door. Impatient, Riggins gave himself the honor of greeting him. The nub of his cigar was just short of burning his lips; though he had enough internal combustion in him now to do it without more smoldering ash. He was infuriated. "About time you got here," he said.

"It was some job—it took awhile."

"Bullshit, these damn things can be pulled off the Internet these days. I don't have time for this shit."

"Well, good evening to you, too, Boss." Barry passed by him, knowing that nothing he said would ever satisfy this rich man. So, he went back nervously to his post like a trained dog already browbeaten.

"Where are they?" Riggins asked.

"What?" Barry responded, sure he had forgotten something.

"The passports?"

"They're in the car."

"I want to see them. Just get them, and I don't want to hear a damn word. Just bring them here," demanded Riggins.

"Whatever. I hope you're feeling better by the time I get back."

Riggins glared at him, but Barry just walked away, thankful that Riggins had not exploded, though he looked like he was fast reaching his limit. Barry was running on empty. When he returned with the passports, he noticed that Riggins was engrossed in a phone conversation. On the other end was Jeff.

"Yeah," Jeff said, "we have everything ready to go. I'm about to call them. We're going to trade the girl, as planned. I'm not anticipating any problem, but we'll be ready. Thanks for sending the additional support—that'll help. I expect it will take us a couple of hours to get to Charleston."

"What in the hell has taken you so long? I thought something had happened," Riggins growled, chasing his words with a drink.

"No, no problem. The other guys just got here. It seems the security has been beefed up on the island. I can't confirm that, it just seemed different. We're okay, I don't think they want a dead girl on their consciences."

"You know they're going to be looking for you."

"I expect someone will be. I'm not going to fuck around with these guys. I know how to play their game. I've been there."

"Just don't let me down," Riggins warned. "I need to rid myself of that chick. What about Paul? Is he behaving?"

"Paul will be Paul. You know what he's like. He's doing his best—ready to kill, as usual. Don't worry Boss, I can handle him."

"Good, Barry and I will meet you as planned. We have everything in order on this end."

"Right, Boss. See you soon."

Reassured, Riggins returned the phone to its cradle and glanced over at Barry. "I guess you heard what I said?"

"I heard what you said. When are we leaving?"

"What time is the flight?" Riggins asked.

"Ten—like I told you."

"I guess you have the answer to your questions, then. Call Dan, he can load up the car and drop us off. I'm going to take a shower. I have to make a few calls before we leave."

"Boss, doesn't this bother you at all?"

"Nothing about this bothers me."

"I mean killing an innocent woman. This has gotten a little bit off track, if you ask me."

"Doesn't bother me a bit. She put herself in the middle of this. She was the one who went to the Feds and told them about me. I never gave her an invitation to my business affairs. She didn't even know who in the hell she was talking about. All hearsay based on that fuck-up, Glen. No. I'm not bothered at all. The sooner that chick is cold the better. I want her to remember me as she dies. I want to make sure she knows who I am. You starting to get soft on me or something, Barry? Do you realize what's at stake if she testifies?"

"I realize, Boss. It's crazy! I'm with you. Let's just be careful."

"I'm not concerned. I trust the guys," Riggins said.

"So do I," Barry agreed, crushing his cigarette.

CHAPTER 22

▼

Tension filled the house. Frank had just confirmed that the Bureau knew Riggins was involved and he was about to travel somewhere. That was all they told him. Frank was ordered to make certain that Sarah would not be harmed; he would be the one to escort Katherine to the meeting place. The kidnappers knew that extra security had been placed on the island, and Frank knew these guys would be on edge. He did not want to do anything to make them trigger-happy.

The phone rang. "Hello," Frank answered. It was the call they'd been waiting for. "Yes, I can hear you...I know where that is...But I need a little more time than that...No, I'm not playing games. It'll take a while to get over to the island...I said I wasn't playing games. Don't harm her...."

"Let me talk to them!" Katherine cried out hysterically. "Please, let me talk to them! Please don't let anything happen to Sarah! I'll go alone!" Frank shielded the phone as the Big Guy pulled her away.

"I know you guys don't give a shit, but that's a mother," said Frank. "She doesn't want anything to happen to her daughter and neither do we. I'll be with her. I'm not letting her go alone. I promise...no games, and I want the same from you. We'll be there," Frank said.

"What did he say?" Katherine demanded to know.

"We're going to meet them under the bridge. They'll exchange Sarah for you. We need to be careful and make sure no one slips up. I don't trust these guys, but I'm pretty sure they will do what they said if no one screws up." Frank looked at Katherine, wanting to make certain she was committed to the end.

"When do we leave?" Katherine asked.

"In about half an hour. Our boat is ready," he said, and then turned to the Big Guy standing behind her. "I'll call the Bureau. Why don't you let the guys outside know what's going on. They need to clear out. I know we're taking a chance, but it's our only option. If the kidnappers suspect anything—"

"I know," the Big Guy interrupted. "Are you sure you don't want me to come along?"

"I'm sure," Frank said, then quickly turned to Katherine. "Are you okay with all of this? We don't have to do it this way."

"We don't have a choice," she said, resigned, "I understand what's going on." She left the room.

"I'm not sure she can take this," the Big Guy said.

"Don't worry—she's tough enough," Frank said. "That's a mother you're looking at. We all need to understand what's going down here. Don't doubt her."

"I understand all right. I just think she's too upset, that's all."

"If you have a better plan, let's hear it," Frank challenged.

"I don't have a problem with this one. Relax, man. You're way too emotionally involved in this. That's not good. I don't think it's what we were sent here for. I could be wrong, but—"

"Cut the bullshit! I really don't have time for your shit. We have work to do."

"My sentiments exactly," the Big Guy said and hesitantly withdrew to the doorway.

"Is everything okay?" the doctor asked, rubbing his face as he headed towards the sink.

"Everything's fine, Doc. How's he doing?" Frank asked, his eyes still on the Big Guy.

"He's doing better than an hour ago," the doctor said. "Now, he's sleeping."

"Has he said anything?" the Big Guy asked.

"No, not yet. He opens his eyes occasionally. The pain medicine and antibiotics are working. That's a good thing."

"Would you like to sit down?" Frank offered.

"No, that's okay, I'd better get back," the doctor said, splashing his weary face with tepid water.

Katherine, ready to go, paused when she heard a moan coming from Sarah's room. She went over and gazed inside at the untidy bed where Nick was sprawled. To her surprise, his eyes opened. A warm silence hovered over the room as their eyes met. She was about to say something, when the doctor walked by her. "Go ahead, he's awake," the doctor announced.

Tears rolled down her cheeks.

Something familiar struck her about this moment—*déjà vu*, so reminiscent of the time, eighteen years ago, when she looked down upon Nick and blew him a kiss just before she ran out of his life.

Nick willed his hand to move, his own tears rolling onto his pillow. Katherine approached. The doctor watched as their hands locked together.

"Nick, I really don't understand why all of this has happened to us. It's said that God places on us only the burdens we can bear. I hope someday we'll have the opportunity to talk about this again. Thanks for trying to save her. I'll make sure she knows that." Nick weakly squeezed her hand, gesturing that it was okay and that he understood.

Frank came to the doorway and looked on briefly. It was time to go.

CHAPTER 23

▼

The two golf carts pulled away from the house and headed towards the dock. Absorbed by the thought of seeing Sarah, Katherine was in her own world. Frank didn't have much to say. He drove on.

The small Haig Point lighthouse seemed larger than life with its lone light shining out onto the ocean. The only thing that flowed was Katherine's blood through her troubled heart. The next phase of this seemingly endless nightmare was about to begin.

Ahead, they could see the H-ferry. Katherine never liked taking this ride, and today was no different. Passing the mansion shook her; it was as if she was saying goodbye. This place had brought such peace into their lives. A solitary light shone from one of the rooms on the upper floor. The soft curtains hanging in the window filtered the light and blew in the quiet breeze. Were they trying to tell her something, she wondered?

The cart bounced along the dock, pulling her closer to the small boat that awaited them. The sound of the waves was strangely disconcerting. Finally, when the cart came to a halt, Frank was the first to disembark. He reached out for Katherine, now keenly aware that he would not be with her as she traveled to the end of this treacherous road. He would do anything to trade places with her.

"Thanks," Katherine said, abandoning her ride. As she looked out on the dark Atlantic, the other island, a journey of only minutes, seemed like light years away.

"You guys wait here," Frank directed. "I'll call you as soon as I have the girl. If for some reason you don't hear from me within the next hour, you know what to do."

Katherine looked at the three men, as Frank started up the engine of the boat. Softly, she told them, "Thank you," and they both drove off. It had been a long time since she had left Daufuskie, but this trip felt every bit like a turning point in her life. Her small island world slowly diminishing in size, she squeezed the pendant resting in her pocket and prepared herself for the ordeal ahead.

In the soft darkness, the water beat against the boat as Frank tried to focus his mind on his role, looking fixedly at the long bridge in the distance. Neither he nor Katherine said anything. They were both lost in their thoughts.

✳   ✳   ✳   ✳

"Let's go guys. You know who's in charge now," the Big Guy ordered, though the agents never doubted his delegated authority. "I want to call the Bureau and brief them. They have to know what's going on. And that sick guy has to go—I'll make the arrangements."

"Kinda like when the President got shot, huh?" one agent joked.

The Big Guy didn't answer. He drove alone—his agenda was set.

And unknown to the agents, their every move was being monitored. A night scope was locked onto them from behind the tall grass, great oaks, and evergreens.

The call to the other side confirmed that the delivery was taking place as directed. Two men in sporty summer attire retreated to their small boat, trailing Katherine and Frank. They were to ensure that Katherine could not escape.

Land was within throwing distance. Katherine and Frank neared Hilton Head, which was eerily quiet, except for an occasional car crossing on the Palmetto Highway that arched above the earth in front of them. Frank anchored the boat and held on to his holster, checking out the dark shadows looming around them. Fighting off his apprehension, he felt like abandoning the mission. He glanced back at Katherine who was trying to steady her own nerves.

Maybe there were other options, he thought, though none stood a realistic chance of saving Sarah. Still, he had to ask her one more time. "Katherine, are you sure you want to do this?"

The men in the boat, close enough to react if necessary, were busy reporting on Katherine and Frank's approach. Frank plied ahead. If they refused to pursue this to the end, there would probably be three graves soon. He helped Katherine plant her feet firmly on the ground. In her hand, she carried Sarah's soft blue cheerleader sweater.

She looked up and said, "I'm ready." Frank wasn't certain he was, though. They walked over to the embarkation center, where they found her car. It was dusty, covered by leaves and begging for attention. Frank cleared off the windows and suggested that he drive. Katherine agreed. They were only minutes away from their meeting place and she had to prepare herself.

Frank's knuckles whitened as he gripped the steering wheel. He looked at her one last time.

"I'm really okay," Katherine assured him. "I don't want anything to happen to Sarah or you. It's me they're after. You know, for some reason I always knew it was going to come to this. That's why I never liked leaving the island. I'm just sorry they didn't just take me and leave the rest of you alone."

Frank found it hard to respond to these words, and his feelings took over. Pulling the car to the side of the road, he stopped and smothered Katherine in his arms. His arms still around her, he said, "Katherine, I'm proud of you. I wish I had your courage. I'm sorry we failed you. We really tried."

"I failed myself. I blame myself, no one else. Years ago I ran away, when I should've stayed and fought. If I had, none of this would have happened. It's easy to look back and say what I should have done, though. Decisions made on impulse create so many regrets. This is really all about me. I've known this for years. Each time I heard myself being called Jenny, each time I called Sarah Amy, I sank deeper. Please don't worry about me. I'll be okay as long as Sarah is alive."

"There aren't many women like you, Katherine. We'll do our best to make sure you and Sarah get through this."

"Thanks, Frank, I believe you. Now, I'd better not keep Sarah waiting."

*   *   *   *

"What's going on?" Paul asked.

"They stopped. Do you want us to move to plan B?" the man in the car responded. "We're right behind them."

"What do you mean they stopped? What are they doing?"

"Looks like they're talking. I'll move a little closer. Wait a minute, the car is moving your way."

"Do you see anyone else?" Paul quizzed.

"Nope. Is everyone ready on your end?"

"Yes. Wait—I can see headlights. I think that's them," Paul said.

"Just be careful," he warned. "We'll hang close and keep a lookout."

As Frank moved closer, two quick flashes from Paul's headlights guided him. Within seconds, the car stopped in front of the vehicle carrying Sarah. The two cars faced each other like sumo wrestlers in the dusk. Blinded by the lights, the occupants of the cars could not see what was happening in front of them. Jeff dimmed his lights, as they anxiously awaited the next move. His eyes peered ahead, waiting for something to budge.

Jeff was the first to step out. The frames of two other men in the front seat were discernable. Frank tightened his grip on his gun, itching to use it.

"Katherine, don't move."

"Where's Sarah? I don't see her," she said in a shrill voice.

"I'm sure she's in there. Listen, I want you to stay in the car. I'll go and talk to them."

"I need to know that Sarah is okay, Frank. What if—" She couldn't utter the word. Panic rose inside her.

"Katherine, you have to listen to me. I know what I'm doing. These guys aren't here to throw you a happy reunion. Just let me handle this. Trust me, okay," his soothing voice said. Katherine was too anxiety-ridden to be lulled again, but she was determined enough to let him do it his way.

"I'll be back." He closed the door. Jeff stood next to the car, one hand in his pocket.

"Listen," Jeff said, "I wanna make this easy. I'm not looking for trouble." He approached the car, confident he was well covered. "I have the girl, just hand her over and we'll be on our way—as promised."

"Where is she? I don't see her," Frank asked.

"In the car. She's okay."

Katherine could no longer control her alarm. She couldn't see Sarah at all. Jumping out of the car, she yelled, "I have to see her. I need to know she's okay. Please, don't do anything to cause them to hurt her, Frank," she begged. Frank immediately tried to restrain her.

"Let me see her," Frank demanded. "I'm not doing anything unless I know she's okay."

"Is that a promise?" Jeff sneered. "I don't think you have much of an option, Bureau boy."

"No, Frank!" Katherine pleaded. "You promised you'd follow through with this. Please, this is our only chance. Please—"

"Bring her out. I'll give you Katherine, but I want to see the girl."

The back door of the car opened. A ragged-haired Sarah stumbled out, escorted by Paul. Katherine was dumbfounded at the way Sarah looked, even in the dark—a weary, panting bundle of misery. "Sarah!" Katherine cried out and sprang forward, but Frank grabbed and held on to her. "Sarah!"

"Mom," Sarah yelled. Her hands were tied behind her back.

"See? We ain't lookin' for trouble," Paul said. "Now you see the girl, so let the mother go. Don't turn this into something it shouldn't be."

Sarah stood forlorn and absolutely terrified, her eyes riveted to Katherine.

"Let me go!" Katherine snapped at Frank and broke his grip. He leaped after her, but it was too late. Jeff quickly overpowered her and Sarah was thrown to the ground. Sarah turned on her side, hands behind her back, watching her mother a few feet away.

"Mom!" she screamed hysterically, saliva dripping from her lips, legs kicking. "Mom, no! Don't let them take my mom," she pleaded. A distraught Katherine wept as she watched her baby lie abandoned on the ground.

"Sarah, I love you. I love you. Don't worry, I'll be okay," she said as Jeff backed her roughly into the car.

"Mom, Mom," Sarah fiercely cried out. She was absolutely devastated. Frank kneeled on the ground, trying to comfort her. His own guilt at being so helpless wrenched him. Next to his knee lay the soiled blue sweater that Katherine had brought for Sarah, but this was small comfort for a girl who was watching her mother being abducted. Frank knew this would happen. Twenty years with the Bureau and he never imagined a day like this one. He pummeled the ground, scraping his skin and causing his knuckles to bleed.

He had fulfilled Katherine's wish. He only hoped it wasn't her last.

As he reached out to help the frightened Sarah, Frank felt a blow to the head. He fell on top of Sarah, who screamed uncontrollably as a horrified Katherine looked on. The man standing over them signaled Jeff to move on.

"Sarah! Sarah!" Katherine screamed, shaking her head violently, but the sound of the engine revving up quickly muffled Sarah's cries.

CHAPTER 24

▼

"That chick has caused me more trouble than she's worth. I'm going to give her something to think about. Hey, be careful up there!" Riggins blurted out to the driver. "I'm not looking to go down croak street before my time." He was bitching as only he could do, his ass glued to the seat. He was prepared to meet the prize he'd been deprived of for years, and he gloated with anticipation, more proud of this accomplishment than any other.

"I don't think he can hear you, Boss. You know how he gets listening to that weird music. Anyway, I don't think you have to worry—God's not ready for you. Not enough room up there," Barry said, grinning.

"I don't find that funny. Wipe that stupid grin off your face. I hope you grow up before we get there; pass me the scotch. Give me the big glass. Make sure it's clean."

"Anything else? I wonder what it would be like if you didn't like me."

"Barry, I really don't have time for your bullshit. Just shut up," he said, and slugged down his drink. Barry chose not to test the waters any further.

"Shit!" Riggins shouted as they passed beneath the LaGuardia Airport sign. The car hit a chuckhole that lifted him and Barry out of their seats.

"Slow down, we have time. Shit, I dropped my cigarette. I smell it, but I can't find it," Barry said and quickly went on his knees in search.

"Dammit, I'm surrounded by a bunch of idiots?" Riggins said, running his eyes across the plush gray carpet.

"Yes!" Barry exclaimed, delicately pinching the dropped cigarette with his index finger and thumb, and parking his rump on the seat—winded and unsure what to do next with the bent cigarette.

*   *   *   *

The darkness deepened as Katherine listened bitterly to the sound of the engine, then scoped out the inside of the car into which she had been thrust. This might as well be a hearse, she thought. She looked ahead of her, between the dark leather seats. The apathetic white face of the driver stared ahead. Shadows fell on her and just as quickly they melted away in endless cycles.

The car sped on.

An empty bottle of alcohol rested at her feet and the smell of its contents emanated from the guy next to her. The uncertainty about Sarah's safety was killing her, but she could only watch, helplessly, the two men in her car, who were both dressed so casually they could have fit in well at the golf club.

Paul lit another cigarette and nervously eyed the cleavage behind Katherine's loosened shirt. Then he hit his throat with another swig of the fiery liquid and hungrily fixed his eyes on a hidden zipper. Jeff was adjusting the rearview mirror to get a better view of Katherine, who had become their priceless piece of nothing, watched more closely than a hunted deer. "I bet you thought you'd never be taking this ride," Jeff taunted Katherine, watching her in the mirror.

Katherine responded by crossing her arms over her chest and inching closer to the corner.

"It doesn't matter. She won't live to tell about it anyway. Let her enjoy the scenery. She's gotta relax a little," Paul said, rubbing his hands along her thigh.

"Get your hands off me!" Katherine hissed, pushing him away. "Is this what you did to my daughter, you bastard?" A quick slap caught her on the side of her face. Instantly, she returned the favor, swinging wildly at Paul, knuckling him upside his head. Her fury was overpowering even for Paul. He struggled to control her and had no qualms about delivering a couple of inaccurate blows that Katherine was unable to protect herself against.

They shook her a little, but she yelled defiantly, "I'm not afraid of you!" She kicked until her leg slipped over Paul.

"Bitch! You better watch what you say. I'll beat the shit out of you," he said, grabbing her wrists one after the other and then jabbing her still clenched fists into her own face.

"Paul, what in the fuck are you doing?" Jeff shouted, slamming the car to the side of the road. "Are you fucking crazy, you son-of-a-bitch! You're about to fuck this up for all of us. Get your ass out and take the wheel. I'm not gonna witness your fuckin' antics. Look at this. Man, you're really fucked up. I can't believe you."

The second car of the abductors pulled up alongside them. A heavy-set man stepped out and walked up. "What in the hell is going on, Jeff?" I thought you were going to fuckin' crash."

Paul had bloodstains on his shirt.

Katherine cradled her nose. Blood was gushing down between her fingers, and her thigh throbbed from Paul's vice-like grip.

Jeff replied, "Just Paul fuckin' up again. He wants to take things into his own hands."

"Listen, Paul," the man said menacingly, "we don't need this shit. It's almost over. I don't want to have to explain anything to the Boss unless I have to. Just cool it, man, he'll take care of her. Okay?" He looked over at Jeff.

"Fuck all of you," Paul replied. He got behind the wheel and shouted, "I'm sick of all of you punk-ass motherfuckers."

"Jeff, I don't think he's in any shape to drive—do you? I'll drive. Why don't you sit in the back with her?" He stared insistently at Paul.

"Not a bad idea," Jeff responded as he twisted himself to look behind him. Katherine, bloodied but still furious, was tending to her throbbing nose. Her yellow shirt was streaked with blood.

"I'm driving!" Paul yelled. His hands locked on the steering wheel. "Don't even think about it," he said to his crony standing next to the door.

Jeff upped his chin to signal to the guy to get in on the passenger side.

"Hey," the man shouted to his partner, who waited patiently in the car, "follow me to the house. I want to make sure they get there before we take off."

"Everything okay?"

"Yeah," he replied, glancing hesitantly at Paul.

"Punks, that's all you all are," Paul said.

"Let's go, and pay attention to the road. I'm not interested in having myself taken out," Jeff said.

"The man's afraid to die?" Paul smirked. "Well, I'm not." His eyes were soon glued to the rearview mirror. Katherine was tending to her nosebleed and over her cupped hand she carefully watched Jeff unwrap a piece of gum. As the car traveled north at an acceptable speed, Paul flicked on the radio and raised the volume high. All the time his radar was on Katherine. His murderous looks chilled her.

*　　*　　*　　*

Sarah sat bewildered next to the dusty tire. Frank was still disoriented, holding his throbbing head trying to feel the spot where he had been struck. He looked around. The darkness was unchanged, but there was an occasional distant headlight. Stumbling, he approached Sarah. "Are you okay, Sarah?" he asked, reaching into his pocket.

She flinched, her eyes as big as flood lights.

"I ain't gonna hurt you. Trust me," he said, backing away. He decided to call for help. While he was speaking into his car radio, something resting on the floor beneath the glove compartment caught his eye. Because of the throbbing pain of his head he had a hard time bending over, but when he did he noticed sadly that it was Katherine's five-leaf clover pendant.

He completed his call, then returned to Sarah. The alarm in her eyes brought him back to reality. His back against the car, slightly disoriented still, he could do nothing but wait. "Sarah, they'll be here in a minute," he said, trying to sound as reassuring as he could under the circumstances. "Hang in there." Never before had his mind been so disconnected from his muscles. It bothered him that he couldn't hold the girl in his arms and tell her that everything would be okay.

The wounds to her person, her dignity, her personality were fresh. Frank could barely hold back his tears. He understood. The sweater on the ground in front of him was the last straw. He rubbed his eyes.

CHAPTER 25

▼

Stacked-up cars waited as the engine-birds rumbled the ground below them from the sky. Everywhere, frustrated drivers blew their horns, baggage was strewn over the sidewalk, and loved ones escorted seniors across the crosswalks, quickening their pace before the thick traffic. Some people were lining up at the curbside check-in trying to beat the crowds gathering inside. Others, too cheap to pay for parking, dashed around between the glass doors and the cars they left behind.

In the chaos, a black stretch limousine slowly pulled up alongside a vacant curb. Soon, curious onlookers were inching their way to the car, some giving up their positions just for a quick glimpse of royalty. Baggers, captain's hats in hand and nodding gratefully for the tips they received, turned their heads.

Barry was the first to show his face, followed by Dan. His thin cotton shirt, which matched his pants, hung to his hips—signaling to those watching that rich Italian money had arrived. Dan was at the back door, waiting for Riggins to exit.

Riggins planted his dark brown imports firmly on the ground without assistance. "Barry, what time does our flight leave? I need to take a piss," he asked, adjusting his pants to loosen the tight fit around his crotch.

"We got plenty of time, Boss. The plane leaves in an hour. Go ahead, we'll take care of the rest. I'll meet you at the gate."

Feeling the urgency of his situation, Riggins marched ahead, toting his leather shoulder bag that perfectly matched his shoes. Bumping shoulders, he shifted his weight through the crowd.

"Sir, you dropped something," a woman called out and reached down to pick it up.

"Much obliged," Riggins replied.

It was his South Carolina map. "Shit," Riggins sibilated, then noticed the line leading to the bathroom. His bladder was close to bursting. "Sorry, I gotta go," he said, beating the waiting men with his bag as he made his way to the urinal, where he released a pressured stream of heavenly bliss.

Barry continued to help unload the car as he watched Riggins disappear into the crowd. Little did he know that Riggins wasn't marching alone. FBI agents were close enough to measure the size of the sweat rings around his armpits. And they were not the only ones who had him in their sights. Directly behind him, an undercover agent, working as a porter, was also observing the scene. "Thanks," Barry said to the airport porter, who lined up the luggage next to the car.

"South Carolina—I'll bet it's real pretty this time o' year," the porter commented while wrapping a label around one handle.

"I sure hope so," Barry said, dropping the man a tip and hurrying inside. With one shift of the porter's head, armed agents positioned themselves like chess pieces on a board.

Having finished his much-needed restroom break, Riggins headed for the gate, followed by the agents.

"Please empty your pockets and place your bags on the belt," a lady instructed. Riggins waited, anxious but oblivious of the identity of the men who had him sandwiched. Following a quick time-check, his bag was ready to travel along the belt, and he made his way through the checkpoints without incident. Barry was nowhere in sight and the crowd was starting to bother him. He fought to maintain his composure, rechecking his watch and searching for his assistant.

Then, Riggins felt a slight bump from the back. His bag swung.

Mission accomplished. A swarthy man gave him a perfunctory apology. Riggins was marked again.

"Shit," he said, but there was no one to receive his killer look. He stepped onto the moving sidewalk, and just then Barry appeared alongside him—his cheeks full, as usual, as he chewed tobacco to sooth his craving for cigarettes. "Goddamn you, where have you been? This place is driving me crazy," Riggins complained loudly.

"Pretty busy out there," Barry responded, trying to avoid a scene.

"Is our plane leaving on time?"

"It's here. So we should be taking off soon. Do you need me to check on things to make sure?" he said, grinning. "You look a little beat, Boss."

"Very funny," Riggins responded. "Let's find a seat."

"Over there," Barry suggested. "Have you heard from anyone?"

"Everything's in order. They have the package, and they'll meet us as planned. I can't wait to see her face when she sees me."

"Why didn't you tell me? I thought you hadn't heard from anyone. It's not like you to keep something like this to yourself," Barry said.

"I really didn't want to talk about it in the car," Riggins said.

"Why? Was that the call you got in the car?"

"That's not important," Riggins said, enjoying Barry's high-strung reaction.

"What else haven't you told me?"

"Cut the bullshit, will you—and grow up. For your information, it appears this agent, Frank, has gotten a little more engaged in this case than we expected, but our man didn't anticipate any problems."

"What about that Nick guy?" Barry asked. "What did they say about him?"

"Don't worry, he'll be taken care of. It's okay, I don't think we'll have anything to worry about in just a few more hours."

"That's good, but it's giving me the creeps."

"What else is new? Just relax, it's all going to be over soon," Riggins said, checking his watch.

Listening, the agent whispered to his colleague, "Did you hear that? Has anyone called Frank to make sure things are okay on his end?"

"Will do," the other agent replied, signaling to the others to move ahead. A female agent pushing a stroller nodded and forged ahead. It was fifteen minutes short of flight time. Everyone was in position.

Barry and Riggins boarded flight 252 to Charleston, South Carolina. "Welcome, we're glad to have you fly with us. This way, sir," the flight attendant said as she directed Riggins and Barry to their seats. "Would you like something to drink?"

"Sure, I'll take a scotch on the rocks," Riggins replied, looking for a place to stow away his bag.

"Let me take that," another flight attendant offered as she passed out pillows.

"Nothing for me," Barry responded, then bit off another chaw of his tobacco.

"Please, fasten your seatbelts, as the captain is about to taxi onto the runway. We have been cleared to take off. In your pocket…" the flight attendant went on with the usual instructions.

First class is a private place to be, but today it was also an armed camp. Heads silently nodded and fingers signaled. Everything was going like clockwork. Better still—the heat seemed to be off.

Barry rested his head comfortably on the seat back and closed his eyes. He appreciated this rare moment of tranquility. The Boss had not been himself lately. He was so different from when Barry first started to work for him some years ago. Back then, parties and guests flowed in and out of the house as if it were a public building. And the virile laughter of Riggins was music to many ears. In fact, Riggins used to thoroughly enjoy laughing. It was something that came easily after so much money was made. These days the laughter was gone. The most common visitor now was a "plain-suit." It was all either money or legal mumbo-jumbo so thick you could stand on it.

The good thing about it was that Riggins was now well protected, despite his acute sense of insecurity. Barry knew that something out there would always prevent him from feeling at rest. Riggins basically had no freedom. Even old friends treated him like a pariah; there were only quick phone calls and then only for pertinent business. Only a few were willing to go on playing his game—the fearful ones that had fallen beyond the point of redemption.

Barry's face flattened. The knock he heard from beneath the plane told him they were on their way.

Mentally disengaged from his surroundings, Riggins plopped his head back, closed his eyes, and thought about what he might say to his worst enemy—that loose spring poking at his butt each time he tried to forget her. Katherine was dangerous as long as she lived. She was a witness to deadly words that could undo him if they were repeated to the wrong ears. His head molded to the seat, he allowed the unintelligible ramble of fears and thoughts inside his head to flow out until he could doze off for a little while before arrival.

The flight attendant, having completed her quick search of Riggins' bag, signaled to the others that they were clear as she marched towards the cockpit.

*   *   *   *

Wrapped in a warm blanket, Sarah was wheeled into the emergency room. Frank was still nursing his head wound, but he tried his best to trail her gurney.

Sarah had retreated deep within herself and her emotional collapse frightened him. Another first, he said to himself—they could easily lose her. He felt a chill in the air. The flurry of bright lights surrounding them couldn't erase it.

People were scattered all over the large waiting room, before the gurney forced the door open. Inside, Sarah was tucked beneath a warm cotton blanket. Her blank stare was that of a beaten, solitary mind. Frank watched as she disappeared behind the drapes. What will they do, he wondered as the curtains moved.

An orderly approached him. "I'm okay, just take care of *her*," he said, pointing in the direction of Sarah.

"Sir, let me take a look at your head. I promise this won't hurt," a nurse said.

"I'll check his blood pressure while you do that," an assistant offered and wrapped his arm in the cuff before he could protest. Frank's head pounded—and Sarah's screams were still fresh in his memory. He looked around as he checked his watch, oblivious to what healing hands could do.

Mom! Sarah had cried. He would never again hear this word uttered in the soothing tone he used to know it by. He thought about Katherine being taken away in that car. "Why her?" he asked himself.

He vowed to find a way to get to her.

While all this was happening, a transport EMS vehicle pulled up, lights flashing brightly. A flurry of anxious people opened the doors.

"Sir, sir, they're here," a young nurse informed Frank. Nick was being taken out of the ambulance and was about to be wheeled into the emergency room. He looked different in the bright lights, his skin colorless as he rocked around on the gurney. A worn-out doctor clung to his side, as if he were the next of kin.

As Nick was being moved, he mouthed something. *"Katherine!"* He called out her name a few times, followed by a long silence, then he repeated her name insistently.

*　　　*　　　*　　　*

"Frank, you did it!" the Big Guy said. "Man, you don't look good. How's the girl?" he asked.

"She's in bad shape mentally. But it's Katherine I'm really worried about! She's in trouble and we need to get to her," Frank said, nursing his headache. He looked like some war hero with his head all wrapped up.

"What's going on with Nick?" he asked the Big Guy.

Glancing over his shoulder the Big Guy replied, "He seems to be holding his own. The doc's with him."

"Where's everyone else? Have you talked with the Bureau?" Frank asked, grimacing at a sharp pain.

"Are you okay, man?"

"Yeah," Frank said.

"I called them after you called me. They're looking for her. I told them to give me a call as soon as they knew something."

"Excuse me, sir," the nurse said to Frank as she made her way around the Big Guy. "The doctor has ordered an X-ray of your head, just to be sure. Someone will be here in a few minutes to take you down."

"All right," Frank replied, feeling a little dizzy, but meeting the Big Guy's gaze.

"I'll give the guys a call and see what's going on," the Big Guy said as the wheelchair entered the room. "Just relax—everything will be fine."

"Just do it!" Frank said while being helped into the chair. "How's she doing?" he asked the attendant.

"They seem to be pretty busy over there. This is one of the best hospitals in the area. I'll see what I can find out while you're getting your X-ray."

"Thanks, that would help," Frank replied as the elevator doors closed.

Meanwhile, the Big Guy was on the phone talking and writing down instructions. He spoke in a whisper as he scanned the room, looking as if he had stolen something. The big room had become a shelter. Ailing bodies hauled themselves through the door and reached

out for relief. There was much coughing, belly holding, and slow shuf-
fling as the walking wounded surrounded the woman sitting behind
the counter armed with information.

CHAPTER 26

▼

Frank was later informed that Nick was badly infected and had to be rushed to the intensive care unit. Frank now awaited word on Sarah's condition. The Big Guy delivered all the details before leaving. He assured Frank that everyone was grateful that Sarah was safe, but Frank just couldn't find it in him to accept their compliments and walk away. He had to be involved in the search every step of the way. The job had become too personal.

In front of Frank stood a petite nurse, dressed in her hospital greens and determined as hell to treat him. In fact, he hadn't seen anyone as determined since his mother whipped his butt after finding out he had accidentally set the garage on fire. A little shaky, he struggled on his heels, almost tripping over a Rubenesque woman dressed in a vivid floral print, bright enough to give someone double vision. "Excuse me," he said to the nurse.

Before he could say anything else, she pulled him aside, removed her blue cap, and placed it in her pocket. "I know you want to find out about that poor girl, but don't be alarmed—she's going to be okay. Is there someone else with you? The doctor would like to talk to you in private."

"No, I'm the only one here. He can talk to me. Where is he?" Frank said, swiveling his head.

"Follow me," the nurse said, having already assessed his ability to walk the distance. Beyond the emergency room, Frank noticed the open curtains around Sarah's bed, but there was no Sarah. He passed several more beds filled with moaning people until they reached a quiet wing, where the nurse said, "Have a seat, please. I'll let the doctor know that you're here. Are you sure there isn't anything I can get for you?"

"I'm fine," he said.

"Dr. Harsha will be here in a few minutes. If you need anything, please let one of us know."

"I will," Frank said. While waiting, he thought that nothing seemed right. The soft lamp on the table next to him cast a soft light on the used magazines.

"Sir, I'm Dr. Harsha." He looked up to find a woman stretching out her hand in his direction.

"Hi…er—?"

"Please, don't get up. I want to let you know that Sarah Oberman is okay." The room suddenly felt warm. On the wall, Frank noticed the hanging cross.

"But what's going on? I know something isn't right. I can tell." He could tell mostly by the way the doctor was acting. She seemed to find it easier to look at the paper in her hand than look into his eyes.

"Sarah…is okay," she repeated haltingly. "She's pretty bruised, you understand, but it doesn't appear to be too worrisome."

"Bruised? Was she raped?"

"No. They might have tried—but, no. We're sure of that."

He jumped up so fast it startled the doctor. "Those bastards!" he yelled, banging his fist on the wall, but this only sent a shooting pain to his head. Grabbing his head, he rested it on his arm against the wall. "Those bastards!"

The doctor stood behind him and said, "I know this is upsetting, but we need to take things one step at a time. Please, have a seat. I really need you to hear this." Frank's anger had disrupted his usual mental control, but he sat down to listen—though not without regret for having failed to unload his gun into every one of them.

He forced himself to listen, catching every other word; but enough sank in to give him the gist of the situation. "I need to get someone over here," he informed.

"We need to watch her for a few days," the doctor explained. "She's been through a lot, but she's a pretty strong young lady. I'll find out what room she'll be in and let you know—okay?"

"Thanks," he answered in a tired voice.

"Are you all right? Would you like me to have someone look after you?"

"Not me—I'm fine," Frank said.

"Why don't you wait here, then? It shouldn't be long."

"Appreciate it." Frank's dull headache left him a little unsettled as he waited.

CHAPTER 27

▼

"*The captain has turned on the FASTEN SEAT BELT sign,* the hidden speaker voice echoed throughout the aircraft, "*so please keep your seat belts fastened until the plane has come to a complete stop. We should be at the gate in a few minutes. Those of you traveling on to other destinations are asked to see the attendant at the gate. For those who will be continuing on with us, our estimated departure time will be approximately ten-twenty-five. As always, thank you for flying with us.*"

"Oh, bullshit," Riggins said, looking over at Barry. "How long do you think it will take us to get there? I'm ready for this shit to be over."

"Not long," Barry responded in an unusually calm voice. He was deep in thought, staring out the window. The flight attendant taking care of the two of them gathered their trash and signaled to all involved to prepare for arrival.

Within minutes the plane was on the ground. Anxious, Riggins was ready to go and demand his bag. "Thank you for flying with us," the attendant said, handing it to him. Riggins was sweating as he stood near the door, almost willing it to open. He wanted out of this claustrophobic prison.

"Step back, please," the flight attendant asked as the door opened. Like trapped gas Riggins exited, and Barry trailed behind him, fighting to keep his bag on his shoulder. They walked swiftly to the reception area.

"Barry, come on, I need to get out of here. Where're the bags? Let's go."

"I checked them, Boss. You didn't think I was going to carry all of them, did you?"

"Listen," Riggins said and stopped in his tracks, his pale face fiercely red. "I don't have time for your shit, do you understand me?" This time, his petulance only left Barry fuming. "Get the bags and meet me at the car. I need to take a leak again," Riggins ordered.

Arguing with him was not worth it, Barry told himself.

Riggins made off but startled by a police officer standing next to the wall, he readjusted his walk. Riggins and Barry didn't know it, but they were surrounded, trailed like stink on shit.

Confident Riggins was about to lead them to Katherine, agents hung close, undetected, until he stepped in the john. Pretending to piss, a couple of the agents stood by, heads erect, eyes covering Riggins. "Shit," Riggins said fighting with his zipper before charging at the urinal. And he almost trampled a man and his little son, who gave Riggins a perplexed look as the father grabbed him.

∗   ∗   ∗   ∗

Things had settled down at the hospital. Sarah was in her room. A female agent sat next to the door watching her. Monitors chirped through the hall as nurses made their medication runs and patients prepared to settle down for the night. Sarah lay in bed restless and cold. She was grappling with her recent memories, her body trembling as she fought notions that only she understood.

The dim light overhead made her bed appear darker than it was. Trapped in her dark corner, she inched ever closer to the wall—terrified. Her eyes gazed fixedly beneath the door, where perverse shadows crossed the light. She tried to will the doorknob not to move. "No, no," she called out.

The female agent overheard her and rushed over to her bed, along with the nurse who had just walked in. "It's okay—try to get some rest," the agent reassured her, rubbing her arm beneath the sheet. "It's all right," she repeated.

The nurse held Sarah's wrist, looked at her watch, and began counting. She took a moment to share a confident smile with the agent, which helped put them both at ease.

That was the scene in Sarah's room. Several floors above, Nick lay in critical condition, his Spartan room adorned by a gaudy wall picture and two green leather chairs, one of which was occupied. A tall, burly man, gun strapped to his chest, monitored Nick's every move.

Frank, deep in thought, leaned against the wall inside Nick's room. He had covered all the details, and yet something still wasn't right. Even the other agents felt it. An eerie quiet descended, interrupted occasionally by beeps from the monitoring and IV machines hanging next to Nick's bed. Frank checked his watch against the wall clock.

Near the nurses' station a man in white clothes with a black belt rested his hand on a wooden stick, which he whipped back and forth as he cautiously moved backwards into the medicine room, where he played with a few bottles. There, he nervously filled a syringe and returned it to his pocket. Fearing exposure, he egged himself on— *Come on!*—before he noticed a nurse headed his way. She came close enough for him to see the flowers in her underwear through her whites.

His hand remained inside his pocket, and he was unsure about his next step. The nurse inadvertently dropped a pill and recovered it. That wasn't very hygienic, but she didn't notice the baby-blues fixed on her.

The clock was ticking.

He was just about to do something unplanned when an uninvited guest put an end to it.

"You'd better hurry, he's in lot of pain," the nurse said, standing in the doorway. It's almost time for the next shift and I'd hate to see Rose have to deal with him all night."

"Me neither," the nurse replied. "She hates the night shift. I'd rather swallow this bottle than have to hear her mouth tonight," she said with a laugh.

"Is there anything I can do to help?" the other nurse asked, anchoring the door.

"No, I'm okay—just need to lock this up. Thanks for asking. Let's go."

The door closed behind them with a long soft squeak. Alone, the man in whites refocused his attention on his mission. He started to swing the cotton strands around the floor. Traveling with his wet sidekick, he headed down the hall. Room 604 caught his eye. He moved cautiously toward the door and listened. The only thing he could hear on the other side of the door were the beeps of the heart monitor.

The agent sat, arms crossed.

*   *   *   *

Base camp on Daufuskie Island had been cleaned and the boys were ready for the next shift. The isolated lights hanging above the Atlantic appeared as little peaceful stars. The boat transported the agents, who were not only in awe of what was going down but determined to see Riggins get his just reward. They filled Frank in with updates over the phone. Frank listened anxiously and kept checking his wristwatch, his thoughts unwaveringly fixed on Katherine. He found it hard not to rush in the direction she was last seen to be heading, but he was smart enough to know that his effort would be in vain.

CHAPTER 28

▼

The smooth Southern air carried a welcome warmth that eased the stiffness of joints.

Barry and Riggins exited. "There he is, Boss. Over there—black car. Let's go," Barry instructed.

"He sees us," Riggins said, hand on Barry's shoulder, "he sees us. Let's go." He stepped off the busy curb. Barry quickly followed with their bags in hand, feeling almost fulfilled.

"Don't pull too close," one agent directed another, who stood so close he could feel the hot air escaping Riggins' body.

"That guy looks familiar," Riggins said about the man they were about to meet. "Let's find out."

"Been a while," Tommy, an Italian-looking guy, said before reaching out to shake Riggins' hand. He was of mixed blood, but his Irish roots were belied by his dark appearance. He was dressed in cloth finer than silk, and his physique had a chiseled quality to it. His teeth—surrounded by a business-like face—glowed richly in the dark.

"That's right," Riggins replied. "Now, let's go."

Wrist wrapped in a heavy Rolex, Tommy greeted Barry. "You're right on time, I just got here. I had a—"

"Let's go, we'll talk in the car." Riggins was impatient.

The three of them drove off—trailed by the agents. Chuck, the lead agent, stopped at the light and asked, "Did you get it?" Riggins' car was the first to pull away; he was oblivious of the heavy mobiles that surrounded them.

"I got it!" the agent blurted out. "That's Tommy Kane. Arrested a few years back as a suspect in an armed robbery, but they couldn't convict him. I'm sure it's him." The agent punched his name into the computer.

"Well, I'll be damned. I think we're about to taste the real thing here. Don't lose them," Chuck ordered. "Wait a minute. Listen. It's Riggins."

It was indeed. "Does she have any idea what's going on?" Riggins asked. "I heard all she was concerned about was making sure the girl was safe."

"She's nervous as hell," Tommy replied.

"Did she tell you anything?" Riggins asked.

"No, not to me, to Paul."

"Paul! What in the hell is he doing right?"

"Nothing," Tommy replied, noticing in the mirror how tense Barry looked. "You know Paul, especially when he's been drinking."

"That son-of-a bitch better not screw this up. I can't wait to meet her. She owes me a big apology," Riggins chortled.

Barry had a strange look on his face. He was too anxious to talk and was waiting to see how Tommy would handle it. Riggins liked having his ego fed, and it felt good for once not to be in the hot seat. Pulling onto the highway Tommy said, "She's a little rough around the edges—with a big chip on her shoulder."

"Yeah, right," Barry mumbled to himself.

"What do you mean by that?" Riggins asked.

"For one thing, she attacked Paul. They almost wrecked the car. I think the woman is crazy."

"That son-of-a-bitch probably deserved it. Is everyone okay?"

"Sure everyone is okay. She's more trouble than any of us banked on, though. You should have let us take care of her," he sighed. "Sorry. I think we're all tired of this scene."

"That's the problem with all of you. You want to do things in a hurry and move on. That's the reason I'm in this situation in the first place. Glen tried to do things in a hurry and screwed up. That chick should have been pushing up daisies a long time ago. None of you has learned a damn thing. I don't even know why I put up with this shit. I need professionals. Someone who knows how to do a job and keeps his trap shut unless he's asked to open it."

"What are you trying to say?" Tommy asked, sullen.

Preparing for the worst, Barry closed his eyes. After all, how could any of them measure up to Riggins—their brains were as small as a pig's without intact sensory receptors; they might as well have been lobotomized. *Yessir—stupid here reporting for duty!*

Barry wondered if that would make him happy. Trying to please Riggins was a thankless task—and it was getting late. He yawned, but then noticed the welcome sign above. Charleston, exit 42, was twenty miles away. They would be there in minutes with Katherine the Great—in person. Should he take another photo of her or just kiss her ass goodbye prior to the execution?

Whatever. Barry just wanted the ordeal to be over. He wondered how he had allowed himself to reach such a low point. Was his lavish lifestyle worth it? His self-esteem sunk ever lower. The snag was that he was inseparable from Riggins. He knew too much, and leaving Riggins was not an option if he expected to live to see old age. It bothered him as he listened to Riggins belittle everyone. Riggins was in full bitch mode, popping his pills.

Tommy was irritated, but he decided not to bite. He was embarrassed that he had allowed himself to be lured into Riggins' self-centered world. Feigning interest in the road ahead, he bit his lip and locked his mouth shut. "I can't wait, I can't wait," he nervously told himself.

Riggins swallowed the little white pills. "Barry, pass me some water. Now!" he ordered and glared at Tommy, who thought, *Five miles to go.* By now, Tommy's shirt was clinging to his skin from all the sweat. This was a hot night.

*   *   *   *

"That guy is sick," one of the agents said as they listened. "He's crazy; did you hear that? I don't know why in the world those guys don't just blow his fuckin' head off."

"Money," Chuck replied. "They can't get to it without him."

"I guess, but what a price to pay. Is it really worth it?"

"It must be to them," Chuck replied. "Be careful, we're getting a little close."

"I will, but where's the 'copter? Should've been here by now," the agent asked.

"Don't worry, they know what they're doing."

Prepared for the worst, the agents had assembled an arsenal. Behind the cars a packed bus trailed.

*   *   *   *

Tommy, his mind burdened, pressed heavy on the pedal. The inside of the car felt like a coffin.

CHAPTER 29

▼

A red-eyed Frank impatiently waited for the elevator, and then when the doors opened he was roused from his thoughts. It was quiet all around. A dark-tanned woman, white blouse above her navel, shared his ride. Her eyes fixed on the numbers lighting up above the door. Frank checked out his dirty shoes and, leaning against the wall, he fought to clear the cobwebs that clouded his brain.

Finally, as he escaped the cold box, he noticed a nurse busy at work in front of him. "Hello, I'm here to check on Sarah. How is she?" he asked, approaching the work station.

"Sarah?" she asked.

Frank reached into his pocket to pull out his badge. "I'm sorry, I should have been a little clearer. Will this help?"

"She's in room 402. I wasn't sure—"

"I understand, say no more. You did the right thing. Thanks." The smell of sickness distended his nostrils as he passed one room after another. At last he quietly entered Sarah's room. She was fast asleep, covered with a thin white sheet.

"How is she?" he whispered to the female agent. "She looks like she's getting some rest."

"She's been sleeping a lot. Talking to herself at times," the agent said, yawning.

"What did she say?"

"'Stop', 'Mama,' that's about it. She repeated those many times before she fell asleep."

Sarah's eyes moved beneath her closed lids. Satisfied by her peaceful appearance, Frank sighed and leaned against the windowsill, arms folded. "It's gonna be okay," he said, directing his thoughts to Katherine. Then he addressed the agent. "Why don't you take a break? I'm gonna be here for a few. You look like you could use some coffee."

"Not a bad idea. Want me to bring you some?" the agent asked.

"No, I'll be okay. I'm just tired."

"I tried. Be back in a few."

"By the way, have you heard anything on Nick Walters?"

"Yeah, he's holding his own. I'll check on him again when you return."

$$* \quad * \quad * \quad *$$

"Frank you really need to get some rest," the agent remarked when she returned with her coffee.

"Don't worry, I'm okay. I'll be back. I'm going to check on Nick Walters."

"Have you heard something?" she asked.

"No," he said and exited. The agent returned to her post with an awkward feeling. She sipped her coffee and took in a deep breath.

Frank passed the cleaning crew, ready to resume his protective mission as he made his way to the elevator. The nightly cleaning was also in full swing several floors above. Edging away from the activity, a pre-occupied man in white, former visitor to the medicine room, slithered his way toward Nick. His sharp eyes captured everything, though no one realized he was looking.

Out of nowhere, a fire alarm went off and lights dimmed as the emergency lights kicked in. Nurses leaped to their feet and swarmed around like hungry bees, wondering what was going. Frank's reflex was to rest his hand on his holster. The elevator doors swiftly opened, exposing him to the seething commotion. He quickened his pace as he approached the nurses' station. At about the same time, the agent covering Nick opened the door to see what was going on. He was immediately met with a knife to the stomach, followed by another deep jab and a twist. "Ah," the agent grunted, hitting the floor. He took a deep breath, then his body was still.

Rushing towards Nick, the assailant pulled out his syringe and injected its contents into the IV, but as he moved away from the bed he collided with the door as Frank burst in. Falling backward, he fought to brace himself against the bed, but he dropped the syringe. Bellowing, he leaped towards Frank, before two shots in the chest stopped him cold. Shifting his attention to Nick, Frank noticed the IV dripping on the floor. He yanked it out of Nick's arm, calling out for help.

"Nurse!" he shouted in an anguished rage while he checked Nick's pulse.

"Oh, Jesus!" a nurse screamed, blocking the doorway. It appeared as if Frank had killed them all.

"I'm a federal agent and these men need help. Quick! I'll explain later," he demanded. "I think he's been given something." Before he could finish, the room was full. Doctors, nurses, agents, and cops scurried around doing what they did best. The doorway was packed with onlookers, many dressed like the killer in white, who now lay motionless, face down on the floor. Frank stepped back before the onrush of medical experts. His alarm brought Sarah back to mind, and he rushed to the exit. "I'll be back. Get him out of here," he shouted, knocking a man into the wall as he flew by.

"Shit," the man yelled, annoyed.

"Sarah," he shouted, heart clanging. He leaped down the stairs in crazed fashion. "Get out of my way! Get out of my way!" he shouted, his gun held high. Screams chilled the halls, like a scene from a horror movie. Frank burst into Sarah's room. The female agent grabbed her gun and jumped to attention. Sarah was asleep. Breathing like a defective engine, Frank fell against the windowsill, weak with exhaustion. Knowing she was safe somewhat settled his rapid heartbeat. "This is crazy. Crazy!" he yelled, holding his head. "That son-of-a-bitch will stop at nothing," he said, looking at the agent.

"What's going on?" the agent asked, anxiously trying to temper her voice.

Frank pulled the agent aside and explained.

Back in the intensive care unit, Nick looked like a human pin cushion as his body fought against the odds.

CHAPTER 30

▼

The sign above read EXIT 42, CHARLESTON, SOUTH CARO-
LINA. The green Jeep pulled off the highway and the Big Guy drove
down a dark, secluded country road. Flicking his cigarette out the window, he swerved to park his car next to another. Perfect fit, he thought,
just like a good screw. The smell of pines and wet dirt skipped in the
air as he got out of the car. "Shit!" he said—the door had caught his
jacket.

The two-story home that stood before him appeared unoccupied.
His only welcome was a single white curtain billowing from the upper
level. He climbed the solid steps. Tired and hesitant, he checked his
surroundings once again and walked over to a closed window. It was
dark and bare. The empty room heightened his concern, prompting
him to take another look at the car next to which he had parked.

His solid hand hit the door, then a muffled noise from the other
side broke the ghostly silence. "Hey, Ralph, come in," Jeff said, glad to
see him. "We thought something happened to you." The two traded
greetings before proceeding into the dark, unfurnished room, which
echoed as they spoke.

"Have you heard from the Boss? We need to get this shit over—
they're onto him. His place has been bugged," he said.

"Bugged? What in the fuck are you talking about?" Jeff asked.

"A couple of guys tapped his place. Listen, they're onto him and we don't have much time. I had a hard time getting out of there. I thought I was going to have to kill the Doc."

"Why?" Jeff asked.

"I think he overheard me talking on the phone after Frank left."

"Where were you?"

"Do you think I'm stupid? I was outside on my phone."

"What did he hear?"

"I'm not sure. I turned around and he was acting kinda strange—a funny look in his eyes."

"Did he say anything?"

"No," the Big Guy replied.

"Shit, man, I don't like what I'm hearing."

"Neither do I. This shit is starting to fall apart. I can't chance it. He'll be taken care of."

"Who?" Jeff asked, perplexed.

"The Doc—who in the hell do you think I'm talking about?"

"What about Nick? Is he dead?"

"Not yet, I tried to give him that shit in the bottle, but the Doc and Katherine kept getting in the way. He's as good as dead, though. Our guy at the hospital will finish his ass. He won't have a problem getting to him. Forget about them, we don't have much time. Where's the Boss?"

Eyes widening, Jeff said, "He's on his way. We need to hold tight until he gets here."

"That's not wise, man. Do you understand what I'm saying?" the Big Guy asked, frustrated. "Listen, I can't sit around here too long. You guys need to get the hell out of here."

"Relax, man, you look like you need a drink or something. I'm not worried. Tommy's with him. Come on, Paul's been waiting to see you." They made their way towards the kitchen, as muffled voices were heard in the background. The radio was on low. In front of it, doing what he did best, stood Paul, drink in hand.

"Hey, Big Guy. I'm happy to see you," Paul said, followed by a solid handshake. "We didn't know what happened to you. The Boss said he lost contact with you. I thought you bailed on us. The last thing we wanted to do was put some lead in your ass," he said laughing. "Why didn't you call?"

"Long story. What happened to you?" the Big Guy asked.

"Ah, I'm fine, have a drink." Paul filled a glass.

The Big Guy kept probing. "Man you look like you've been beaten." Jeff, breaking a grin, held off and waited for Paul's explanation.

"Fuck you!" Paul shouted. "I'll give you the same thing we gave that punk buddy of yours."

"Relax, Paul," said the Big Guy. "Let's get serious. I saw what you guys did and it looked painful."

"Serious my ass, that punk motherfucker deserved it. I should have put a bullet in his ass."

"Man, you're talking out of your head. You been drinking too much of the wacky shit?"

"Fuck you! You punk-ass Bureau boys think you're so fuckin' smart. Kiss my white ass," Paul shouted, pouring himself a drink, "I don't need you. If you fucks are so smart why in the hell are you here? Can't be that good in your private club. The last thing I need is a goddamn student shoving his bullshit up my ass. Fuck you!" He scowled and finished his drink.

Checking his watch, Jeff placed his hand on Paul's shoulder. "Come on, Paul, relax. This is not the time to go postal, we have a job to finish. Relax, man—I mean it." He turned to the Big Guy and said with a wink, "Hey, tell him you're just fucking with him."

"Get the fuck away from me," Paul said, dropping his shoulder. "I don't need either of you. I could have done this myself. You see this?" He spun his gun in his hand. "This is all I need. The two of you don't mean shit!"

"Hold on," the Big Guy said, hands in front of him as though he was waiting to be hit. "We're not fucking with you. I know you're good, just relax—okay?" Returning Jeff's wink with a cherubic smile on his face, he went to join his angry companion in a glass of crazy juice. "You guys are tense, this shit must be getting to you. This has been one scary fucking day." He emptied his glass. "Where's Katherine?"

"She's in the back. That bitch thinks she's tough. I was within a cunt hair of beating the shit out of her," Paul said in a slurred voice. She ain't right."

Puzzled, the Big Guy turned to Jeff for an explanation.

"He's always thinking about pussy," Jeff said in a hushed voice. "That's his problem, he needs some."

"Who in the fuck are you talking about?" said Paul, lifting his bottle. "My dick is bigger than a sausage link. Yours is so short it's ready to blow."

"Hey guys, this will be over soon. Calm down. This is not the scene we want the Boss to walk into," the Big Guy said.

"Take your ass somewhere and save that peaceful bullshit for church. I'm not afraid of him. Shit, he couldn't do this without us. I'm the man!" Paul yelled. Staggering, he pushed the bottle into the Big Guy's chest.

"Maybe later, guy," the Big Guy responded, pushing the bottle right back. "Hey, I think she'll be pleasantly surprised to see me. I can't wait to see the look on her face."

"Do you think that's a good idea?" Jeff asked. "We shouldn't do anything until the Boss gets here."

Hooking his arm around Jeff's shoulder, the Big Guy quietly said, "I'm not like your friend over there, trust me. I've come too far to blow it, I promise. Now, where is she, really?"

"In the backroom, like I said, but watch yourself."

"Thanks," the Big Guy said.

"But I'm still worried about that guy Nick," said Jeff.

"Don't be. He'll be taken care of, as planned. Tomorrow will be a new day, trust me."

"I've heard that one before," Paul said sardonically.

"Let's stay positive; we'll know pretty soon," Jeff said. "News travels pretty fast around here."

"Don't worry," replied the Big Guy, winking as he walked away.

"I'm gonna check to see what's taking those guys so long. Hey, man, you need to lay off of that stuff," Jeff said.

"Fuck you! Why don't you go play in the fuckin' traffic," Paul blurted out.

"I think I'll do that. Thanks for the tip," Jeff replied.

"He needs to take his big ass back on the island and resume his babysitting job. He ain't worth the clothes on his fucking back. Maybe I need to apply for his job. You think they'll take me?"

"Yeah, they'll take you all right," Jeff replied. "To the fuckin' crazy house," he muttered. But it was getting late, and Tommy should have called. Jeff peered into the dark where there was nothing but faded shadows looking back at him.

CHAPTER 31

▼

His feet heavy on the floor, the Big Guy swaggered down the short empty hallway. How ironic, he thought. This reminded him of her place. He paused, imagining the look on Katherine's face when she saw him. His feelings were the same as when he was first given her case. It read like a who's who—most of whom were more rich and powerful than he ever dreamed.

And he remembered thinking how easy it would all be. So, how could have Detective Glen blown it? But the money was too dazzling even this time around. All these guys with wealth thicker than quicksand had nothing more to do with their money than toss it to Riggins. When the Big Guy realized that none of them were wealthier than Riggins, it intrigued him even more.

His hand on the doorknob, he ended his moment of reflection and stepped inside.

Katherine's eyes had widened in fear as she saw the door open. Her hands were numb. Then she set her eyes on Big Guy and relief brusquely replaced her dread.

"Oh, thank God you're here. Is Sarah okay?" she asked, expecting to be untied. But the Big Guy was taciturn and just grinned.

"What's the matter?" She was puzzled. His face bore an expression she had not seen before.

Proud of the drama he was creating, he continued to toy with her. "I bet you never thought you'd see me again. Heard you had a little trouble on the way," he said, amused, standing close enough for her to smell his sweat.

"What are you doing? Is she okay? Please, untie me," she begged. Frightened, she searched his eyes. He circled her chair, glancing at her hands, one on top of the other and twisting.

"Why are you doing this?"

"Doing what?" he smirked.

"I can't believe I trusted you. What have you done with Sarah?"

"Shut up! I don't owe you any explanation. You're lucky you made it this far. No screw-ups this time."

Desperate, she implored, "Why?"

"None of your fuckin' business. I said shut up! You and that boyfriend of yours will meet soon. The two of you deserve each other. I'm glad he found you, it made my job easier."

"You bastard!" she yelled.

"Scream, no one can hear you. Ever wonder what it feels like to be buried alive, choking on dirt?"

Katherine burned him with her angry look, then fought to hold back the tears pooling in her eyes. What had she done to deserve this?

His strong hand gripped her chin. She flinched but was locked in his grip. "That pretty face of yours is too nice to mess up," he said.

Katherine's sweaty neck ached, but she thought of Sarah and she didn't care anymore how much this big ape treated her like dirt. Nothing mattered but Sarah.

Finally, she broke his grip. "Kill me, why don't you. Just tell me Sarah is okay."

"Don't worry, she'll live. I'm not into killing kids. You needn't worry."

Relieved, she asked, "Is Frank in this with you?"

"Would you like him to be? Maybe we could play 'good cop, bad cop.' Oh, that sounds like fun. Would you like that, huh? Would that make you happy?" His hot breath warmed her ear.

"Why? Why?" She felt flustered.

"Don't look at me like that!" he demanded. "I'm not the one who'll stuff your ass." But she kept up her look of defiance. "I said don't look at me like that!" he yelled. "Tell you what, make a wish. I'll deliver it for you. What do you want? Say it, I'm listening."

"Get your hands off me!" she shouted. Betrayed by her innocent trust, she now felt the hot empty room threatening to bury her in her grief. But she held her tears.

Why me?

Her first impulse was to suspect Frank. But, no! She had to control her thoughts better. Only two men had ever held her warmly—her father and Nick. And then Frank.

By this time, the Big Guy had positioned himself at the window. It was quiet and dark, allowing him a dim view of the back woods. "It'll soon be over, I promise," he said in a diffused voice. Katherine chose not to reply. Then the Big Guy stepped out and closed the door.

Overwhelmed, Katherine collapsed in her tears, wishing someone would end her pain. How could this be happening? "Sarah," she cried out. "I'm so sorry." The thought of her beautiful daughter being treated like a piece of meat was unbearable. "What have they done to her?" she asked. She wanted Sarah to hear her.

A dim light shone beneath the door, but this time no shadows.

Death row was a long agony.

What would it take to have someone come in? She was entranced by a doorknob that wasn't moving.

∗   ∗   ∗   ∗

In the dull hot wind, not far away, a well-polished car pulled off the highway. Tommy was within a couple of miles of the house, focused but afraid to say anything. He wanted out. His feet were heavy on the pedal—he was pushing the clock.

Barry sucked up the smooth road. He was more or less familiar with the whereabouts of their captive, an area he knew well, but he couldn't help contemplate the lurking strangeness of the night. The hefty trees seemed taller than he remembered. He twitched his nose anxiously, trying to sniff out the honey-like smell wafting in the air.

Riggins was thinking only of Katherine, having rehearsed his lines many times for their fateful meeting. But for some reason they escaped him just now. It had seemed so simple a few hours ago—revenge awaiting delivery. He stuck another little white pill to his tongue and grabbed the bottle of water from Barry's hand.

CHAPTER 32

▼

The news was out and reporters surrounded the hospital, snapping shots of anything that moved. A veil of security had descended. Everyone was suspect. An armed, secret service-looking brigade rushed inside. "Move out of our way, please," the agent ordered. The men under his command following close behind began to scatter, as if they were familiar with the place.

The Hospital CEO, after a quick briefing, locked himself in his office to prepare for the media barrage. The main thing on his mind was protecting the reputation that he had worked so hard to build. Breathing heavily, his pen moved faster than he could think. Then, he looked up at one of his executives. "Why?"

"It's not that bad, just don't look nervous," the Vice President said, looking down on his boss. "You know how these guys get. Anything for a story,"

There was a rap on the door. "Shit, who's that?" the CEO asked. "Tell them I'll be there in a minute."

"I'll find out," the shaky Vice President replied.

It was one of the agents, who had got fed up trying to calm the media crowd. When he saw the Vice President, he inquired, "Is he ready?"

"Almost. He needs a couple of minutes."

Impatient, the agent said, "If you like, I can talk to them. But some-body had better start filling them in soon."

"No, that won't be necessary."

"Let me know if you change your mind. I do this all the time."

"Thanks, but that won't be necessary. He'd rather do this himself."

✱   ✱   ✱   ✱

The questions inside Frank's head were not much different from those of the hungry crowd below. He stood next to Sarah's door, his weary eyes watching the rapid traffic of armed men and confused nurses. He was just about to open the door when he noticed a woman wearing a navy-blue suit and a man in similar attire. She was walking hastily in his direction before she and the man, who was about triple her size, were joined by several police officers.

"Are you Frank?" the woman asked.

"Yes," he said, releasing the door.

"Allow me to introduce myself. I'm Vivian Jones, Director of Secu-rity. I've been asked to brief you on Mr. Nick Walters and some other matters. I was told you're responsible for bringing him here. Please, come with me. These men will take over. Don't worry, the young lady will be adequately protected."

Frank looked in awe at the triple-sized wonder beside Vivian Jones who was scrutinizing him. The man reminded him of the Big Guy, except his belt had fewer notches open.

"This won't take long," she added. "There's a private room around the corner where we can talk." She signaled to the police officers to take position. "I'll be right back," she told them.

"There's already someone in there with her," Frank explained.

"I'm aware of that," she replied. Frank followed her and her hefty sidekick, who led the way.

Once inside, he began, "So, what's happening. Is Nick Walters dead?"

"No, he's not. I think he'll survive. He's in the intensive care unit right now. Whatever was in that needle never entered his system. I was told it's possible he might have been given something else, based on his earlier blood test, but at this point that is only speculation. We're still waiting for the lab results."

"What do you mean by something else? I'm confused."

"So am I, but it appears Mr. Walters has a toxic substance in his blood. Quite unusual from what I've been told. As I said, they're still running the tests, but he should be okay."

"Toxic, what in the hell does that mean?" he asked.

"I'm not a doctor—just delivering the message. Are you all right?" she asked, concerned about Frank's blank expression.

"Sure, just tired," he responded.

"When I hear anything else I'll let you know."

"Thanks, I'd appreciate that," Frank said. "What about the other guy—who was he?"

Suddenly, she chose to sit down, with a crushed look on her face.

"I'm sorry, did I say something wrong?" he asked. Something was wrong; he knew it.

"No, you didn't..." she answered, her eyes sweeping the floor. Composing herself, her voice dropped. "The man you shot tonight has been with us for over twenty years. He has a wife and three kids. It doesn't make sense," she said, struggling to control her feelings. "I know him, and he would never do anything like this."

"Why not?" Frank asked.

"That man...would never do anything like this, not even for money." She looked as certain as could be.

"Mister, you don't understand," a deep voice interrupted them. "The man was her brother *and* the head of hospital security."

Frank watched her dejection grow. Uncertain of how to respond, he traded solid looks with the man standing before him. "Brother?"

"Yes, my brother," she said. That's partly why I needed to talk to you. I'm hoping you can help me understand. Do you know these guys?"

"But are you positive it's your brother?"

"That's what I've been told."

"Where is he now?"

"They've taken the body to the morgue. They didn't want me to see him just yet. My family is on their way here."

Somehow it all started to make sense. Picking up the tempo, Frank said, "Show me. Come on, let's go."

"What do you mean?" she asked, startled by his changed expression.

"Let's go to the morgue, something is not right," he said, holding the door.

The floor was filled with agents and polished police officers as Frank and the hospital officials headed for the elevator. When the elevator door opened after their descent, the first thing Frank noticed was several police officers standing outside two large stainless-steel-like doors. "Is he in there—the guy that was shot?" Frank asked.

"Yes," a young officer replied. "Right in there." The green was still hanging from the young officer's ears as Frank walked past him. It made him think back on his earlier days.

Noticing the director's hesitancy, guilt wore his knees. "You can wait if you like. I need to do this," Frank told her.

"I'm okay," she replied looking at the doors. "I need to do this, too. It will be easier on my family if I do."

"Are you sure?" he asked.

"I'm positive." A chill pierced them as they entered. Before them lay a body draped in a white sheet. In this sterile milieu, silver tables lined the room like bakery racks. The tools of life and death were arranged on a table in the center of the tiled floor. They lay there, waiting to be turned on, with their jagged, frightening blades and hoses that dangled like bungy-cords from the ceiling.

The director held her hand to her mouth in horror.

Frank folded back the sheet, exposing the man's artificial countenance. "That looks like the guy I shot," he said, though not entirely sure. Is that your brother?" Frank asked.

"Looks like him, but his hair…it seems different," she said, eyes widening.

"What do you mean different?" Frank studied the corpse.

"I mean, he looks different. Maybe…"

Frank himself began to notice something peculiar—a thickening around the man's neck.

"What are you doing?" she asked, as Frank put his hands to the corpse. The skin began to peel away, which stunned Frank.

"Oh God!" Vivian screamed. "It's *not* my brother!"

Frank stood in disbelief.

"Who is it?" she questioned. "Do you know him?"

"Actually, yeah," he said. "It's the doc. He worked with us and was taking care of Nick Walters. Those bastards!" Frank's hollow look frightened her. "The guy I shot—he's not dead. When was the last time you saw your brother?"

"Ah, yesterday, I believe. Yes." She gave him a troubled look.

"Did you actually see or talk to him?"

"I spoke to him on the phone. It's been a couple of days since I saw him."

"Was he at work when you talked to him?"

"No, he was at home getting ready to go to work. What does this all mean?" She was desperate for an answer. Frank glanced at the large man beside her, ignored the director's alarm, and dragged his eyes sadly over Doc's body.

Why? What did he do? he begged to know. The pieces of the puzzle did not fit. He turned back to Vivian, who was as bewildered as he.

"Let's go. I'll send a few men to check on your brother; we need to find him. Why don't you give him a call? What's his address?"

She told Frank the address, and wrote it down as well. "I'll call him, I need to call my family also," she said, before pausing. "Do you think he's okay?"

Frank ignored her question. She already knew what he refused to say at that moment. "Please, call him." He stood by as she picked up the phone to dial. He took another look at the doc.

Frank found another phone and dialed.

Hello, two voices at the other end of the line said in unison. Frank, sighing, pressing on his eyes, had his connection. "It's me—Frank. I need you to go over to this address." He read Vivian's handwritten note. "Yeah that's right. Call me as soon as you have something. Thanks," he said. Just then, he observed the ghostly look on Vivian's face.

She hadn't made a connection. "Please take her upstairs," he ordered the large man.

"Sure," the big man responded.

When the door closed behind them, Frank fully exposed Doc's body and made a few mental notes. Then he rushed out, passing a few men and then waiting for the elevator door to open. His unsettled thoughts conjured up names and images faster than he could comprehend. Katherine weighed heaviest on his mind. He could still smell her perfume, but it was her big brown eyes that haunted him.

No, he refused to allow himself to go down that road. "Come on!" He coaxed the elevator and pounded his fist on the wall. Never in his nineteen years with the Bureau had he fallen into a pit so deep. Finally, the door opened. Within seconds, he was in Sarah's room.

CHAPTER 33

▼

"I see where they're headed," the helicopter pilot informed the others as he hovered nearby. "There's a house about half a mile away. A couple of cars are parked in front. Do you read me?"

"Yeah, we do," Chuck said. "Do you see anyone?"

"Not a soul...Hold on. I see light."

Chuck asked, anxious, "What is it?"

"There's a short road leading to the back of the house. Send the bus. I think the guys can get pretty close. I'm gonna back off for now?"

"Hold steady, move with us," Chuck instructed, observing the car turning into a tree-lined driveway.

"I'm with you," the pilot responded.

"Fellas, this is it, turn off your lights. Remember, no one goes inside that house. Do you understand?" Chuck asked.

"Yeah, we got you," several agents responded. Guns clicked like loose teeth as each agent prepared for the worst.

*   *   *   *

Riggins, poker-faced, looked ahead at the unfamiliar house tucked behind the big greens. Anger and fear tugged at him—neither getting the upper hand. He tapped nervously on his knee while scanning

Tommy, whose every move made him even more nervous. Tommy, clammy hands glued to the steering wheel, refused to get rattled by Riggins' microscopic dissection of him. He fought to keep his feet and mind in sync. He willed the car to its final destination and anxiously breathed air from outside, untouched by his ill-tempered passenger.

Barry calmly observed the two men, then directed his thoughts to New York, which seemed so far away. He tried to imagine how to tell Riggins that he didn't want any part of this. Desperate, he wanted to order Tommy to make an about turn, but he knew that he was not in control and was pretty well stuck on this path. But what would happen if he didn't get out of this mess? He was afraid and uncertain of what Riggins might do. He wanted to say something, but he couldn't force a word through his clenched teeth, and his stomach just tightened.

*   *   *   *

"I see them," Jeff yelled. "Guys, they're here," he shouted. "Paul, get Ralph!"

"Fuck him! His big ass is in the bathroom. Can't you smell? You let him know." He staggered toward the window.

"Man, you'd better get your shit together, and fast. He's not going to like this."

"To hell with him. We delivered, haven't we? He better be happy and pay me my money."

The Big Guy came in. "Hey, what's going on in here?"

"What happened, did she blow ya?" Paul asked.

"Jeff, what's going on?" the Big Guy repeated, ignoring Paul.

"They're here, I saw their lights," Jeff said as he observed Paul, who was heading back towards the kitchen, singing the blues.

The Big Guy looked out another window. He seemed bothered. It was dark and calm—too calm. Something didn't smell right. Rushing over to where Jeff was standing, he took another look. A flash of light constricted his pupils. Hesitating, he backed away from the window, signaling Jeff to do the same. Tommy had just pulled up the driveway. "Wait a minute, Jeff," the Big Guy whispered, pushing Jeff back. "Oh, shit! he yelled, looking up. Helicopter lights flooded the scene.

Blinded, Tommy shielded his face. "What da fuck!" he said. "They found us!" He reached for his gun.

"No fuckin' way!" Barry said, incredulous. "We have to get the hell out of here." He shielded his eyes. Beyond the bright light, he could see nothing but trees, grass, and brush.

"Shoot," Riggins demanded. "Blow that shit out of the sky. Give me the gun, you idiot. Give it to me!"

"*Get out of the car*," Chuck yelled through his blow-horn. "*This is the FBI. You're surrounded. Hands up—and slowly.*" As he spoke, agents positioned themselves behind their cars, all guns pointed on the polished beauty. They were on high alert, directed to shoot at anyone except Katherine.

"*Listen to me, Riggins. I know you're in there. Come out. You're surrounded.*"

"What the fuck," the Big Guy said, his back against the wall and his neck extended forward. His eyes and mouth were wide open. "Jeff!" he called out. "We're surrounded, man, I have to get out of here."

Frightened, with his gun in hand, Jeff asked, "What are we going to do?"

Paul burst into the room. "You fuckin' cowards!" he yelled and headed for the door. But the Big Guy brought him down in a flash. Paul swore like he never did before. "You punk-ass motherfuckers…I'm not afraid…Get off me…I'll blow some smoke up their ass!" he raged, finally pushing the Big Guy away.

"Shut the fuck up and listen," Jeff said. "They know he's in the car."

"I'll give those fuckers what they want," Paul said. He was unstoppable and rushed out the room. Unsure of what to do, Jeff and the Big Guy held their positions. The car was still in place. Nothing moved around it. The two men traded quick peeks. Within seconds Paul had returned, pushing a defiant Katherine in front of him. Before either of them could say anything, her body hit the floor like a limp noodle, hands tied behind her back. She fought to get up, legs kicking, but to no avail.

"If you're wondering how this is going to end, I think this slut is about to find out," Paul said, hovering over her.

"Wait, Paul!" Jeff yelled out. "We're going to need her. Hold on, man!"

Trembling, Katherine looked up at the Big Guy. "Is it worth it?" she asked. "Might as well—"

"Shut up, bitch!" Paul shouted. He held his gun high up in the air, as Katherine crawled like a snail at his feet.

"Wait, something's happening," Jeff said.

Barry had just stepped out of the car with his hands held up high, and Riggins was yelling at him, "You bastard!"

"Don't shoot, I'm unarmed," Barry pleaded, blinded by the bright light. "Please," he begged, his legs unsteady.

"Step away from the car. Keep your hands in the air. I mean it," an agent ordered.

"The rest of you get out of the car—*now*," another agent called out.

Paul, noticing Barry's surrender, opened the door violently and fired several shots, hitting Barry. His shots were quickly returned. "You want me, motherfuckers, come and get me. I'll blow her brains out. Come on!" he challenged.

"Are you crazy?" Jeff shouted.

"Yes," Paul responded, then he turned his attention to Katherine. Once again the four of them were locked in the dark shadowy room. Paul's cold murderous eyes chilled Katherine the most. *This is it*, she told herself. Drained and hopeless, she prayed. She bid final farewell to Sarah and closed her eyes. Paul fired another shot through the window, causing her to flinch. To protect herself, she rolled to the wall, breathless. The smell of the Big Guy was too close for comfort. He was within a hair's breadth of stepping on her.

"Paul, what the fuck are you doing? You're going to get us killed. This isn't some fuckin' game," the Big Guy said.

"Quiet!" Jeff demanded, straining to hear what was being said outside and ready to piss in his pants.

"Back away from the car," an agent instructed Barry, who was clearly hurt. But the agent kept him at bay because of the scattered shots coming from the house. Holding onto his bloody leg, Barry backed against the car and yelled out for help. The agents were ordered to maintain their positions, even though the risk from whoever was stirring inside both the car and the house was mounting. Certain that Katherine was still alive, Chuck kept his ear to the phone. His men were poised to enter the house. "One more time," he directed. "We have to be ready to make our move as soon as those guys hit the door."

"Affirmative," the agent responded, and in a firm voice, he called out to Riggins and Tommy, "Get out of the car—*now*!"

This time several agents quickly surrounded the back of the house and accompanied a few who had taken up position beneath the window, close to where Jeff was standing.

"Tell them to let her go; we're trapped," Tommy said to Riggins. "We don't stand a choice."

"You punk, this is all your fault. Get the hell out!" Riggins shouted. His hands were shaking, and several of his pills hit the floor. "Get out!" he shouted. . This time his words were followed by a full bodily assault on Tommy, who, infuriated, held onto the door and fought to protect himself. He searched for his gun, but it was knocked away.

"You're fuckin' crazy," Tommy said, as he hung onto the door. Next to the car, near the rear tire, sat Barry writhing in pain, one leg outstretched, his clothes bloodied. He exhaled slowly, his face etched in pain. He feared that any false move would earn him another bullet, so he just watched Tommy struggle.

"Hold your fire," Chuck directed. "Someone is getting out."

"Please, don't shoot," Tommy pleaded, dragging himself out of the car. "You're crazy!" he shouted back at Riggins for the last time. It was hot and the rough surface he rested upon was starting to tear into his skin. "Please," he begged, his arms crossing his face. "I'm unarmed." He backed away from the car.

"Don't move," an agent called out. Tommy, arms outstretched, face fixed to the ground, and certain he was about to meet his maker, hoped he had done the right thing.

"Tommy, don't move," Barry said in a hushed voice. "It's over...I don't want to die."

Riggins tarried in the car, his eyes fixed on the open door abandoned by Tommy. A soft wind blew inside and an eerie quiet settled around him. Overwhelmed, he hurled himself towards the door and slammed it shut. Once again, he was entombed, only this time he was alone, smothered in his wet cottons. Breathless, he sucked up a few pills from the moist carpet and then touched Tommy's gun beneath the seat.

The agents were all in position, waiting for the go-ahead. With a concerned look on his face, Chuck hung up the phone and nodded lightly. The men were ready to enter the house.

Paul impatient with the silence, recklessly fired off several shots. Jeff was so furious he was ready to attack him, but several bullets melted into Paul's back before he could do anything. Horrified, Katherine screamed as Paul spun away from her.

"Drop it!" an agent shouted. By this time an army of other agents was lined up like skeet-shooters. Jeff and the Big Guy were surrounded.

"Drop it!" the agent yelled again, ready to use them as target practice. Dazed, Jeff watched Paul spew blood and then fall heavily to his knees, defeated.

"Don't shoot," Jeff pleaded, holding his heavy trembling arms high above his head to signal that he and the Big Guy were surrendering. The Big Guy found it difficult to keep his eyes off the FBI insignia of the agents rushing all around him. *I'm one of them*, he thought, as the cold steel cuffs locked his arms together. He tried to say something.

"Shut up!" several agents ordered. Choking for air, Paul remained face down on the floor.

In the corner, Katherine had collapsed in one of the agent's arms. Several men picked her up to escort her to another room. "Sarah," she cried out, confused.

Assured that everything inside was taken care of, Chuck spoke. "This is your last warning. We have Katherine. Your time's up."

Chuck's words sickened Riggins, who listened, hoping for a magical break. "What should I do?" he asked himself, his stomach dropping farther. Then, a fleeting thought occurred to him about something that Tommy had said earlier: *They'll never catch me alive. I would never survive prison.* Riggins was trapped in the web of self-destruction he had created. He caressed the gun in his hand and looked up at the bright light. It made him think of heaven.

The false quiet was interrupted by a single shot.

CHAPTER 34

▼

A half-opened screen door was the first thing the entourage of men noticed as they pulled up in front of the home of Jesse Brown, Vivian Jones' brother. Cautious, they called out his name as they approached the door. John, the lead detective, instructed his men before pushing the door open. He wanted to make sure the creaks in the floor didn't alarm anyone inside. "Mr. Brown, are you in there?" he called out, gesturing the others to cover him. It was dark and a radio set on low sat on a small table in the corner. The furniture in the living room appeared in order. "Check upstairs," he whispered. Quickly, he and several men headed in the opposite direction, down to the basement. "Jesse," he called out again, his words punctuated by the creaky wooden steps. The basement was empty, except for several boxes, an old bike, and a few tools resting on the cement floor.

"Hey!" one of the men shouted, standing at the top of the steps, "He's upstairs...in the bedroom." John didn't have to ask any more questions; the man's eyes told him all he needed to know.

They all rushed inside the room. Sprawled on the bed, face up, eyes open, was Jesse, his head resting on blood-soaked sheets. Except for the open drawer of the nightstand, everything seemed to be in place. "Call homicide," John instructed. He gloved his hand and rummaged through several papers. "Guys, something's not right," he said, walking over to the closet.

"What do you mean?" one of the men asked.

"I'm not sure, but somebody was looking for something," he said. He checked out the closet, where several short-sleeved shirts and pants hung neatly. On the floor were several of Jesse's dirty hospital uniforms. "I don't see his badge," John remarked with a strange look on his face. "Look around. I'm going downstairs."

*   *   *   *

Back at the hospital, Frank waited outside of Sarah's room, talking to a few police officers. Sarah was still resting comfortably, oblivious of all that had happened. The sedative was doing its job. This pleased Frank, who now knew she had nothing else to worry about.

"Sir, you have a phone call over at the desk," an attendant informed him.

"Thanks," he said. "You guys make sure no one goes in there, I'll be right back."

The call was from John, who wanted to discuss his findings.

*   *   *   *

The intensive care unit was busy. Bells sounded from every room as nurses marched, frantically trying to do their best. Nick was fast asleep. The antibiotics seemed to be working and his color had returned. Sitting in the room, a tired agent struggled through the early morning newspaper.

A Caucasian man dressed in white was heading toward the room, carrying a tray filled with surgical supplies. Hanging from his shirt pocket was a badge that read, "Jesse Brown." Everyone was busy at work as he approached the nurses' station. "Yes, how can I help you?" the clerk asked.

"Just bringing up the supplies that were ordered. Kinda crazy around here tonight?" he inquired.

"Yeah, but it's quieting down. I don't think we need any more entertainment. There has been enough to last the rest of the year."

With a false smile the man agreed. "Where do you want me to put these?"

"In the supply room would be fine, thanks."

"Okay," he said and walked away. Dropping his load on the countertop, he pulled a gun from beneath his shirt, topped it with a silencer, and headed towards Nick's room. He was determined to finish the job. His pace quickened.

"Excuse me," he heard a nurse say as he approached her in the hall. Immediately, a silent bullet pierced her chest, and he dragged her into an empty room. The thump of her body hitting the wall, however, caught the ear of the agent inside Nick's room. Unbeknownst to the agent, the assailant was no more than ten feet from where he sat, and before he could even look outside the room, he was met by a shadow. Two bullets ripped into his chest.

The intruder then fired two shots towards the bed, but one ricocheted. But before he could check on the success of his handiwork, two bullets in quick succession ripped into him from the rear. One of them hit him in the back of the head.

Breathless, heart pounding, Frank stood over the fallen man.

For the second time a frantic scene erupted. Screams of terror echoed down the halls. Aware that Nick had been shot, Frank shouted out for help and pulled back the sheets to assess the damage. Breathing a sigh of relief, he applied pressure to the bullet hole in Nick's leg. "Hurry," he ordered, refusing to take his eyes off the man who lay lifelessly on the floor.

"Oh my God!" a nurse screamed, her hand covering her mouth.

"Get me some help, now! He's been shot in the leg," Frank shouted.

"Are you all right?" the first officer on the scene asked.

"Yeah, I think so," Frank answered. "I think we'll be fine this time." He gazed at Nick, who grimaced as the nurses repositioned his wounded leg.

"It's going to be okay, Mr. Walters," another nurse said while placing a towel on his forehead. "The doctor will be here in a minute—just hold on."

Frank clipped off the badge attached to the dead man's shirt, after checking his pulse. In the doorway stood Vivian Jones, her eyes filled with tears. He walked towards her and, with his hand outstretched, told her, "This is yours."

"I don't understand," she protested.

"I don't, either," he replied in a somber voice, moving aside to allow the medical crew to pass. Nurses were lined up like pallbearers on each side of Nick's bed. "Take good care of him," Frank directed. He and Vivian watched as the group disappeared. "I'm sorry," he said to Vivian.

"Why my brother?" she agonized. "And who is this man?"

"Everyone's asking the same questions. The only thing I can tell you at this point is that a man with a vendetta was out trying to shut a few people up. Somehow your brother got caught in the traffic. I know most of this doesn't mean anything to you, but believe me, the man responsible for this will pay. I'm sorry, I wish I could have done more."

"Thanks for saying that, but that doesn't help bring back my brother. He was an honest man. I don't want anyone to think differently."

"I'm sure they won't. You need to get some rest, it's been a long night," Frank replied, refusing to tarnish her trusted memories. This ordeal has already taken a grievous toll on everyone, and Frank found it difficult to look into her tear-drenched eyes any more than he could Katherine's. He understood what death meant, although he never had to suffer the pain of losing someone close. Life had not yet taken him down that path.

But he thought of his family. His parents were aging, but young at heart. They constantly challenged Frank to persevere in the face of adversity. He attributed this to their Irish blood. Bob, his younger brother whom he was very close to, had never been more than a phone call away. They had both entered the law enforcement business around the same time. Frank always thought of Bob as the crazy one, but it was Bob who had made it and was now a prominent police chief. Frank, on the other hand, had inherited all of the family's wit and knew when to use it.

A soft smile crossed Frank's face. It all seemed so far away now. "I'm very sorry," he said to Vivian.

CHAPTER 35

▼

Shattered glass sprayed over Riggins' hair. The agent who fired the single shot gazed down upon him, his smoking gun in hand. Riggins writhed in pain. He held onto his bloody hand as agents surrounded the car. The bright light and eerie silence were gone, replaced by voices barking out instructions.

"Get him out of there," Chuck said, approaching the car. "We've been waiting for this honor for a long time, Mr. Riggins."

"To hell with all of you. You don't scare me. I want my lawyer," Riggins said, glaring defiantly at the men.

"You'll get your lawyer," the agent responded.

"Get this pathetic piece of shit out of here," Chuck ordered, pushing through the crowd of agents, each hustling in a different direction in the knowledge that they had just earned some interesting notches for their career.

"Get your hands off me!" Riggins shouted as the men hoisted him from the car. "Be careful!" he yelled, pitying his wounded hand.

Like a rich widow being escorted from her husband's funeral, Riggins was buried under a thousand gazes—a mere curiosity. "What are you looking at?" he challenged the onlookers. No one said anything, but everyone knew that this was the end of an ordeal that few people truly comprehended. The New York investment scandal had mystified so many that the victims had become household names. Everyone was pleased to see the man behind it all captured. The badges of courage had never shined so brightly.

Pushed along by a stabbing nudge in his side, Riggins was led away.

The front door finally opened, exposing several agents draped in their heavy vests. The men on the porch stepped aside as others trailed out of the house. They unveiled what had become known to all as "The Find."

It was Katherine.

Katherine was wrapped in a thin blanket barely covering her scars and her anguish. Her eyes bloodshot, her hair disheveled, she looked out calmly into the crowd before her. And it stared in turn at her. Then, spontaneously, all the men one after another began to applaud. It was a salute to Katherine's courage.

Katherine made her way cautiously down the steps. "Careful," a young agent said, feeling the urge still to protect her and to watch her every step. As she planted her feet firmly on the ground, a sudden chill seized her. Riggins was nestled in a car in the distance. She couldn't clearly see him; she just knew he was there. No one besides Riggins provoked such revulsion in her. Knowing he had been captured was not enough.

She forced herself closer. She wanted to see him. It wasn't enough that she had survived and that his failure had come to this, for he would never acknowledge his guilt.

She saw herself running in the woods with a beaten Sarah. She remembered Sarah's horrific screams in that dark basement followed by a blow to her face that dulled her senses. And then, the two single shots from the handgun of a heroic detective, as her tormentor fell dead before her.

Katherine's memories were more real than the flesh. She felt anger, but now also blessed relief.

Riggins sat broken and still. Then he noticed Katherine standing nearby, farther than ever from his reach. She was so frail. How could such a frail chick cause him such enormous pain? She should have been dead a long time ago.

How could I have let this happen to me? She looks so stupidly innocent, he thought. For a moment he felt cocky again. "It's not going to end like this," he vowed, shaking his head.

But Katherine was now protected better than the First Lady. She moved on, too tired to look him dead in the eyes or to deliver him one of those Hollywood slaps.

Was she really safe now? Was Sarah? After all, she had been under protection before, and look what had happened then.

Katherine struggled with these doubts. But she also knew that if she didn't let go, she would never find peace to live her life again.

Leaning his large frame into the car, Chuck reassured her, "He'll never bother you again."

"Thanks," Katherine replied.

Smiling, he turned to the driver and said, "Take her home. We have a lot to do around here." He tapped on the roof of the car and the car pulled away.

Katherine took a last look into the eyes of the man she would never forget. Tightening the blanket around her shoulders, she sat back and thought of Sarah. Sarah's suffering at the hands of their captors haunted her. However resilient, Sarah was still vulnerable and no match for these guys.

Why hadn't they just taken me? she asked.

She had failed as a mother and she knew it. This was her punishment for running away years ago, when she had the opportunity to stay and tell the truth. But could it really have been different? she wondered.

And Nick? Would he have left his father and given up the Walters millions just for her? She thought about the last time she was with him. His pleas for forgiveness then had begun to break through as if her mind was paper-thin. "I never learn," she accused herself. "Maybe I'm evil—and just plain accustomed to bad decisions."

The car made its way onto an unfamiliar highway.

"It won't take long," the agent assured her. "We'll be there in a couple of hours."

"I'm fine. I just want to see Sarah."

"We'll get you there. Don't worry," he promised.

"Worried? Ha, ha!" she said, and then murmured, "You don't have a clue." She looked out at the homes in the distance. *What I wouldn't give to trade places with any of them!* she told herself. She took a deep breath, convinced that none of the agents understood what she was feeling, and held on to her blanket.

Her world had changed forever again.

CHAPTER 36

▼

A tired Frank inhaled the early morning air, trying to revive himself as he waited in front of the hospital. He knew that he had a strong, masculine smell about him, but he didn't care. He wasn't sure how she would react upon seeing him so soon after the recent events. He had no choice about the matter. There was just a little more to go, and he prayed that Katherine could handle it. Pacing like a father-to-be, he watched a couple whisking their sick child away—it reminded him of the time that he took his daughter to the hospital. The worried look on the mother's face was familiar. She wiped the child's forehead affectionately and the man held him close.

Frank's eyes followed them until they disappeared. They were a family, unique yet like so many others. He always had trouble relating to this, chiefly because his job was his life. He never had much to talk about with his daughter. Working to protect Katherine, whatever that meant now, gave him a great deal to think about. He hadn't planned any of this.

"They're here," a refreshed police officer said to him. With his hands in his pockets, Frank watched two cars pull up to the curb. They were identical, unmarked black Suburbans. An agent in the front car was the first to get out. He approached Frank cautiously. By this time, another agent had exited the vehicle and walked toward the car following behind.

Frank extended his hand. "Hi, I'm Frank, with the Bureau. I've spoken to—"

"That would be me," the agent said. "Pleased to meet you. It's been rough, but I think she's going to be okay. I heard you had some trouble last night. Does it ever end?"

"I think it has, finally." Frank's eyes were glued to the door that was about to be opened.

Inside, Katherine placed her blanket on the seat and peered through the window, where Frank filled her view. She stepped out, flanked by the two men.

"I never thought I'd see you again," Katherine said.

Frank found it difficult to reply. "I told you it would all work out."

"I didn't believe you," she said, embracing him and soaking his shirt with her tears. Frank put his machismo aside and held her tightly.

Nodding his head, the agent backed off to give them their space, and then said, "There's someone inside who needs to see you."

"How is she?" asked Katherine.

"She's fine, Katherine," Frank replied.

"I can't believe this is over."

"It is," Frank replied. "Let's go." He guided her through the automatic doors. Wading through the curious onlookers, agents and all, Frank squeezed her shoulder, trying to imagine what it must have been like for her.

The humming of the elevator soothed their souls. Neither of them said much, but Katherine clearly took comfort in his presence, and he confessed to himself the deep respect he had for her.

"She's down there," Frank said. "You need some time together. I'll be here; I'm not going anywhere. So, go ahead, it'll be okay."

"Thanks," she whispered, letting go of his hand. Fighting to control his feelings, Frank watched her go. A miracle was about to happen. His promises, which had seemed just wishful thinking earlier, were about to become a reality.

The guard stepped aside as Katherine approached nervously. She took a deep breath and walked at a good clip towards Sarah's room. As she set eyes on her Sarah a flood of emotions overtook her. Sarah was asleep, and looking more peaceful than an angel. Katherine, cheeks salted with tears, stood over her. Sarah looked much older, she thought, as she reached out to touch her pale skin. "Sarah, dear, I'm here—it's me," she said, stroking her forehead just before kissing her cheek. "Sarah, I'm really here."

At first startled, Sarah was quickly soothed by her mother's familiar scent. This was just another dream. She fell into Katherine's frantic embrace, as Katherine cried out in joy. "Mom," Sarah answered. "I love you." She refused to release her from her tight grip.

"Oh, Sarah," Katherine choked, "it's going to be okay. I'm so sorry, Sarah." She could not stop herself from weeping.

"Mom, I never thought I'd see you again."

Running her fingers through Sarah's hair as she sat up, Katherine assured her in a broken voice, "It's over." They held each other, eyes closed, for a long time in the quiet murmurs of their injured hearts. Katherine checked her senses to make sure she hadn't just woken from a nightmare. Tears dripped as she rocked Sarah like a newborn baby. Sarah was now miles removed from her horrible reality of the last couple of days. She focused all her attention on Katherine. In time, the gaping hole in her heart, created when she lost the hope of ever seeing her mother alive again, would heal itself.

Meanwhile, Frank was receiving an update. Barry and Tommy had been taken to a nearby hospital and Barry was being prepped for surgery. Riggins was mentally out of control. He saw things that weren't there and shouted out words that made no sense. He has been placed under heavy security at the state jail and, from what Frank could decipher, was under a suicide watch.

But the Big Guy's involvement troubled Frank, who was informed that his former colleague had been separated from Jeff and was undergoing heavy interrogation. Everyone hoped he would give them enough information to put Riggins away forever. "He was basically a good man," Frank tried to convince himself, but there were also Doc and Nick. He never imagined the Big Guy would some day walk along the dirty fence. He scratched his head.

Murder had been committed.

Frank was determined to devote all the time he needed to connect the pieces. He headed towards Sarah's room. His body was aching for rest, but that could wait.

Outside the room, he leaned against the wall and stared at the solid door, imagining the sheer happiness on the other side. He, too, wanted to take in the scent of her hair. And he needed to protect Katherine.

He stood there for long moments. Neither he nor the guard said anything.

CHAPTER 37

▼

One month later...

Katherine had completely devoted herself to Sarah, but things were not moving along as she hoped. Sarah had become a recluse. The more her mother tried to get her to talk about what had happened the more withdrawn she became. Not knowing what else to do, Katherine decided to enlist some professional help—against Sarah's will. So, she and Sarah traveled across Calabogue Sound every other day to meet with Sarah's counselor. After a long evaluation, Katherine was informed that Sarah was suffering from post-traumatic stress syndrome and, in time, she would work through it. Katherine blamed herself, and she devoted every waking moment to Sarah.

It was hard, but Frank, though on another assignment, kept in touch. He had assured her that he would be there when it was time for her to testify, and he enjoyed sending her post cards. He didn't scribble down many words on them, but the pictures spoke for themselves. Katherine just enjoyed hearing from him. She wrote several letters to him but decided it would be best to keep them in her possession for now.

After their most recent session, the therapist recommended that Katherine consider moving. She was told this might help Sarah let go of the horrific nightmares that she continued to have, nightmares that always ended with a man breaking into the house and killing them both.

These thoughts were heavy on Katherine's mind as she listened to the squeaks coming from the old porch bench. Sarah was into her daily ritual on the back porch, rocking her life away while looking out upon the royal greens and pines as she listened to music. There was little to smile about these days, but Katherine forced herself into accepting this ambiance for now, and just looked on. It was true—she had once fallen in love with Daufuskie, where the ocean wind, wild birds, and pine needles were all joined in a natural harmony.

She placed her cup of coffee on the table, and as she watched Sarah, she listened to the pine needles tapping on the roof in the soft winds. She knew she must come to a decision about this place, and was ready to do anything to save Sarah.

There was a tapping sound at the door.

It was Jila, thank God. "Jenny, how's she doin'? I bin worried."

"Hi! Come on in, Sarah's doing better. We talked a little more this morning. She's trying. I just wish she would tell me what's going through her mind."

"Jus' needs time, I guess. It's bin rough on ya both—I know. Y'all celebrities by now. Pretty soon, I be needin' an appointment jus' to get to see ya." Jila was smiling.

"Believe me, I'm not proud of that."

"I didn't mean to—" Jila said, embarrassed.

"At least it's getting quieter and that's good, believe me. I know once the trial is over she'll be able to relax a little more."

"Is the trial set?"

"Not yet, we're expecting it to take place in a month or two. I'll be ready whenever. She's on the back porch. She'll be glad to see you."

"Well, I'll do ma best," Jila said. With Jila's every visit, Katherine hoped for a change in Sarah's mood. Jila was the only person, besides herself, that Sarah could confide in.

The back screen door closed behind Jila, and Katherine watched silently as she sat down in front of Sarah. She could tell by the smile on Sarah's face that Jila was still welcome.

She picked up her cup and took a seat on the sofa.

*　　　*　　　*　　　*

Katharine darted into the kitchen when the scent of the stew was thick enough. She threw a glance at the porch, where Jila and Sarah were prattling on. A quick taste told her the stew needed more pepper. As she was reaching for the pepper shaker, someone knocked at the door. *Who could that be?* she wondered. She dropped her towel on the kitchen table and went to the door.

Behind the screen, like a lone vagabond, stood Nick, carrying a basket of goodies. He and Katherine had spoken several times since their rescue, and to see him in the flesh was a pleasant surprise. She took a second sneak look at the porch and went to greet him, rather apprehensively.

"Hi," he said, smiling nervously.

"Hi."

"I tried to call, but the line was busy."

"So you decided to cross the Atlantic," she humored him.

"Yeah, and take a chance," he added. "Keith thought it would be a good idea. He arranged for me to get a ride over. I hope you won't be upset with him. These are for you and Sarah."

"Thanks," she said, and then looked over her shoulder. "I hope you won't be upset if we went someplace else to talk."

"Not at all," Nick replied. He was just glad she didn't slam the door in his face.

"Give me a second."

"I'll wait right here. If you prefer that I go someplace else, I will."

"No, that won't be necessary. I have something on the stove. It will only take a minute." Anxious, Katherine set the basket on the table, took care of the stew, and was ready to go. Jila and Sarah were still engrossed in their talk—which was a good sign. Katherine smiled.

Closing the front door behind her, she said, "I'll drive," and placed the key in the golf cart.

"That's fine. You seem a little nervous, though. If my being here bothers you...I just wanted to make sure the two of you are okay. I know with the trial and all it can't be easy."

"I'm fine. The sooner this is over the better. The one good thing is that Sarah will not have to testify. I made them promise me that. They have all the information they needed from her."

"That's good; how's she doing?"

"Better, I guess. It's going to take some time, but I see a little improvement each day. She's strong."

"She gets it from her mom?" he said, hoping to avoid sounding as if he was flattering her. Katherine chose not to respond. "I found it difficult coming here. I thought about it over and over, but it was the right thing to do."

"Why today, Nick?"

"I just felt you both may need me, and with the trial approaching. I hope I'm not being presumptuous?"

"You're not. It's just the timing," Katherine said.

"I'm sorry this isn't a good time, then."

"No, its okay—really."

"Hey, I remember the first time I stayed on this island. I was in my golf cart and saw Sarah and Jila playing in the waves—just two ordinary girls I didn't even know. Seems such a long time ago."

"It is," Katherine replied and turned off the cart. "This is one of my favorite places on the island. It's the best view of the two lighthouses. Sometimes I sit here and try to imagine what the lighthouses are saying to each other, as I look across the ocean. It's so peaceful." She gazed at the hypnotic motion of the waves.

"I like that thought, Katherine. You know I always liked the way you think. It's been a long time since we talked like this."

"I know," she replied, in a distant voice.

"Katherine, I know I've said this a thousand time, but I have to say it again. I'm truly sorry for all the trouble I've caused you. I never meant for it to be this way. I'm paying for my faults, and I don't have anyone to blame but myself. I wish I could—"

"Nick, I know what you're going to say. You can't take it all back. All of this has happened for a reason. I don't know why, but it has. Our lives have changed and none of us will ever be the same again— never. I've stopped searching for definite answers. I just know there's a future ahead for us to plan for. You need to look to the future, too. The only thing that matters to me now is that Sarah is okay, that's all."

"What can I do to help her? Anything—you name it."

"I'm not sure, Nick. There may come a time when the two of you will have the opportunity to sit down and talk. I don't know—maybe that's just wishful thinking. She's in therapy and we are talking about all kinds of things, even moving."

"Is that what you want to do?"

"It doesn't matter what I want. I want whatever is best for Sarah; I owe it to her."

"You, too, have to stop punishing yourself. None of us could have predicted this. It still seems unreal to me. If I could just help in some way."

"I'll talk to the therapist and let you know, okay?"

"That's all I'm asking. I just want a chance to help. I may never be a father to her, in her eyes, but that's okay. I mean, not really okay, but I accept it. I understand why. I can deal with it for now. What about you? Where are you with all of this?"

Taking a deep breath she replied, "I'm not sure, Nick. The only thing I can think about right now is what's best for Sarah."

"I'm with you, and I'll be here whenever you need me, I promise. I need the break from the big city anyway."

"Thanks, that's good to know. I can't make any promises, though."

"I'm not asking for anything, as long as you know you can call on me anytime."

Sighing, she replied, "I know."

"I'd better be getting back. I rented a small house on Hilton Head. Here's my new phone number. I hope you don't mind."

"I don't mind, but try not to surprise us again. With everything that's gone on, it's better to plan things from here on. I hope you understand."

"Katherine, I do, and I appreciate your honesty. I'll do that, I promise—no more surprises. Just having this time with you today is more than I dared dream. It's a start. Don't worry, no more surprises, I promise."

They returned to the house. Katherine said her goodbye and watched Nick drive off, her back against the door, thinking about what they hadn't said. She fought to redirect her thoughts, which were so easily thrown off course. It was quiet all around, except for the muffled sound of music from Sarah's room. The volume level told her that Jila had left. Sarah wanted to be alone again, and Katherine could see only darkness underneath her closed bedroom door. Katherine placed her ear against the door and hand on the doorknob to listen. It took every bit of strength she had to refrain from intruding on Sarah. Any interference now might be ill-timed. She had misgivings about the reception she might receive if she decided to exercise her parental authority and walk in unbidden.

Sitting in her bed, Sarah stared at the shadow cutting the light beneath her door and pulled the sheet closer to her. She knew who it was outside, but horrible memories returned—as if it was about to happen again.

CHAPTER 38

▼

As the weeks passed, Katherine regained some of her hope. The old Sarah was revealing herself sporadically. One day, Jila had prepared Sarah's favorite, Jerk Chicken, before they both eagerly strode their way toward the beach, deep in their usual conversation. Jila was having a great time swimming in the water and then lying on the beach, feeling the warm sand between her toes. It seemed like years since the two had felt so relaxed, although Jila always tried her best to cheer Sarah. The sun, not yet ready to call itself high noon, nevertheless demanded respect, so they hurriedly applied suntan lotion to their dry skin. Jila was up to her usual. Having brought along several of Sarah's favorite tunes, she decided that they were going to dance on the beach, if it killed them.

Surprisingly, Sarah was the first to rise and dance her way to the water, as if she needed to be baptized. And soon enough, the sounds of male whistles flowed like honey. Several guys in their sails stopped to flag their T-shirts at the bathing beauties. Jila was incorrigible. She strutted her stuff without missing a beat. And Sarah, for once, was giddy. She laughed as if there was no tomorrow. Inside, she just wanted to make everything seem like old times. The uncertainty of whether or not she and her mother would be staying on the island had dominated her thoughts for too long. She had to live for the present for a change.

After a swim, Jila shook the water from her hair, satisfied that Sarah was enjoying herself.

The hours passed, their skin glistened in the hot sun, and the wind blew in their ears. It was all quiet again. Only the sound of the waves and an occasional seagull greeted them. Then Sarah, who had seemed so content only a moment ago, made a three-sixty. It was hard to miss.

"Sarah," Jila solemnly addressed her, brushing the sand off her arms. "We need to talk. I know ya bin through a lot and ya gettin' better an' all, but somethin' still ain't right. Bin too long already. I'm ya friend—please tell me what's eatin' ya."

Unsettled, Sarah remained looking at the sky. "Nothing," she began. Somehow she hoped Jila would move on to another topic.

"Sarah, I know ya better than that. Ya can be honest with me," Jila persevered.

"It's not you, it's me," Sarah said.

Jila's lack of an immediate response surprised her. But Jila was more surprised to see the tears trickling beneath Sarah's sunglasses.

"What's the matter?" she asked.

Sarah didn't answer.

"I stay 'wake at night wonderin' if I…if I done somethin' wrong, blamin' maself for not bein' with ya that day. It's bin hard, Sarah. Ever' time I see Mike I think 'bout ya. I don' even enjoy bein' 'round 'im no more."

"Mike? What does he have to do with this?" Sarah asked.

"A lot. I blame 'im," Jila choked on her words, "knowin' it was me who lied to ya and said I had to work that evenin'. I jus' can't go on pretendin' everythin's fine. I know it ain't." She sniffled and wiped away a tear. She deserved to be locked away, she thought—no visitors, and a diet of just bread and water.

"Jila, it's not your fault," Sarah said, shedding her own tears as she reached out for her. "There was nothing you could do. I decided to go over to the island. It's not Mike's fault either, don't blame him. You can't blame yourself for something."

"I do," Jila lamented.

"Well, don't! I knew you were going to be with Mike that evening, it was obvious. But that didn't bother me. You deserve to be happy. He's a nice guy and I know he really cares for you." Sarah held a half-shell in her hand and thought about all the things Jila had taught her. The fading lines all over the shell seemed to talk to her. She brushed away the sand. "Jila, it's driving me crazy keeping this inside."

Jila waited intently, the hot sand needling at her feet. "What have I done?" she asked, dreading the undoing of their friendship.

Chin on her chest, Sarah languidly said, "Jila, when it happened, I saw Nick running my way and was sure he was after me, just like before."

"Sarah!" Jila said, astonished.

"And, when they grabbed me, I kept waiting to see him. I knew he was there, but he never came. He never came," she sobbed.

"I'm sorry I didn't—"

"It's just that when I found out later that he was trying to save me, I felt so guilty. It wasn't supposed to be this way. I hate him!" Sarah shouted.

Jila wrapped her arms around her. "Ya gotta tell Jenny. Talk to her, tell her what ya bin tellin' me. She loves ya, she'll understand, I know she will."

"I've tried, Jila, and I'm still trying, but I know she wants something from me, something I can't give her."

"All she wants is to know ya okay."

"She wants me to talk to him. I heard her on the phone. She thinks that'll make everything okay. But I can't do that, I can't. I hate him."

"Ya listen to me and talk to her," Jila ordered.

"I'll try, but you have to promise me one thing," Sarah said, wiping her face.

"What's that?"

"You have to promise me you'll talk to Mike again. Don't blame yourself or him."

Pausing, Jila looked out upon the big blue, deep in thought. "I'll try," she said in a distant voice.

"No, Jila, you have to promise me."

"Okay, I will," Jila agreed.

Relieved, Sarah rubbed her face and took a deep breath. "Jila, you know that place where we go and everything is so peaceful? Let's go there. Here," she said, reaching out, "hold my hand." Sarah displayed the shell.

Jila placed her hand over Sarah's, closed her eyes, and chanted in a soft voice. Their minds harmonized with visions of the beautiful blue sky above—smiles rich as silk. People began gathering around them and the soft drums of time came to life in celebration. As Jila and Sarah danced in sacred water, a man in a wrinkled white shirt and gray pants sprinkled more water above their heads. They were free, and they danced without a care.

Crowds hovered around like honeybees returning nectar to their frayed souls. Singing and shouting freely, water against her face, Jila shed her poisons—cleansed, pure to the world, and free. Sarah felt as if there was no tomorrow. She mimicked Jila's movements and celebrated in her turn. The air was light, the touch was soft, the sky so bright. Floating, they looked down upon the world. It was beautiful—velvet pastures, rich blooms, and people all so happy.

Finally they awakened; their fears had faded like yesterday's news. Their calm was so complete nothing could spoil it. Only earnest smiles remained on their cheeks, along with the rich warmth that the man's outstretched arms had generated for them. This was the world they wanted to remember forever, one lifted by a power mightier than all.

"Jila," Sarah called out, exhausted; but Jila's face was filled with tears of joy. "I felt it Jila, I really did."

CHAPTER 39

▼

"Katherine, how you doing? We have a date," Nick talked excitedly into the receiver and sipped on his cool coffee. "Hello, are you there?"

"I am," Katherine said, taking her seat.

"You don't seem sure. You okay?"

"Fine."

"How's Sarah doing?" he asked, and took a quick sip.

"She's much better now—getting back to her old self. But she's so young, Nick!"

"You're both survivors."

"Thanks for saying that," she said, looking at her father's picture on the mantle.

"You sound kinda down?"

"Today's my father's birthday and I really miss him."

"Maybe you should go to Alberville. You said you wanted to visit his grave. Think about it."

"Maybe I'll do that."

Silence.

"Katherine, are you there?"

"Yeah, yeah—I'm here. I'll see you tonight, Nick?"

"At the boat."

"Sure—bye." She hung up the phone.

*   *   *   *

Two agents outside were about to get into their car, one flipping the keys to the other and joking. Frank looked on from his cluttered office. He was thinking of the Big Guy, hoping some good would come of it all. He pinched the bridge of his nose, closed his eyes—unsure of what to do next. He decided to call Katherine.

"Hello, it's me—Frank. Katherine?"

"Hi. Who did you think it was?"

"I thought it was Sarah. You sound so much alike on the phone."

"I'm glad you called, Frank. I was thinking about you."

"Really?"

"Yeah, it's the trial. I can't stop thinking about it. I know you said it'll be okay, but, I—"

"It will be." He tried to sound reassuring as he filled his cup with coffee.

"Frank, please be honest. Will I have to see him again?"

"He'll be there, but you have nothing to worry about. He won't be able to see you. We won't put you through more than you can handle."

"I'd rather swim in the ocean and forget about it all."

"It'll be okay."

"I think I *will* go to the ocean side today."

"Sounds good, but I sure hate to have to come and rescue you, again."

"I don't know, let me think. Big ocean, two people—sounds like a movie in the making to me." She let out a faint laugh.

"You never know," he replied. "I'll be there. Everything's fine, Katherine."

"Thanks, Frank. Guess I just need to hear it—again and again."

Just then, Sarah stumbled into the room. She was winded and her arms were filled with clothes. "Sorry, I didn't know you were on the phone," she said, gathering her breath and placing the clothes on the table.

"It's Frank," she whispered.

"Tell him I said hello."

Katherine did and said, "Frank, I better go. Talk to you soon." She hung up and looked admiringly at Sarah's spurt of energy.

"Sorry, I wanted to get some washing done before Jila came over. She's gonna give me some tips on making her favorite curry dish. I had a hard time finding some of the ingredients. The man in the store thought I was crazy when I asked him for kernel powder." she said with a laugh. "It wasn't until I told him the other things I needed that he realized I meant curry powder. I felt so stupid, Mom."

"I've done that before," Katherine said, carefully placing dishes in the dishwasher.

"So-o-o," Sarah said expectantly, standing by the table.

"So…"

"So, it's him—you're gonna see him again tonight?"

Dreading the imminent conversation, Katherine exhaled slowly and gave a makeshift answer. "We're just talking, nothing more. I can see the look on your face every time I mention his name. I just didn't want to upset you."

"No, it's not that. There's a lot you aren't telling me. I'm an adult, you know. I can handle it."

"Sarah, I'm not hiding anything from you. I've been very honest with you. You know that."

"Then why didn't you tell me you were thinking about leaving the island? I had to hear it from Tom. He thought I knew, Mom. What's going on?"

"I wasn't hiding anything from you. You and I discussed the possibility. You know that. The therapist suggested it might be better to move someplace new—get a fresh start. I thought it would make you feel better."

"If you really thought that you would have told me, not try to hide something like that from me."

"I'm sorry, Sarah," she said walking over to her. It was frustrating. "I'm just trying to do what's best. I would never do anything to hurt you."

"I know, Mom. That other day when you talked about going back to Alberville to visit Grandpa, I thought that was a good idea. I wanted you to go."

"Don't you want to come with me?"

"I think you need to do this alone. I know *he* offered to go with you, but I'm not going to say anything about that. Not right now."

"Sarah, why don't you talk to him? Tell him how you feel, if nothing else. I think it would help everyone, especially you."

"I really don't have anything to say to Nick," Sarah said firmly, grabbing her clothes and rushing out of the room.

"Sarah," Katherine called out, but Sarah had already closed the laundry room door behind her, determined to ignore her mother.

Sarah was now seriously distressed again. She wrestled with what she had just done, because she never did like to see her mother's hurt look. She poured the blue liquid over her dirty laundry and thought of the ocean.

In the other room, Katherine wiped off the table thoroughly, as if to purge her life of all its sins and faults—once and for all. She naturally empathized Sarah, but she also felt for Nick. They were so much alike it scared her. But now she was torn between Sarah and Nick—the man she used to love so passionately.

CHAPTER 40

▼

Jila contacted Mike, as she promised, and they made a date. But Mike felt queasy about getting together alone, so he suggested his friend Raymond join them along with Sarah.

Jila, feeling a little awkward herself, agreed. She pranced around playing with her hair, and having a terrible time deciding what to wear. At one point, the pile of clothes on her bed equaled whatever remained in her closet. But her favorite music was playing in the background. That always helped.

Jila knew nothing about Raymond, except what Mike had told her, that he was handsome and a "really" nice guy. Who knows, maybe he and Sarah could hit it off. Finishing her eye shadow, she stood looking at the clothes spread out on her bed and at the clock. It was almost six. The guys were coming to pick them both up at Sarah's in less than an hour.

"I've got to get maself together," she said, holding her orange two-piece pants outfit in her hand. She was excited and hoping against hope that she had picked the right outfit.

*　　　*　　　*　　　*

Sarah waited nervously at the window for Jila. She had just got off the phone talking to Katherine, who was busy at the mansion. Katherine had wished her a good time and apologized for not being there when her date arrived. But it was ladies' night at the mansion and she and Keith were at their best entertaining the guests.

Afraid to sit and wrinkle her white sleeveless dress before it was admired, Sarah kept pacing, fearing she might do something stupid and ruin the evening for Jila. Her image of Raymond had gone from dark and handsome to fat and short, then to plain and tall. But she finally shook her head and chastised herself about her silliness. Seeing Jila driving up put a smile on her face and she stepped out on the porch. Jila's orange outfit glowed against the green backdrop.

"Jila, you look nice."

"Wow, I like that dress. You bin hidin' it, huh," Jila said with a grin.

"No. I bought it when we went shopping together a long time ago."

"I don' remember, but it sho' is nice."

"Thanks," Sarah replied.

"The guys should be here any minute," Jila said.

"Yeah, let's talk. Tell me about this place we're going—"

"They takin' us to Marshside Mama's, it's on the far side of the island. All I heard is the food is real good. Never bin there maself, but I hear it's the best place to go if ya want to try the local flavor and experience the true culture of the island."

"You've never been there?" Sarah asked, surprised.

"Bin pass it. It's like eatin' Mama's food. Trust me, ya have a good time. Now, let's get ready. I need a mirror, they'll be here any minute—"

"Jila, did Mike tell you anything else about him?"

"Who?" Jila responded, while prancing in front of the mirror. "Oh, don' look at me like that. Raymond," she emphasized, "is a knockout!"

Sarah's eyes widened. "Really? You're pulling my leg. I can tell by that smirk on your face."

"Sarah, ya know me too good. But, if he hangs out with Mike, I'm sho' he is. Of course, that means he ranks second to Mike."

"Stop kidding—is he, really?" Sarah asked again. Jila was about to answer, but Sarah interrupted her. "Wait, I hear a golf cart. I bet it's them."

"It is!" Jila said excitedly, almost knocking Sarah over trying to get a sneak preview. "Sarah! He's real cute, and he's wearin' white jus' like ya. If I didn't know better, I'd say they is twins. How's ma hair? Quick, go open the door." Jila adjusted her clothes.

Sarah did just that. Jila waited in the background, chuckling and anxious.

"Hi, Sarah," Mike said in the superb, controlled voice of a true gentleman. "It's good to see you. Been a while, hasn't it."

"Hi, Mike."

"You look real nice. This is my friend, Ray."

"Come on in. Nice to meet you, Ray," Sarah said, extending her hand.

"Same here." Ray flashed a perfect smile.

Before Mike could move Jila had edged closer. "Hi," Mike said, kissing her on the cheek. "Ray, this is Jila," he said proudly.

"Nice to meet you, Jila. Heard a lot about you."

"From whom?" Jila quipped.

"I told you, man—prepare yourself," Mike said, smiling.

"Ya tol' 'im what?" Jila asked.

"Oh nothing," Mike quickly responded.

"We'd better go," Ray said, displaying a gleamy smile. "Are you ready, Sarah?"

Sarah was mesmerized. "Yeah," she said, and grabbed her purse.

"Like your outfit, Jila," Mike said in a sexy voice as he held her hand and headed out the door. Witless, Jila winked at Sarah.

The four of them prattled the entire way. Jila, smile pasted to her face, winked again at Sarah as Ray assisted Sarah off the golf cart. Sarah tried to hide her big smile, but it was difficult.

"This looks like one of those down home joints," Ray remarked. "I know the food will be great."

Pausing, they all looked up at the hand-painted Marshside Mama sign.

Predictably, Jila said, "I like the music," and walked in. The decor was alive. It looked like Christmas. Strands of small light-bulbs dangled from the windows. Old concert posters hung on the walls. Jila watched, shaking to the music as the people in front of the Jukebox line-danced. There was a solid roof above them, but the spirit of the place was one of fresh-air celebration. Picnic tables held up their extended umbrellas and tabletops wore vintage plastic covers.

"This is like an indoor picnic," Ray concluded.

"The food smells good," Mike said, looking at Sarah for confirmation. But Sarah was on sensory overload, waiting to sit down.

"Come on in. Find a seat," the waiter said, holding a tray of food high above his head.

"Where do you want to sit, ladies?" Mike asked.

"Anywhere—don' matter to me," Jila said, mimicking the dancers.

"Sarah?" Mike asked.

"Anywhere's fine."

The place was full of happy people drinking and eating all kinds of food. Huge crab legs extended from buckets. The four of them eventually decided on a spot near the juke-box.

"Sarah, you all right?" Ray asked, noticing Sarah's distracted manner.

"Yeah," she laughed it off. "Just trying to get used to the place."

"I like it," Jila said, dancing in her chair.

"They got nothin' like this on Hilton Head, I'll tell you that," Ray said.

"We're in for a treat," agreed Mike.

"When was the last time you were in a place with folding chair?" Ray chimed in.

"Actually yesterday, at your Mama's house," Mike replied, amused.

"Funny, very funny," Ray said, embarrassed. Sarah burst out laughing, hoping that Ray wouldn't take it the wrong way.

"Hi, this your first time here?" the perceptive waiter inquired.

"Yeah—that goes for all of us," Mike said.

"That's great—welcome! I'm gonna be your waiter. The food is great. Can I start you out with a drink, while you check out the menu?"

"Sounds good," Jila said.

There was some commotion two tables over, and the waiter had to excuse himself. "I'll be back in a jiffy," he said.

"What menu?" Sarah asked in a low voice, scanning an empty table, where a lone salt shaker stood.

"It's over there leaning against the pole. I saw it when we sat down," Mike said.

"You mean that blackboard in the center of the room," Sarah remarked, surprised.

"Yeah, over there," Mike said.

"I still can't see it," Sarah protested.

"Me, neither," Ray said.

"Oh, don' worry, when the waiter comes back we'll have 'im turn it 'round," Jila said, not missing a musical beat. "I don' believe my ears—first they play country and now we're into seventies songs. This place is sho' full of surprises."

"I can't get over their jukebox—it plays real CDs," Mike remarked.

Sarah wasn't saying much. She and Ray listened to Jila and Mike enjoying themselves, talking about everything and everyone—from the small bar with a few bottles waiting to be poured, to the couple sitting in the corner cracking crablegs and kissing. The place was unique and the smell of food from the kitchen was out of this world. Sarah quickly noticed the screenless windows and the wide-open doors, wondering why the place didn't have air conditioning.

When the food finally arrived, all of them drooled. Sarah and Ray had ordered the flounder, Mike the steamed seafood platter, and Jila the ribs. The four of them continued their small talk while eating, until Sarah yelled out, "Oh, my God, its a pig!"

"Pig?" Ray replied. His back was against the door, and he refused to turn around. The shocked look on Sarah's face acted like a mirror. He knew she wasn't kidding.

"Oh shit!" Mike screamed, laughing hysterically. "It *is* a pig! A big-ass black pig. You gotta see this, Ray. Turn around!"

"Oh," was all Jila could say. Her mouth dropped.

Tears of laughter streaming down his face, Mike said, "And he's coming after you, Jila. You're the one eatin' ribs."

"I don' believe this," Jila remarked in a stunned tone of voice.

"Look, Ray, look!" Mike shouted.

"I can see it out of the corner of my eye," Ray said. "I don't need to see any more of it."

"I have to get a picture of this," Mike said. "No one will ever believe this ever happened."

Ray saw the waiter coming his way with a tray of food held high above his head. He wasn't at all sure what to do. The big black pig went right past him and moved quickly in the waiter's direction. The next thing they knew the pig was squealing as the waiter tried to push him away.

"Oh shit," Ray screamed, ready to piss in his pants. Mike, overcome with laughter, fell backwards in his chair.

"Get outta here," the waiter shouted at the pig, while holding his tray steady.

While Ray came unglued, Mike howled on the floor, holding his stomach tightly. "What's the matter, man?" he said to Ray. "it's only a pig!"

"Man, that shit ain't funny. I thought he was bitin' the waiter."

"Biting the waiter! When was the last time you heard of a pig bitin' anyone? Pigs don't bite—right Jila?"

"Oh, now she's the expert! Guess you two have been around pigs all your life!" Ray replied.

"Tell him, Jila. Do pigs bite?"

Jila forked the last tidbits from her plate and said, "I ain't sayin' a thin'. Thas' 'tween the two of ya."

"This place is wild. I knew we were gettin' local flavor, but this takes the cake," Mike said. "I love it!"

"I think it's time to go," Sarah said.

"I agree," Ray said. "Let's get the check."

Mike was enjoying the scene, though, wishing for another show. "This is better than *Animal Farm*—a pig walkin' about like a patron. I can't wait to tell my folks 'bout this place."

"I'm ready," Jila said with finality, looking askance at Mike. Sarah looked ashen even in the dim lights.

CHAPTER 41

▼

A few days later, Jila was feeling good as she adjusted her skirt. A rabid dog could not have been more excited. Her perfume overshadowed nature's best, and after a quick check of her watch, she approached Sarah's house.

Sarah was her casual self. "You're looking good," she greeted Jila. "Don't tell me; you're going out with Mike again."

"Oh, that was fun, wasn't it? I really didn't mind the entertainment. And, ya gotta admit, the food was great! Mike crazy, ain't he? Ya know, he tol' me he met the guy who owns that ugly pig while waitin' for the check. That pig is eleven years old and drinks beer. Can ya believe that? A pig drinkin' beer!"

"I'd rather not discuss it tonight. Come on in and have a seat if you have time."

"Ya know I do," she said. "I came by to check on ya. Did Jenny go out 'ready?"

"Yeah, she did."

"Ya kinda down 'gain, ain't you? Everythin' okay?" Jila asked, leaning against the sofa. Sarah looked as if she had something to say, but the words weren't coming out. "What's botherin' ya? I don' have to go, ya know. Want me to help ya cook the curry?"

"No, please, I'm not up for cooking. I'll be fine, just feeling sorry for myself," Sarah said. She sat down and directed her eyes at a picture of Katherine taken shortly after their arrival on the island. She was standing next to Keith. "Really, I'm fine," she repeated.

"It's Nick, isn't it? What ya fixin' on doin', Sarah?"

Sarah's face was painted in agony; her beautiful browns glistened in the soft light. She couldn't hide her tears.

"Jila, I can't. I've tried, but I can't," she said, shaking her head.

"I don' think ya bein' asked to love 'im, or even like 'im. Jenny jus' askin' ya to talk to 'im, thas' all. I ain't all that sho' he meanin' to say a whole lot to ya. 'Course I ain't in ya shoes, either, but if I were, I reckon I'd at least talk to 'im. Thinkin' of my father the other day. I'd do anythin' to be talkin' to 'im 'gain…"

"A father would never try to kill his daughter. Why should I talk to him?"

"I know this ain't the same—at all. All I'm sayin' is: he ya father. Do ya think it's easy for Jenny? She still tryin' to understand all o' this, especially knowin' how ya feel. All, I can say is: Think 'bout it. Sho' ya don' want me 'round today?" Jila checked the clock.

"No, I want you to have a good time, and tell Mike I said hello. Where are the two of you going?"

"Out to dinner and then for a nice long ride on his fancy boat."

"Sounds nice. Get out of here. I'll be fine. Stop by tomorrow; we can work on the curry then." Sarah walked over to the door.

"Okay, but ya think 'bout what I said. See ya tomorrow." Jila kissed her friend and strutted off the porch.

Sarah felt like a captive, with no escape in sight. She folded herself on the sofa, pulling at her roots. "Why me?" she cried. The room was quiet, but the noise in her head was deafening. She tried to untangle her thoughts, but images of Nick's face, past and present, came to her one after another and pulled at her heavy eyelids. "I don't need this," she protested. Her mind was too foggy, fighting to find her place in the world. Sarah longed only for her bed. She plopped down on it and buried her face between the scented sheets.

*   *   *   *

It was quiet—just before two in the morning. Katherine lay in bed, sheet pulled to her waist. Sarah stood in the doorway listening to the short pants of air from Katherine's sleeping frame. Half-doubled over, one hand clutching the doorframe that supported her, she took a deep breath, but she found it hard to move in her pain. Slowly, she made her way to the bed, her hand pressed tight to her stomach. "Mom," she groaned and grimaced.

Katherine's eyes opened wide.

"Sarah, what's the matter?" she asked, vaulting from the bed.

Sarah face was enveloped in thick sweat, gasping. "I'm not sure…it hit me…all at once," she said. "Cramps. I've never felt anything…like this before."

"I'm calling the doctor. You don't look good at all." Katherine shuffled through some papers and dialed the number.

"Doctor'll be here in a few minutes. I'll get a towel. Do you feel like throwing up?" Katherine asked.

"No," she replied, "Not any more. What time is it, Mom?"

"After two."

They sat in silence for a few minutes until the doctor, black bag at his side, arrived. "She's in the bedroom—follow me," Katherine said.

The doctor took his time to examine Sarah properly. Rubbing her hands nervously together, Katherine kept hitting him with a barrage of questions. "Is she going to be okay? I've never seen her like this before. Do we need to take her to the hospital?"

The doctor finally withdrew his stethoscope and focused his eyes on Sarah. "No. Must be something she ate. She said she feels better, I think you just need to watch her. I'll give her something for her stomach; she should be fine in the morning" He reached into his bag.

"I'll keep a close eye on her. Sorry to get you out of bed, Doc."

"Don't worry about that. Helen's used to it. If you need me again, call," he insisted. "I'd better be going. I'll check on her again in the morning."

Katherine thanked him and waved goodbye. Within seconds she resumed her motherly vigil. "Sarah, are you sure you're feeling better?" Sarah gave her a lame nod, and Katherine lay next to her. Her eyes were fixed on Sarah and she refused to turn off the lamp. She pushed Sarah's hair gently out of her face and monitored her slightest move. It had been a while since she was mother-doctor. It reminded her of the time Sarah swallowed a penny. Katherine stayed up all night worried to death about her.

CHAPTER 42

▼

Wakened by the morning light, Katherine was the first to rise, while Sarah slept on peacefully. She inched her way out of bed, searched for her slippers, and headed for the bathroom.

Birds hummed along as she brushed her teeth and ached for her cup of coffee. Ready to start her day, she returned for another look at Sarah and then made off for the kitchen. She was searching for a spoon and preparing her coffee when a lone figure in the yard distracted her. "That's strange," she said as she peered outside.

But it was only Keith and he seemed troubled. Katherine knew how he hated getting up early, and immediately began to worry. He was acting strangely, moving slowly up to the porch. She went out to greet him but when she looked at him, he avoided her eyes. He didn't have to say anything—something was terribly wrong. She stepped back, almost instinctively. "Keith, why are you here so early?" she asked.

Clearing his throat, his face on alert, he replied, "Katherine, there's been an accident."

"Accident? What happened?" When he hesitated, she shouted, "Keith, what happened?"

"It's Jila. She and Mike had a boating accident. They were both killed last night, around two this morning!"

"Oh, no! That can't be true," Katherine said, overwhelmed. "Please tell me it's not true."

"Katherine, I wish I could. I'm sorry."

"Oh, God! How am I going to tell Sarah?" Katherine was shaking. Keith pulled her into his arms and they both wept. "How did it happen?"

Wiping his eyes, he said, "I'm not really sure. I was told Mike had a little too much to drink and the boat overturned while he was racing someone. He and Jila were killed instantly. I know this is the last thing you and Sarah need to hear after all that you have been through, but I had to be the one to tell you." He began to sob.

Heartsick, Katherine looked down the hall at the closed door. Her hands cupped her face as she shook her head. There were no words to describe what had happened. "I'm here with you. You don't have to do this alone. Let me tell her with you," Keith offered.

"This will kill her. They were so close and she's never been through anything like this before."

"She's strong. It won't be easy, but we have to tell her."

"She hasn't been feeling well; she was sick last night. I had to call the doctor. Oh, I can't do this, I can't—"

"Sit down. Here, wipe your face." He handed her his handkerchief. "You have to gather yourself." But Katherine kept moving about. "What are you looking for? Sit down. I'll make the coffee. Where do you keep it?"

"Over there—bottom shelf," she said, thinking about the last time she saw Jila. It was a couple of days ago. They had spent most of the time talking about Sarah. Jila offered her advice; she made her feel better. And she had promised Katherine she would talk to Sarah about Nick. Katherine knew if anyone could break through Sarah's stubborn will, it was Jila. She remembered her confident smile when she left that day. Jila was the only one who could break through Sarah's depression after her kidnapping. And that first time the two girls had met—Sarah was more excited about life than she had ever been. She always felt that way after she and her new-found friend returned from the beach. Jila was the sister that Sarah never had.

"It'll be all right—we'll get through this together. Here, take a sip of water, the coffee is almost ready. This will help."

Katherine wiped her swollen, reddened eyes. "Thanks for being here," she told him and blew her nose. "This is going to be one of the hardest things I've ever had to do."

"I know. I promise I won't leave you. Drink this before we go in," he said, handing her some coffee.

Katherine blew lightly over the hot liquid before sipping it. Keith watched her as she drank. He had already convinced himself that he needed to be strong when they entered that room. Katherine suddenly put aside her cup, and he helped her to her feet. They headed for Sarah's room. The short hall seemed a mile long. Katherine's feet felt leaden and her heart heavy.

"It'll be fine," Keith tried to sooth her before placing his hand on the doorknob. When they opened the door, Sarah lay asleep on her side, sheet spread over her. Katherine looked hesitantly at Keith, but he gestured to her to move on. She felt a rush of heat and her legs were about to give way.

"We have to do this," Keith whispered grimly.

Gently, she called Sarah's name. Her voice was so low she could barely hear herself. "Sarah, Sarah, wake up," she said, shaking her. "Sarah."

Sarah, grunting and taking a deep breath, rolled onto her back and rubbed her eyes. "What time is it?" she asked.

"It's early—about seven," Katherine said, her face bearing the strain of what she was about to announce. Sarah noticed Keith hovering over her, which immediately told her something wasn't right. Her eyes returned to Katherine who, unable to conceal her tears, fought to maintain her composure.

"What's going on?" she demanded, eyes darting between Keith and Katherine. Keith forgot what he had told himself earlier and instead covered his mouth as tears flowed down.

"What's the matter, Mom?"

"Sarah, it's Jila, she's been in an accident." Relieved she had made it this far, she tried to take Sarah in her arms, but Sarah quickly broke away.

"Is she okay?"

"No, she's not. Jila…Jila and Mike were killed last night, a boating accident. I'm so very sorry."

"No!" Sarah screamed. "No! It can't be!"

"Sarah!" Katherine fought to hold on to her.

"Jila, no!" she called out, hysterical.

"Sarah, please! Stop her, Keith," she pleaded, but Sarah had scrambled out of bed and, gripping her head, kept screaming uncontrollably. She fell against the dresser and knocked everything to the floor. "Jila! Jila!" she shouted in a crazed voice and ran out of the room.

"Keith, please," Katherine begged.

"Jila, Jila! Jila!" Sarah screamed and fell to her knees, her hand griping the front door.

Keith and Katherine surrounded her. "Jila!" Sarah howled.

They all wept, hoping that God would show them it wasn't true.

CHAPTER 43

▼

The old white wooden Union Baptist Church—without air conditioning—was filled to capacity, as Sarah and Katherine entered with Jila's
family. Mama wouldn't have it any other way. The sweet smell of flowers reminded Sarah of Jila. Jila's white coffin was draped in a vivid bed
of red roses and surrounded by colorful vases of flowers. Shining
through the simple glass windows, the sun's rays darted down at the
large wooden cross hanging in the front and on Jila's simple coffin.
God had come to take Jila away, just as she would have wanted it,
Sarah thought. Revering the beauty but overwhelmed by grief, Sarah
was certain her best friend had made it to Gullah Heaven.

The minister, who had known Jila well, delivered a fitting eulogy.
This was followed by Gullah rituals and songs. But, it wasn't until the
choir sang Jila's favorite song and the coffin was being rolled out of the
church that the magnitude of the loss hit Sarah. The words *daylight
come and me wanna go home* confounded her. It was too much for her.
She cried out, begging for her dear friend to return. Katherine, herself
almost inconsolable, held on to Sarah. Mother and daughter were
united in grief.

Keith was right next to them as they made their way down the aisle.
Standing in the doorway, they all looked out at Jila's coffin, which sat
on the back of a horse-drawn wagon. The sun was brighter than they

could ever remember. The singing continued, as people walked behind the cortège; behind them were lines of golf carts filled with mourners. Everyone celebrated the precious life that had been taken away so early.

Finally they reached the cemetery, with its colorful headstones. Many of the names engraved on them were unrecognizable. Sarah closed her eyes, breathing deeply as Jila's coffin was taken off the wagon. A woman standing next to the wagon sang a heart-heavy spiritual.

"Please follow me," a tall black man in a white short-sleeve shirt said to Katherine and Sarah. Mama waited in front of them. Jila's coffin was ready to be lowered into the brown hole next to her father's. The minister said a final prayer.

Mama, a study in pain, was the first to place her white flower on Jila's coffin. Sarah clutched a seashell in her hand. It was the last one she and Jila had held when they visited Gullah Heaven.

As the crowd dispersed, Katherine stood behind Sarah, rubbing her arms. She knew Sarah needed to say her final farewell in her own way. "Go ahead," she told her.

Sarah knelt in the hot dirt, tears streaming down her face. Then she placed her hand, shell enclosed inside, on top of the coffin. "Jila, I'm gonna miss you so much. I can't believe this has happened. It hurts," she cried. "I hope you're happy in Gullah Heaven. I can still see the smile on your face and smell your scent all around me. I wish I had made you stay with me that night. I can only blame myself," she said with a heavy sigh. "I'll never forget you, Jila." She closed her eyes and squeezed their shell. As she did, she felt Jila's hand on hers. Listening, she heard the mounds of earth whispering to her. Unfamiliar voices told her Jila was at peace. She saw Jila join the celebration in Gullah Heaven and smile radiantly. Jila was placing her hand in the hands of the man standing in the middle of the crowd. Floating on her knees, she looked up at the sky. When Sarah opened her hand, the shell fell away and buried itself among the flowers.

"I'll never forget you, Jila," Sarah vowed and slowly backed away.

"Are you ready, honey?" Katherine asked, sobbing.

"Yeah," Sarah responded, refusing to look back. "*Daylight come and me wanna go home*, Jila," she whispered to herself.

CHAPTER 44

▼

Alone, Sarah walked along the beach carrying a pail. She searched for seashells. Her frequent visits to Gullah Heaven seemed to help her as she tried to cope with her loss. Jila was everywhere. Not an hour went by when Sarah didn't think of her on this sun-filled day.

The wet sand covered her feet and she played with the shells that rested on her skirt. Then she went for a walk, stopping for a while to watch the sails pass by. She wanted to sort out, for just a brief moment, what happened the night Jila died.

She sat down. Her legs withstood the burning sun as only hers and Jila's used to before the two girls traveled to Gullah Heaven.

Someone waved from afar. The person looked distressed.

Sarah squinted.

Mama was approaching. It was rare to see Mama on this side of the island, but it was clear she wanted to say something to Sarah. Out of breath, she approached Sarah and said, "Chile, I bin look'n fuh oonuh. You'own murrah tol' me oonuh gwine tuh de beach. Chile, duh oonuh okay?"

Sarah quickly understood her. "I'm doing better, Mama. Can't get Jila off of my mind, though. Everywhere I go, everything I do makes me think about her. How are you doing?"

"I miss 'e berry much. Dat farruh ub hab gwine haffuh tuh ansuh tuh I," she said.

They shared a smile.

It was curious. Mama was carrying a brown box that reminded Sarah of a piece of furniture. Something was on her mind. "Chile, Oonuh 'membuh dat box Jila alltime crack 'e teet?"

"Yeah, Mama, I remember. She told me she kept her thoughts in there."

"Dat's right, I nebbuh ax 'e 'bout de box. Dat chile bin writt'n all da time en lock t'ingss away in d'a box 'bout de time 'e farruh de't'. Attuh 'e met oonuh, 'e don' writ' ez much. 'E lub oonuh," Mama said, her voice quivering. Slowly she opened the box with her trembling hand. There were several envelopes inside, all opened. Sarah moved closer and placed her hand on Mama's, letting her know it was okay. "I bin gwine t'ru 'e tings and I notus 'e hab writt'n tuh oonuh. Uh thought 'e bin sump'n 'e wan oonuh tub hab," Mama said, placing the envelope in Sarah's hand.

"Thank you, Mama," Sarah said nervously. She held the envelope, wondering what Jila had written.

Mama smiled, a solid tear beading down her cheek, as she stood up. "I gwine leabe oonuh," she said, brushing off her flowered skirt. "Come by en see me. I mek' som' ub dat fey chickin oonuh luk, okay?"

"Thanks, Mama, I love you." They traded kisses and a deep hug, and then Mama was on her way. Sarah followed with her eyes her footprints in the sand, wishing they were Jila's. A swift wave washed up against her feet and surprised her. She stepped back, holding the white envelope tightly. Then, she placed it against her nose and inhaled. It smelled like oak. Walking over to their favorite spot, she sat down. With the soft ocean breeze in her face she read.

Dear Amy,

It's bin a long time since I sat down and wrote a letter. Ma last letter was writtin' years ago to maself. It remains locked up in ma secret box. I wrote it after ma Father died. I remember that day as if it was yesterday. As Gullah people, we fought fo' our freedom to keep this land in remembrance of all those who picked cotton and nurtured this earth for others to enjoy. That day, I was walkin' 'long on the dusty trail now known as Haig Road. It was a beautiful day. Earth was so hot I could feel it through my sandals. I remember seein' the chickens crossin' the road. They always made me smile. I think it was the way they walked.

Far 'way, I saw ma Mother and Brother walkin' towards me. Ma body ached all over, especially ma stomach. It started early that day, I could barely walk. I knew someone was tryin' to tell me somethin' that I was not prepared to hear. The worry lines on ma Mother's face doubled and tears covered her face. Ma Brother stood silent, his pain trapped, as ma Father would expect. I knew before ma Mother spoke that ma Father had gone to Gullah Heaven. I fell in ma Mother's arms as we comforted each other. I'll never forget the smell of her pain-sweat or the warmth of her tears droppin' on ma neck.

It took me years to feel what I felt that day. A loss that touched ma soul in a way I could never imagin'. Ma Father was the family's rock. He taught me how to share ma soul. The day he died, I swear, he took those lessons I learned from 'im with 'im. I searched fo' years to find where he had hid 'em, because I knew ma Father would never truly rob me of a gift so precious. Ya see, when I met ya, I found somethin'. At first I was not sure; the feelin's had bin foreign to me fo' such a long time and ma heart needed some time to adjust. Amy, ya friendship has given me somethin' I thought I'd lost forever. I needed that.

That night on ma porch when ya shared ya secret with me, I felt like I had lost ma Father all over 'gain. It was at that moment that I knew ya would not be 'round fo' long. I really didn't know what to say. Havin' the opportunity to say goodbye to someone I loved was new. As I held ya in ma arms that night, I prayed. It was not a selfish prayer to have ya with me forever. I prayed fo' ya safety.

So much has happen since then. Ma prayers have bin answered, because I feel ya are finally safe. I'm not sure where ya will go. I know in ma heart we will never be separated. If I could follow ya I would, but I can't imagin' livin' anywhere else. This island is the only home I've known. Ma Father and his family souls are buried beneath this earth. I can feel their power each time I rest my feet on the ground. And there are others like maself that continue to enjoy this sacred grass between our toes.

I share all of this with ya because I see ya are hurtin'. I know Nick will never be the perfect Father to ya, but at least he's 'live, and ya have a chance to do somethin' with that. I would give anythin' to have ma Father with me 'gain. All I'm asking is that ya don' give up on 'im. Try to understand, not only what ya are feelin' but also what Jenny is feelin'.

I guess what I'm tryin' to say is "thank ya." I'm glad ya safe and ready to move on. Ma pain was lifted when I heard ya were okay. One pain lifted only fo' 'nother to surface. The heaviness I feel as I think 'bout ya leavin' is difficult, but I know I have to let go, because I know this is best fo' ya.

I'll never forget the first day we met, like I will never forget that last day I saw ma Father. His dingy white shirt, gray ankle-length pants and gullible smile, lives with me. It protects me. I remember our last words. He said, "Goodbye, I'll see ya tonight." I replied, "I love ya. I'll see ya later." I never knew how much strength those last words would give me. They were the last words he heard from a family member that day.

I share this with ya because I have grown to love ya. Ya the little sister I never had; the friend I've always wanted. I guess what I'm really tryin' to say is "goodbye." I know I could never say this to ya face without fallin' 'part. But, I hope ya understand. Thanks for blessin' ma life. I love ya, Amy.

Ya sister forever,

Jila

Sarah looked up to the sky, clasping the letter next to her breast as the tears flowed down her cheek. Trapped between every line was a meaning that only she and Jila understood. They had shared so many precious moments, yet this was the greatest. She fought to hold herself together. Jila had reached beyond her grave to give her something to cherish.

Sarah read the letter again, and felt Jila's warmth reaching down from Gullah Heaven. It was the same feeling that she and Jila had experienced each time they visited that holy place. The primary colors of the big blue had never been brighter. The warmth of the sun had never carried so much energy. Sarah picked up a half-buried shell in the sand. It was perfect, not a crack or line out of place. She held it close to her, and closed her eyes and began a quiet chant to prepare to visit a place she had come to love.

CHAPTER 45

▼

Back at the mansion, Katherine and Keith were busy solving the problems of the world, before taking an afternoon break and waiting for the next flow of hungry and alcohol-thirsty patrons to gather. Business had really picked up with all the new residents on the island.

But Keith was miffed again. Katherine had just informed him that the owners of the club were thinking of having a big golf outing. He was too quick tempered to give her a chance to talk about staffing.

"I'm gonna call in sick that week. If they think we can do all of that, they're full of it. You know, Katherine, I really like my job, but sometimes I think those idiots are sunstruck," he went on, puffing defiantly on his cigarette.

"Keith, you're overreacting. I spoke to Tom and he told me they were going to put together a planning committee. It's obvious—we'll need help. Don't let it get to you. Believe me, we'll get some help."

"We'd better," Keith said, flicking out his cigarette. "I refuse to work like a Hebrew slave. Both of us are overworked as it is. Look at you—you're here as much as I am, if not more. You need to be at home with Sarah. She needs you. Your lives have been put through hell."

Reaching for her pop, Katherine didn't say anything at first. She looked over the picnic table at Keith, who was ready to explode. That

Italian blood in him always reddened his skin when his temper was turned up. "Keith, don't worry about me," she responded with a sad look on her face. "Jila's death has been hard on all of us. But Sarah's doing fine."

"I'm sorry. It's just that you've been slaving to keep this place running and so have I."

"We have and it's worked out okay so far. I'm not gonna get all worked up unless I have reason to, and I want you to do the same. Maybe you need to take a few days off. I can get someone to come in while you're gone. You haven't taken a break in a while."

He reached for another cigarette. "Na, I'm not ready for a break. I plan to take some time off in the spring to visit my family. I'll take a break then."

Smiling, she replied, "You may have solved your own problem."

"What do you mean?"

"Well, think about it. They're talking about having the tournament in the spring. If you play your cards right, you might be away on vacation."

Keith gave her a crazy look as they both burst out laughing. Grinning, he said, Katherine that's what I like about you. You know exactly what to say to make a guy feel good."

Katherine laughed. "I try, it just takes me time to get there." With that, they moved on to planning the rest of the week's menus. But when Keith saw Tom was coming their way with a couple of prospective clients, he took the opportunity to leave. He didn't want to hear anything else that would upset his day. As usual, Katherine prepared to be the host-*du-jour*.

She took another sip of her pop.

Lately, Katherine had become as much a part of selling Haig Point to people as the realtors. The last couple of months had forced her to rethink whether or not this was the best place to stay, especially after everything that had happened. Since Jila's death, she had had difficulty deciding. She and Sarah had spoken about it several times. Each time

Sarah said she wanted to stay, it bothered Katherine, because she heard Sarah's cries at night.

And Nick was appearing more often, even though his relationship with them remained strained. Sarah wasn't rude to him, she just wouldn't go beyond hi and bye. Her attitude was pretty forced.

"Katherine, I want you to meet Mr. and Mrs. Moss," Tom said, shattering Katherine's musings. "They're thinking about moving to the island. I was telling them all about you and the mansion. Mrs. Moss would like a tour. Do you mind?"

"Not at all. I was just taking a break, I would love to."

"Thank you, Katherine."

"Mrs. Moss, let me show you around," Katherine said.

"Please call me Barb. I'm too young for that Mrs. Moss stuff," she said with a curt laugh.

"I know what you mean. Tom, where do you want us to meet you?"

"I'll be back in about thirty minutes. I'm taking Mr. Moss over to the lighthouse. He wants to see the upstairs."

"Call me Joe, I can't let my wife get one up on me," Mr. Moss said, grinning, as he and Tom drove off.

"Thanks for doing this," said Barb. "I really needed a break. My butt was starting to ache, if you know what I mean—I'm sick of hearing about golf. I felt like taking one of those balls and stuffing it into Joe's mouth just to get him to change the subject."

"I know," Katherine said. "I always tell the women who don't like to golf to go out and spend money. That seems to get their attention." She grinned.

"You're so right. I think I'm going to enjoy this tour," Barb said, still following the guys as they sped off in the distance.

"Oops, don't trip," Katherine said, reaching out to grab her. "Watch that first step."

Embarrassed, Barb replied, "Oh, I can be so clumsy at times. I've fallen going upstairs more than I have going down. I'm so glad God has given me a few bumpers for protection."

As the two women walked up the stairs, Keith, who was now fuming at Bob, walked by. Katherine returned his agitated smile without skipping a beat. Giving this guided tour was just what she needed today. Opening the door, she and her guest escaped inside the old house as Katherine began relating the history of the mansion like some fascinating story. Intrigued, Barb hung on to her every word.

They ended their tour in the lending library, where they sat next to the massive fireplace. The smell of old burnt wood filled the air. Barb talked at will and Katherine, always the dutiful hostess, listened, before she noticed Keith peeking through the door. He was up to his usual antics, and Katherine tried her best not to laugh. Luckily, Barb was convinced that Katherine was reacting favorably to the stories she was telling.

*   *   *   *

Meanwhile, Sarah was sitting on the back porch, rocking. She held Jila's letter in her hand. The view of the greens and golfers made little impression on her. Removing her headband she fluffed her hair and nestled into the corner, as if she was about to read a good book. Repositioning herself again in the creaky old chair, she closed her eyes, searching for inner peace as the fine pine needles tapped on the shingles.

CHAPTER 46

▼

The trial was only a few weeks away.

Katherine stood next to the window, arms crossed. A soft breeze relaxed her soul. Impressive pines and oak trees obstructed her view, and squirrels raced carefree up their barks.

The Calabogue Sound was filled with happy sails. But the enchanting view could not soothe the void in Katherine's heart. Not yet. She was just beginning to find spare moments for herself. But she still had to testify. Too many certainties and uncertainties still entangled her life. Months ago, the thought of testifying was nothing more than that—a thought. Now, her stomach tightened at the thought of the meeting with her attorney, which was only a couple of hours away.

The honey fragrance in the air grew with each breath she took. She leaned against the wall. Nick was inside, Sarah having finally indicated her willingness to talk to him. Katherine needed all the support she could get. She was prepared to overlook virtually every past sin committed against them. But why was Sarah willing now? Katherine did not know. She was just thankful for Sarah's change of heart.

She walked back into the kitchen and searched through a drawer. Sarah was still sleeping in her room.

Nick joined Katherine in the kitchen. "Excuse me," he said. "What are you looking for?"

She pulled a black leather book out of the drawer. "I need to call Beth."

"Beth?" Nick was puzzled.

"Yeah, she's an old friend; used to take care of my father. Nice lady; reminds me of Mama—you know, Jila's Mom. I'm sure you saw her at the funeral."

"Mama, funeral—what are you talking about?"

"I know you were there. You didn't want to be seen—was that it? Maybe someday you can share that with Sarah," she said flipping through the book. Nick chose not to respond. It wasn't worth denying.

Katherine laid the phonebook on the table and reached for the phone.

"Beth—she's got your attention, I see," Nick said.

"Yeah, I'm sure she must be worried sick about us. I've been meaning to call her, but I knew I couldn't. My father loved her and I know Sarah misses her. She's Sarah's Godmother. I promised her that I would always keep in touch. I need a few minutes."

"Take as much time as you need," Nick said. His thoughts turned to his daughter, who shared his blood but not his love. He still longed to be a true father, not just a victim of a night of passion. Fatherhood was an honor and involved a trust that he did not want to breach. Things needed to be different—they just had to be. He wanted hugs, smiles, and paternal bonding to be as much a part of his life as their blood tie. Sarah's distance paralyzed him. He thought about the useless years during which they had been separated. Getting to know Katherine again was only part of a new beginning. Still he was eternally grateful to Katherine, who had taken the trouble to plan their first sit-down dinner that evening—just the three of them.

Hearing voices, Sarah woke up and stood with her back flat against the door to listen. It was all so heart-wrenching to hear this man again. She was torn, and kept floating in a world of indecision, staring at the flat white ceiling for answers. It seemed so obvious: she and Nick marched to different drummers.

She walked over to her nightstand and opened the drawer. It was filled with shells but smelled fresher than potpourri. Holding her favorite shell, the one that she and Jila thought was the most beautiful, she went to sit on the bed. She stared at their picture and the envelope that sat next to it. A smile surfaced before her eyes sorrowfully closed again. She begged for someone to tell her what she needed to do.

There were footsteps outside. Someone was at the door.

Katherine was by now engrossed in her joyous telephone reunion with Beth. Seeing this, Nick had pondered before deciding that it was time. He now stood, half-frozen, next to Sarah's door, his hand raised for a knock.

Sarah stayed motionless. Feeling trapped, she could only whisper to herself, "Jila." She needed her best friend more than ever now.

There was a knock and then silence.

"Sarah, are you in there?" This was followed by a timid tap. "Sarah?" His heart raced. There was no turning back now.

"Yes, who is it?" she replied mechanically.

"It's me, Nick. I need to talk to you. May I come in?"

There was no answer. Slowly, Nick opened the door.

"What do you want?" Sarah asked. "Are you here to beat up on me again?"

"No, Sarah. I just want to talk to you before dinner. I want…I want…to get to know you…and to say how sorry I am. I was such a disappointment. I never wanted things to be this way. I'm not sure what to ask of you, Sarah. I know this isn't easy for either of us, but I want to find a way."

Sarah returned a piercing look as she took mental stock of the stranger before her. He was dressed like a sailor, white pants bagging over his sandals. A thick mustache added power to his lips, and he had slick, speckled hair highlighted at the temples. "May I sit down?" he asked. His shaking hand reached for the chair next to her desk.

"What if I say no? Would you leave and never come back?"

"I'd leave, but I won't promise not to come back. I know I've hurt you, Sarah. I was wrong and, for whatever it's worth, I'll have to pay for it the rest of my life. It hurts, but I accept my faults. All I want is for us to be able to talk and try to get to know each other. That's all I'm asking for; nothing more right now."

Sarah looked at her picture with Jila. She listened to Nick, but she was burdened with immense sadness. Throwing a few jabs and backing away would suit her just fine, but she was too tired. Besides, Jila wouldn't let her. Contemplating such actions made her uncomfortable. Here she was speaking for the first time, for whatever it was worth, with the man who was something more than just a man in her life.

"What do you want from me? I'll tell you right now I don't want anything from you. I don't care about your money. Mom and I are happy just the way we are. I don't even care if—" She couldn't complete her thought.

"Sarah, I respect your feelings and I can live with what's happening. This is a start. I won't push any harder than you'll let me. I owe you this. Can we just try to talk and get to know each other a little? I'd like that," he said as he stood up, not wanting to make her uncomfortable.

Hoping he wouldn't approach, Sarah answered, "Yes."

"Okay. I won't push anymore today. I know when I've reached the limit, Sarah. You'll never know what this means to me. I dreamed about this so many times." Nick's eyes were moist, and he fought to regain his composure. "I'd better go, thanks." Drained, he exited the room.

Sarah breathed a sigh of relief and buried her head in her hands. Jila's words were heavy on her mind.

CHAPTER 47

▼

The days came and went. Katherine struggled to maintain a cordial relationship between Sarah and Nick. Nick never said much to Katherine about that day he walked into their daughter's room; only that he thought things went well. Sarah had given him more than he ever thought she would—a conversation. He knew he had his work cut out for him. But he allowed himself to think like a father. He took this as a challenge—definitely his greatest challenge. But he felt he could handle it. He imagined a happy family returning home to Alberville, as Katherine had been planning. Although he had no assurance that either Sarah or Katherine would ever want to be a family with him, he refused to stop trying.

Katherine had decided she needed to return to Alberville for a few days. Jila's death and the time away made her long to be close to her father, Al. She'd invited both Nick and Sarah to join her, hoping to add another patch to their relationship, but Sarah made it clear that she wanted to stay behind and pack, in preparation for their permanent move.

At the mansion, Katherine was busy checking the day's receipts, little old Alberville prominent in her mind. She even longed to see old Detective Ganelli, who had saved them from Detective Glen. But as she closed the lock on the safe, she heard Keith fighting again with

Bob. She headed towards them, ready to assume her refereeing duties, and had got near enough to see poor miffed Bob, hand on his hip, rolling pin in the other. He was daring Keith to add another pinch of salt. But Katherine was saved from having to intervene by the ringing telephone. It was her attorney.

"Yes, this is Katherine," she said, throwing a stern look as a warning to the two men. "Oh, I was expecting your call yesterday. No, I'm not busy…Yes, I have a moment…What time? Will he be there, too? Okay, I can handle that…That's good, I'm ready to get this over. I'll be away for a few days; not too far away…I'll give you a call when I get back…Yeah, that will be fine, I'll look for it…okay, bye." Without skipping a beat she began to resolve the squabble between the two men.

She had a couple of hours before the dinner party was to begin.

*   *   *   *

Sarah was still flustered from her face-to-face encounter with Nick. She needed someone to talk to. Since Jila died, Keith has been the one to fill the role of family friend. Darting around the house in a T-shirt tied in a knot, her blue jeans cut well above her knees and brunette locks in a ponytail, she needed something else to do besides packing. She picked up the telephone and dialed from memory.

"Hello, Keith, can you come by?" she asked, phone locked to her ear and praying he could.

"When?"

"Now would be great."

Keith was watching over a pot that wasn't even his. His eyes flitted around looking for Bob. "Hold on," he told Sarah. Spotting Bob, he signaled for his help.

"All right, Sarah, I'll be there in a few," Keith said. "And Sarah—"

"Yeah."

"You're beginning to sound like your old self—whatever the problem is at the moment."

"Thanks, Keith," she replied.

They hung up. Bob was cursing again, but Keith ignored him as he untied his apron.

Sarah continued her packing, half-heartedly, struggling with the thought of leaving Daufuskie, knowing Katherine had made the decision because of her. She reached into her dusty chest and stumbled upon a photo album. Inside were pictures of her and Jila. They were dressed like angels for Sarah's first Halloween party at the clubhouse. It was a moment frozen in time, never to be forgotten, she thought. She rubbed her fingers across Jila's cheerful face. In the background stood Katherine, the strains of life showing on her comely face. Sarah was reliving the dread that she and Katherine felt their first year on the island. She struggled to stay positive, but thoughts about Nick resurfaced.

There was a tapping at the front door. Trainer, her favorite deer, was up to his usual, eating out of the flowerpot. The first day she and Trainer met, he had lost his way and somehow got trapped in the soft earth near their house. She remembered freeing him with a prayer that he might learn quickly the rules of survival. Ever since that day, Trainer had been coming to visit her; although it had been months since his last visit. "You must know I need a friend, don't you, Trainer," Sarah said.

Watching him made her think of Alberville, because he had come around only weeks after their exile to Daufuskie had begun. He was her first friend, when Alberville was still fresh in her mind and the pain of her young life seemed so unbearable. They had grown up together, one might say—maybe too quickly.

Being loved could not make up for the loneliness that had befallen her so quickly after her ordeal with Riggins. Her eyes blind to the world, Sarah went to the porch. The sun shone brightly. She lifted her head and drew a deep breath. The soft winds whispered sweet nothings in her ear as the smell of the salty Atlantic seeped into her blood. "I belong here. I belong here," she said with conviction.

When she opened her eyes, Trainer was gone. She looked at the old lighthouse, which had a churchly facade. "What's God trying to tell me? What's my future gonna be like?" she asked.

She looked at the palms of her hands. The lines were probably a palm-reader's nightmare. She couldn't tell which line to follow. They were so different from each other and yet had this common feature: they all belonged to her. Sarah brought her hands up to her face as if to pray.

She went inside. The haze in her head had somehow dissipated. Amazingly, the storm had passed. She was ready for the next step.

"Sarah...Sarah." Keith was knocking at the door.

CHAPTER 48

▼

A week later...

The well-traveled vehicle slowed down as it neared a dusty hair-pin turn. Up ahead, the numbers "768" welcomed an old veteran thought to be extinct from these parts.

Katherine took a breath as raspy as cowhide. It has been years since she was here. The aroma of dead roses was as welcome as the chess-like marble and granite slabs around her. Each was as unique as the history they told.

She had finally arrived at Alberville's place of rest. There were many new neighbors, so many that the direct view to her father's grave from the dirt road was obscured. Al always had a way of surrounding himself with the best, though. On this day, Katherine wore the broadest of smiles and the saddest of tears. She wanted to familiarize herself with the new neighbors, and one step felt like twenty. Her handkerchief glued beneath her eyes, her every emotion fighting to dominate the rest, it was the memory of Al that she felt most strongly. And clasped tightly in her hand was the five-leaf clover pendant he had given her on graduation day. The more she walked on the more her muscles relaxed—until she reached her most sacred place. And there she stopped to brush away the dirt that had gathered on Al's headstone.

Her tears dropped to the parched earth.

"Daddy, I'm back. I've come home," she whispered as she rested her head on his pillow. "I wish you were here, you don't know how much I miss you. You'd be so proud of Sarah. She's a lot like you. She's beautiful. It's been so long since I felt so close to you. I hope Mama is enjoying having you around." Katherine's words faded until an eerie silence filled the air. Even the birds stopped their gossiping.

She knew what she had to do. The world was standing still as if to acknowledge her strength. She held on to the five-leaf clover pendant in her hand, and after gently digging at the base of Al's headstone, she planted it like a mother laying her baby to rest.

"I will always love you, Daddy," she said, leaves crunching beneath her feet. Her eyes were fixed on the little mound that rested on the ground. Only she and Al understood the significance of the pendant. It would forever be safe and so would she.

She was ready to let go. Her steps were easier now, whatever the burden she carried.

Once inside the car, she closed her eyes and rested her head on the leather seat. "I love you, Kate. I love you, Kate," came a voice inside. She was certain it was Al. She took a deep breath, opened her eyes, and gazed down the dusty tree-lined road. "I'm ready to go," she said, and threw a quick glance to Nick, who had been waiting alone in the car while she paid her respects. For a moment their eyes locked in a spiritual embrace.

He started up the car and they drove off.

CHAPTER 49

▼

Daufuskie Island was like a greenhouse; the sun's warmth hung overhead like a blanket. Trapped beneath the clear sky stood Sarah on the wooden dock overlooking the Calibogue Sound. She knew she had to decide, before Katherine returned from her trip, if this island was meant to be her permanent home. She watched the H-ferry abut the dock. People waved from their sails and glided by like deer in mid-flight.

This beloved paradise and its inhabitants has been her home. It was here that she had a semblance of family. She watched as a little girl with sun-bleached hair stepped off the ferry carrying a straw purse with a bold sunflower motif. A man held her hand.

Sarah envied the girl and the tranquility of her tiny soul. Having a father yet not having one distressed Sarah. But she had Katherine. And their relationship was strong, despite the turmoil in their life. She looked ahead at the royal-blue water with its white caps and the waves that sang their songs. The scenic beauty captured her heart, maybe for the last time, and she struggled with her thoughts.

Staring back at the mansion, she could see Keith moving around in his usual regal manner. His Hawaiian shirt and unorthodox crooked smile were woven into the soul of this old house. He gave it character, one that everyone loved, especially Katherine. Keith had a special gift, a human flair so infectious that customers often demanded his presence, and kept returning to the mansion because of it, again and again. Never had meals been so simply yet so eloquently presented to guests.

Sarah recalled past social events at the beach club. She felt again the handshakes, the warm hugs, the tugging at her heart. Everyone had welcomed her and Katherine when they first arrived, and it was the same now. Nothing had changed. It was their home. **And yet** they were supposed to leave Daufuskie Island for their other home. In time...

"All aboard!" the H-ferry captain called out. "All aboard!"

It would soon be her turn, if leaving was what she really wanted.

Sarah was grateful that her best friend had left her a letter, because now Jila's thoughts would carry her forever. She folded the letter, her thoughts floating like Styrofoam pellets, her heart torn by the emotion of the parting. So many uncertainties. But for the love between her and Katherine, there would be no hope in this world, nor will to go on. Yet love also brought friction. Sarah didn't want to be marginalized in the new relationship that Katherine had found with Nick.

"All aboard!" she said as she lifted her shoulder-bag and walked away—towards the mansion. She had made her decision. The solitary sounds of the H-ferry's engine grew fainter as she reached the steps. And she grabbed the glistening brass door handle. Looking through the window, she saw Keith prepped to serve an elderly couple. His eyes connecting with hers, he flashed her a reassuring smile.

"I'm already home," Sarah whispered, as she opened the door.

E P I L O G U E

▼

Three months later...

"Please rise."

Behind an iron curtain Katherine waited. Taking a deep breath and rubbing her clammy hands together, she steeled herself. Al would be proud of her on this day. She needed his strength. She closed her eyes and said one last silent prayer.

In front of her, the room was filled with unfamiliar faces but, just as Frank had promised, no one could see her. Her greatest comfort was knowing that Sarah and Nick were waiting in the wings. The three of them were anxious to return to Daufuskie Island and get on with their lives.

As Katherine looked around the room, a husky, professionally dressed man was sitting between two men dressed in similar fashion. He stared relentlessly in her direction. It was Riggins. He tapped his pen on a pad of paper, and hatred flared from his eyes. It was overpowering. Although protected, Katherine felt exposed. But she remembered all they had been through because of him.

This was the beginning of her and Sarah's healing. Yes—their healing.

Riggins was not in a position to buy his way out this time. He was about to get what he so richly deserved. Ralph, the Big Guy, had already testified, and all of Riggins' cronies were behind bars. Ralph had done everything he could, hoping for leniency. His testimony about his and the others' involvement, from beginning to end, was truly chilling. But it wasn't until he spoke of the plot to kill the doctor that he lost it. He became like a child, weeping uncontrollably, searching for someone to tell him that it was going to be okay. The jury listened, unsympathetic.

Then it was Katherine's turn. "Are you ready?" the judge asked the bailiff, as those who were standing took their seats. Her legs weak, Katherine rose, but she took heart—she was about to regain control of her life. Her mind's eye refocused on the man to whom she was forever indebted. From the grave, her father had helped her turn her life around. She let out a long sigh, bracing herself on the arms of the chair. She thought again of all she and Sarah had suffered. Their wounds needed to be healed. And this was the medicine the powers of which were yet to be proven.

"Raise your right hand. State your name."

"Katherine Oberman," she said proudly, a surge of energy traveling through her body.

"Do you swear to tell the truth, the whole truth…"

"I do."

Sarah listened to each word that escaped Katherine lips. Then, something happened. Her face distended into a clement smile as she looked over at Nick. Their eyes connected. He had taken a concerned stance near the chamber door, listening intently. Something was born at this moment that had not existed before.

Sarah pulled her favorite shell from her pocket and closed her eyes. She saw a bright, beautiful day. Music began to fill her ears and people gathered. In the middle of this majestic gathering stood the ginger man. At his side was Jila, and above Jila's head shone a light brighter than the brightest star. Jila's face glowed as she waved cheerfully to Sarah, who was finally at rest—standing next to Nick.

"Stay happy, ma friend," Jila softy whispered and blew Sarah a kiss.

"I will," Sarah responded, her face washed with tears. "I'll never forget you, Jila."

Sarah's wilted lids began to open. Katherine's voice surrounded her and the calm of knowing Jila was safe and happy warmed Sarah's inners. She took in a deep breath. She was ready to move forward with a life just beginning.

Other novels written by Author

SILENCE

Author's e-mail address
Silenceijm@aol.com

0-595-27018-2